When I Fall in Love

When I Fall in Love

Iris Rainer Dart

William Morrow and Company, Inc.
New York

Grateful acknowledgment is made to the following for permission to reprint excerpts from:

"Let Me Be There" by John Rostill. Copyright © 1973 Petal Music Ltd. (UK) All rights in U.S. and Canada assigned to and administered by EMI Gallico Music Corporation. All rights reserved. Warner Bros. Publications, U.S. Inc., Miami, FL 33014.

"When I Fall in Love" by Edward Heyman and Victor Young. Copyright 1952 Victor Young Publications, Inc. Renewed, assigned to Chappell & Co. and Intersong-USA, Inc. All rights administered by Chappell & Co. All rights reserved. Warner Bros. Publications, U.S. Inc., Miami, FL 33014.

"When I See an Elephant Fly," words by Ned Washington, music by Oliver Wallace. Copyright 1941 by Walt Disney Productions. Copyright renewed. World rights controlled by Bourne Co. All rights reserved. International copyright secured. ASCAP.

"You Are So Beautiful" by Billy Preston and Bruce Fisher. Copyright © 1973 Irving Music, Inc. (BMI), and Almo Music Corp. (ASCAP). All rights reserved. Warner Bros. Publications, U.S. Inc., Miami, FL 33014.

"You Make Me Feel Like a Natural Woman," words and music by Gerry Goffin, Carole King and Jerry Wexler. Copyright © 1967 (Renewed 1995) Screen Gems-EMI Music Inc. All rights reserved. International copyright secured.

The Little Prince by Antoine De Saint-Exupéry. Copyright 1943 Harcourt Brace & Company. All rights reserved.

It is the policy of William Morrow and Company, Inc., and its imprints and affiliates, recognizing the importance of preserving what has been written, to print the books we publish on acid-free paper, and we exert our best efforts to that end.

Library of Congress Cataloging-in-Publication Data
Dart, Iris Rainer.
When I fall in love : by Iris Rainer Dart.
p.   cm.
ISBN 0-688-16034-4
I. Title.
PS3554.A78W48   1999
813'.54—dc21   98-45074
                                                  CIP

Printed in the United States of America

First Edition

1 2 3 4 5 6 7 8 9 10

BOOK DESIGN BY BERNARD KLEIN

www.williammorrow.com

*This book is dedicated to Ryan Martin and Chad Saffro, two extra-
ordinary young men who showed me the world through new eyes. I
am so grateful to both of you.*

*And to my brother-in-law, Justin Dart, Jr., whose battles for equality
are legendary.*

Thank You

Dr. Kimberly DeDell
Dr. Thomas Hedge
Dr. Jeffrey E. Galpin
Dr. Howard Allen
Brad Freeman
Arlene Saffro
Elaine Markson
Ron Bernstein
Mike Lobell
Cathy Schulman
Joyce Brotman
Betty Nichols Kelly
Sharon Kuperman

And, always, my unending gratitude to my family: Stephen Dart, Rachel Dart, Gregory Wolf, and Stuart Little, for giving me the love, inspiration, and encouragement to spin my stories.

When I Fall in Love

One night after she'd been working late at her desk, she went to the window to close the blinds and was startled to see the dented white pickup truck parked across the street and the outline of a man sitting very still behind the wheel. She moved away quickly to turn off the light, then nervously crept back to the window again. But the truck was gone, and she wondered if maybe she'd imagined it. When she saw the truck and the man out there the next night, she knew she had a reason to be afraid, so she called the police, trying to sound rational as she told her story. The officer sighed, annoyed by her complaint, and told her to call back "if the guy tries anything."

That same night, after she double-checked all of the locks, she slid into bed and finally drowsiness tugged at her and pulled her down into a trembling sleep. But the jangling of the phone awakened her, and she grabbed for the receiver only to hear her heart beating in her ears and silence on the other end until the click of the disconnect.

After that she was awake for hours, startled by the slightest creak of a floorboard. In the morning, while she stood at the sink brushing her teeth, the memory of the call made her stomach lurch. In her office at her desk she tried to work but she couldn't shake the panic of the night before or the exhaustion from the interrupted sleep.

The day she ordered caller ID was the first time he didn't call, as if he knew, and that made her more afraid. That night her dreams were filled with ringing phones and panicky chases with a white pickup truck pursuing her as she ran breathlessly down unrecognizable streets.

When she didn't see his truck outside for a few nights, she prayed that something had happened to make him decide to leave her alone. But then she drove around the corner on that dark, rain-slicked Friday after dinner and her headlights caught the white pickup in front of her building again. Terror broke over her and she let out an involuntary wail of despair.

Even as she stepped out of the car she knew it was a mistake not to simply drive away to the police station or to her sister's apartment. But some vain hope made her hang on to the idea that if they looked at each other face-to-face, if she could convince him she wasn't hiding anything, he would stop the torment.

The rain was coming down more heavily now and the street-lights made white pools on the shiny black street. She could feel her hair matting to her scalp as she closed the car door, trying to breathe deeply and summon some shred of equanimity. As soon as he saw her he opened the truck door, stepped out, and moved toward her, his shoulders hunched against the rain, his eyes glaring. She heard her voice quaver as she tried to tell him she didn't know the answers to the questions he spat at her.

From behind her she heard her own car door open and close and she saw the man look over there to see who was with her, but his gaze quickly moved back to her because he was sure she was the one who had the·information he needed. Once again she tried to explain but his expression was glazed and she could tell he wasn't understanding the things she said. Even from a few yards away she could smell the sour alcohol on his breath. She felt the panic in her chest and tried to think of some way she could back down and hurry inside.

But then she heard the warning cry, and that was when she saw the glint of the gun in his hand and from what seemed like very far away she heard the blast. "No!" she screamed. Then there was another blast. For a helpless moment she was unable to move, undone by the stunning realization of what had happened as she watched the man stagger back to his truck and drive away.

Her own horrified screams filled the night. Lights flipped on in neighbors' windows. Dozens of people, faceless, well-meaning people, hurried out of their apartment buildings, and a woman she didn't know tried to calm her, but she pushed the woman aside and dropped to her knees on the wet ground.

"Somebody help us! Please do something!"

Then she leaned forward, keening in sorrow and grief until the shriek of a siren became louder and mercifully, blessedly, the ambulance arrived, parting the crowd.

Her life, her love, her hope for the future had been destroyed. Unless there was some magic that could turn the horror around.

And here is my secret, a very simple secret. It is only with the heart that one can see. What is essential is invisible to the eye.

—*Antoine De Saint-Exupéry,* The Little Prince

1

Harry Green was on his deathbed in Cedars-Sinai hospital, which to him was no reason to stop being funny. Every day Lily and the other writers came to his room at Cedars, which Harry joked was "a kidney stone's throw away from CBS," and there they stayed all day to write *Angel's Devils,* a sitcom whose prognosis was nearly as bad as Harry's. Though the doctors were sure this was his final hospital stay and that it would be only a matter of days until he died from the cancer that was invading what was left of him, Harry was determined to hang on until the end of the season.

So every morning he pushed the button that made the head of the bed deliver his cadaverous body into a sitting position. Then he welcomed the writers with his skin-and-bones arms open wide and a whole slew of thoughts he'd had in his drugged haze of the night before.

"A rabbi, a priest, and a Buddhist monk walked into chemotherapy," Harry offered as the writers looked askance. Then he shrugged. "Hey, they say you should write what you know."

"That's funny," Marty said, and with his foot he positioned Lily's chair closest to the bed since she was the only woman on the staff—and a hot-looking one—and Harry was not dead yet.

The daily pilgrimage of the *Angel's Devils* writing staff to the hospital had become a natural part of their lives since Harry had announced to them one dreary, rainy morning, in the middle of a pitch meeting, that he was too cancer-ridden to come into the office anymore. When the bozos at the network got the news of Harry's illness, they wanted to replace him immediately, but Marty went to their offices and swore to them that "even while he's croaking, Harry Green is funnier than anyone else out there." And incredibly, they bought it.

So Harry stayed on the *Angel's Devils* payroll, continuing to be a beneficiary of ongoing Writer's Guild health insurance, and instead of working in the bleak little offices at CBS, the writers wrote the show crowded into a circle around his hospital bed. All of them were oblivious to the monitors and the IVs and the visits from the nurses who wound their way through the group to provide Harry with his pain medication. And they all rose obediently whenever the nurses came to shoo them out when Harry needed some procedure that required privacy.

Even Dorie, the show's typist, came to the hospital every day, plugged in her laptop, and clickity-clacked away, taking notes on all the story ideas and keeping track of the jokes that were flying around the room. And from time to time, Harry's wife, Rosie, peeked in and smiled, because she knew this was the way Harry wanted to go out—doing shtick.

When the workday was over and the other writers left, Lily made a point of staying for a while to be alone with Harry. Not to talk or joke anymore, just to let him know she loved him. Most of the time he had already fallen asleep from exhaustion; but now and then his eyelids would flutter, and he would see her there and manage a smile.

"Is it too late to take herbal remedies?" he asked.

"Never too late," she said, moving closer to hold his bony, veiny hand.

"I guess I shoulda listened to all that shit you told me about nutrition. When you warned me that guacamole wasn't a vegetable."

"Harry, get some sleep," she said, not wanting to leave but knowing it was time.

"Don't stay on this shlocky show after this season's over," he said. "Next year you get on a classy sitcom."

"No such animal," she said, using one of Harry's own expressions. Even though his eyes were closed, a smile fluttered across Harry's lips.

She didn't say what everyone knew, which was that after Harry was gone there would be no more *Angel's Devils*. Harry Green was the King of Jokes, and he kept the ideas coming and the show treading water.

"I'll think about changing," she promised, not even sure that any other show would want her.

It must be late, Lily realized. The black night had turned the hospital room window into a mirror, and she wondered as she caught a glimpse of herself in it how Mark could love her as much as he said he did. Her fine, dark, straight hair lay lifeless against her head. Her heavy-lidded eyes looked sleepy. She was tired and looking more haggard than a thirty-eight-year-old woman was supposed to, and she was overwhelmed with sadness.

As soon as it was clear by Harry's breathing that he was asleep for the night, Lily gathered her legal pad and purse and headed for the door, looking back at him, her beloved mentor, knowing each time that this might be the last.

Tonight as she drove her Jeep west on Beverly Boulevard, she promised herself that tomorrow she'd get to the hospital earlier than the others so she could be with him when he was alert and awake. That way she'd have a few private minutes to recite the speech she'd saved all these years: the speech in which she would thank him for all he'd given her.

To properly let him know how grateful she was for all he'd done for her, the way he'd taken her in when she was that too-dumb-for-words girl who had found her way to his office building and, seeing that his secretary was away from her desk, marched into his office, pumping with the adrenaline of terror and bravado. People did these things in books and magazine stories all the time, she remembered telling herself all the way there. Why couldn't she?

"Mr. Green, I want to work for you," she'd said, her voice noticeably shaky. She was clutching her folder of material to her chest like a sixth-grader about to make an oral book report.

"I got the same secretary for twenty years," he said, not looking up.

"I'm a writer," she tried. "My agent's Bruce Brown. He told me to drop off some of my jokes." She was struck by the gall that had allowed her to come out with a lie like that. What if Bruce Brown was Harry's agent too? What if Harry picked up the phone now and called him? She didn't even know what Bruce Brown looked like. It was a name she'd seen in the trade papers.

"Who'd you write for?" Harry asked. Now he was looking up at her over half glasses. Not the way a man looks a woman over, but with that semi-sneer she'd seen people use when they picked up the on-sale day-old fruit at Hughes Market.

"My sister, Daisy." She cringed as she realized she'd actually said something that moronic to a man who had written for every big comic on the planet.

"No kiddin'? How 'bout your uncle Phil? Ever write anything for him?"

"Daisy is an aspiring stand-up comic," she explained, making it worse. "She gets up at the Improv sometimes," she'd added, marveling now that after that remark Harry hadn't called security to have her removed.

"How lovely for her," Harry said. It was clearly the first time he'd ever used such an innocuous word in his life. "But I'll be honest with you. And you can take me to the union with this. These guys on my staff," he told her, "they don't want any girl writers here. These putzes have no filters between their sick minds and their foul mouths. Every grungy piece of garbage dirtbag thing they think, they gotta share. They get raunchy in a way a nice human being like yourself can't even fathom. And having some chick in the room, if you'll excuse my slang— which compared to what they'll call you is nothing—that's gonna get on their nerves.

"So you can run out and blow the whistle and bring on the women's committee of the Writer's Guild and the National Organization of Women can march up and down picketing my office. But I'm giving you the full-out truth, doll."

That was when the phone rang.

"Yeah?" Harry said as he picked it up and listened. Then he smiled a toothy Cheshire cat smile, which Lily realized later was because he was certain the phone call was arming him with a way of being obnoxious that would have to make her run screaming from his office.

"Do I have a sperm bank joke?" he said like a vaudeville comic setting up a punch line. "Let's see," he said into the phone. Then he smiled. "Hey, doll-face, you got any sperm bank jokes in that folder?" But he wasn't really asking her; he was proving to her that working for him was not her style, that writing on the staff of a show with a bunch of down-and-dirty men would be way too rough for her. Now he was back on the phone, pitching with the person on the other end of the line, "Sperm bank? Withdrawal? Uh, let's see . . ."

Lily really felt like a jerk now. The man clearly couldn't wait to get rid of her. And he was right. She didn't fit in. Not because she was a woman, but because she was overqualified for some dumb writing staff job. She had been a film major in college, had listened to lectures on the art of making film from Martin Scorsese and Sydney Pollack. She had planned and told everyone that her goal was to make small, important films and take them to places like the Sundance Film Festival, where the real filmmakers were.

Then, just out of sisterly devotion, she'd written those jokes for Daisy. Self-deprecating Daisy jokes, observations-about-relationships-with-men Daisy jokes, and when the jokes got big laughs at the small clubs, it was Daisy who convinced her she was funny enough to try for a job on one of Harry Green's shows.

Harry Green sat there in his high-backed chair looking munchkinlike, then he turned to face the corner. He was jabbering away into the phone pitching sperm bank jokes, and Lily knew that turning the chair to the wall was his way of telling her to get out of his office.

Okay, I tried, she thought, moving toward the door. I'll tell Daisy I tried, big-time. Didn't send some polite little letter the secretary would have tossed. Didn't try to reach him by phone to have some secretary say, "Will he know what this is regarding?" I actually balls-out stormed into the office building and into the man's face, for God's sake. So he said no. I can handle it.

She was a step from the door when she decided that maybe

she should leave her folder of material with him just on the off chance that he'd actually look at it. And as she turned back she had a silly brainstorm, which she addressed to the back of the big leather chair since Harry was too short to be seen over it.

"There are sperm banks in Los Angeles where you don't have to get out of your car to make a deposit," she said, then paused for a beat. "They give new meaning to the term 'drive-by' shooting!" Her own raunchy joke made her laugh an uneasy laugh, and Harry Green obviously didn't even hear her, so she dropped the folder on his desk, muttered a barely audible "nice meeting you," and turned again for the door.

But just as she crossed the threshold, she heard the squeak of Harry Green's chair, and his words stopped her.

"You got a job."

"Thank you," she said breathlessly.

"What's your name?"

"Lily Benjamin."

"See you tomorrow at nine."

That was thirteen years ago and she'd worked with him ever since. On every show. And every time, she was the only woman on the staff. "Guess I outraunched the raunchy," she said to Daisy the night before her first workday as the two sisters celebrated over pizza and beer.

"Don't forget to put the seat back up," Bruno Waldholz said to her the first time she used the unisex rest room in Harry's offices. Bruno was a teddy bear of a man who had five kids under the age of ten and a wife who came to all of the tapings.

"Shut the fuck up, you assholes—there's a lady present," Marty liked to say to the writers to tease Lily. Marty and Bruno had worked on all of Harry's shows too. Their little group was a family to her. They had come to change the locks when her husband walked out, and they invited her and her son, Bryan, for every holiday. They had introduced her to her fiancé, Mark, a few years ago, when Harry had had a heart attack and Mark had been the attending physician. Harry had changed her life. And she had thanked him many times, but probably not enough. Tomorrow she would change that.

2

Lily's housekeeper, Elvira, always sang while she worked. Beautiful, lilting songs, with a cry in her voice that made her sound like early Linda Ronstadt. And when she moved around Lily's kitchen preparing a meal, every move, from chopping to serving, was done tenderly. Lily's son, Bryan, loved her enchiladas and quesadillas, but most of all he loved her company. In the thirteen years that his mother had been in the television business, Elvira had been his lap for reading time, first on the car pool line, provider of first aid, and fierce competitor at board games.

"You cheating," Lily would hear Elvira shrieking at Bryan. Then her blast of a laugh would follow. On the nights when Lily was late coming in from work, she'd find Elvira and the now fifteen-year-old, nearly six-feet-tall Bryan camped on the living room floor playing a game.

"I am not."

"You land on my street and don't pay no money."

"You didn't ask for money."

"I ask now. Give me money."

"Okay." Bryan laughed and handed over the rent for Atlantic Avenue to the steaming Elvira. Usually they were so engrossed in their game that neither of them looked up at Lily as she breezed by to the kitchen.

Bryan and Elvira had private jokes, and they both loved football, a sport Lily had never been able to understand and thought of as simply a gang of goons crashing into one another. Bryan bought Elvira flowers on her birthday, insisted that she pack his lunches, and every morning before he climbed into Lily's car to head for school he gave Elvira a good-bye hug. Lily felt stupid about being jealous, especially when her sister, Daisy, who had a knack for knowing her weaknesses, teased her about it.

"When Bryan gets married, Elvira will give him away," she said.

"Meaning?" Lily knew something bitchy was about to fall out of Daisy's mouth.

"That she's his real mother."

"That's cruel. She's there because I'm working my ass off to feed him and send him to private school."

"Don't get mad. That's how it is with working mothers. Their kids know the maid better than the parent."

The night Daisy said that, Lily had stayed awake, haunted by the insane thought that she should fire Elvira—hating that her child would certainly look back on too many of the highlights of his childhood as times he'd spent with Elvira. Maybe, she thought, she should change her lifestyle. She could freelance and work out of the house. But all of the freelance writers she knew were struggling and wished they were on a show the way she was.

Drifting off to sleep she remembered all the times Elvira had been there for her. The times she had nursed Lily through the flu, bringing hot tea and Tylenol. The times she had stayed late to serve her a hot dinner. The way she offered friendship on those nights when she was baby-sitting for Bryan and Lily had collapsed after a taping.

The conversations they'd had were priceless. Two women from such diverse cultures talked endlessly about life and particularly men, and they found that they agreed on everything—especially that men were impossible. Lily describing with a shudder how it had felt when Donald left her and Elvira shaking her head sadly as she talked about her own husband, Ernesto's, foul temper.

Tonight, when Lily came in from work, she could hear Elvira singing "Blue Bayou" as she chopped cucumbers for the salad. Mark was humming along with her as he stood at the stove adding a little more oregano to the pasta sauce. Lily thought he looked particularly handsome with his dark hair falling in his face, and she felt a rush of love as she watched him. He was always so happy in the kitchen. At his own house he had a large Wolf range and he called it "my Ferrari."

Now he was in shirtsleeves, still wearing a tie, and he had a dish towel secured in the waist of his pants as an apron. Lily was sure all his cardiology patients felt lucky to have such a compassionate man as their physician.

"Hi, hon," he said sweetly as she gave him a quick hug in greeting.

"Mmm. Smells so good," she said, grabbing a slice of cucumber just as Elvira turned the knife to chop them into cubes.

"Missed me," Lily joked.

She was about to tell Mark about Harry Green's condition, hoping to get him to stop by the hospital room tomorrow, but before she could, he gestured to her to look at Elvira's face. Something was wrong. Her eyes were unusually puffy, and there was a black-and-blue mark high on her right cheek that was so long it extended around to her ear.

"Elv," Lily said, putting her tote bag down and moving more closely to look, but Elvira hurried away from her to open the refrigerator as if she were hoping to step inside and hide there.

"You okay?" Lily asked.

"Me?" Elvira said, not looking back though Lily was looking right at her. It was a technique Bryan used too. "Me?" he'd say, though she was looking right at him and couldn't possibly have meant anyone else. It gave him a moment to vamp while his mind raced to find the correct response.

"You. Your face is black-and-blue."

Elvira laid the knife on the counter and wiped her hands with a dish towel. She was sweet-faced and short and pudgy, and she was almost always smiling. But tonight her eyes looked defeated and resigned and much older than the eyes of a forty-year-old woman. Lily had never seen her so devoid of animation.

"I have to quit this job. I have to leave tonight and get far away from here."

"Not tonight," Bryan said, and Lily turned to see that her son was standing in the kitchen doorway. "You can't leave us, Elv." The boy made his way toward her and extended his long arms and Elvira moved toward him to let him wrap them around her. Then the tiny woman put her sad face against him.

"My husband is very bad. He hurt me many times. Now I have to go far away to be safe. And I can't never come back," she said.

Mark turned off all the fires on the stove and now the four of them stood in a pained little circle in the middle of the small kitchen. Lily had suspected for a long time that Ernesto was physically abusive to this dear, gentle woman, but Elvira had been closed-mouthed about any violence. Now the evidence was all over her sweet face.

"Elvie, there are programs, women's care centers where you can go. Let me get on the phone and find one of those for you now," Lily offered. "I can have you at one of those places in a matter of hours."

"Please," Elvira said, looking afraid. "Let me do this my own way without any questions."

"What about the police, Elv?" Bryan asked, releasing her from the hug but still keeping an arm around her shoulders.

"They don't do no good. I tried to get them to help last year and the year before and they don't come. Once I tried to call them and Ernesto cut the wire and tied my hands with it." Her hands, Lily thought, those beautiful, tender hands. "You go and eat your dinner," Elvira urged them. "I get ready to leave. I have plans, and it will be okay."

"Just have dinner with us," Bryan said, tugging Elvira toward the table. "Please."

Mark reached into his pocket, pulled out his money clip, removed a pile of bills, and, without counting, handed them to the frowning Elvira.

"Please take this just in case," he said. Lily wanted to throw her arms around him for his kindness. Elvira moved his hand with the bills in it away.

"I have savings," she said.

"Let this be for extras," he said. "Please. In honor of all the nights we cooked together, allow me."

Elvira took the money tentatively, then looked at Lily. "Doctor Mark is the best man in the world. I'm so glad you're marrying him. I wish I could be here for the wedding."

"Come on, Elvira. You're the guest of honor," Mark said, escorting her to his chair and pulling up a step stool for himself.

As Mark served the dinner, Lily lit the candles, and when they were all seated Elvira looked at the three of them. "Pray for me," she said. Her face was quivering to keep the tears inside.

"Let's hold hands," Bryan said, and in the soft light of the candles the four of them took hands around the table as the candlelight cast eerie shadows on the wall.

At the end of dinner, Bryan and Mark cleared the table and Lily walked Elvira to the garage in the building, where her old blue Pontiac station wagon was parked.

"Can you tell me where you're going?" Lily asked.

"Better for you not to know," Elvira said.

"We'll miss you so much," Lily said, leaning into the car to give the doughy woman a hug.

"You be strong and love that boy," Elvira said into her neck. "You're giving him a good father, and that's what he needs more than anything."

Lily nodded, wiping a tear from her eye, and stepped away from the car as Elvira backed out of the parking place and through the garage doors into the night.

3

◇◇◇◇◇◇◇◇◇◇◇◇◇◇◇◇◇◇◇

Lily knew the news was bad the minute she stepped off the hospital elevator. Marty was waiting for her, and she could see his face was pale and that he was struggling to maintain his composure.

"He's gone," he said, taking Lily's hand and moving her toward the sterile furniture in the waiting room at the center of the eighth floor. It was the spot to which the group of writers had retreated when the nurses sent them out of the room so they could minister to Harry.

"About four in the morning. Rosie was with him. He knew he was going. Still he was doing jokes. She said 'Harry, how do you feel?' And he managed to croak out, 'With my hands.' And those were his last words."

Lily emitted a puff of a laugh, then leaned against Marty's tubby body and cried. "I know. I loved him too," she heard him murmur. "He was the King of Jokes, and nobody will ever take his place."

The night before she had been awake for hours, worrying about Elvira and where she could possibly go to hide from Ernesto. Was it some random place she had chosen for herself? Why hadn't Elvira allowed her to call up one of those abused wives protection programs to help her? No, Elvira was too proud and ashamed to let anyone do that for her.

"I hate to tell you, but we have to work today," she heard Marty saying, and she realized he was right. They had a show to put together that had to be shot on Friday, and they didn't have the luxury of falling down on the job just because their beloved friend was gone. And Elvira. How could Lily stop worrying about Elvira? Early this morning she had noticed what looked like Ernesto's white truck parked outside her house.

How did people do it? Surgeons had to operate no matter how they felt. Pilots had to fly jumbo jets even after they fought with their wives. But neither of those professions required funny, whimsical, witty words. No chance there were any of those left in any of the writers this morning.

In the writer's reception area at the office the TV was on, and Bruno and David were playing video games. Dorie the secretary was reading a Danielle Steel novel, and Marty was on the phone talking to agents, looking for a replacement for Harry.

"We thought Norman Steinberg was replacing Harry, but Steinberg said he didn't want to wait around for Harry to die, so he took the Cosby show and moved to New York. Now who do you have for us?" There was a long beat. "Are you kidding? We'd kill to have him." Marty listened and muttered, "Yeah. Yeah. So the fuck what?"

Now he seemed to be fighting to get someone named Charlie Roth, and she heard him arguing about him with what was probably one of the network executives.

"Harvey, is *your* record so clean?" she heard Marty ask. "The guy likes pretty young women. Who doesn't?" He was obviously talking to that network bozo Harvey Meyers. A forty-year-old bachelor who had come on to Lily a thousand times, even when she'd held up her engagement ring to remind him that she wasn't on the market. "I say we make the guy an offer." Whoever the guy was, Marty was pushing hard to get him.

When he got off the phone, he called them into the conference room for a meeting, but when the others straggled in they sat morosely around the table and all any of them wanted to do was tell stories about Harry. The chair at the head of the table from which Harry had always presided was empty. They tried halfheartedly to pitch story ideas but everything fell flat.

Lily loved these men. Over the last few years on this show they'd become her closest friends. Marty Blick was an insane, wild-eyed, witty former stand-up comic whose ideas were always off the wall. Bruno Waldholz was an adorable, pudgy man who dressed only in overalls and T-shirts, and David Gorman, reed thin and hawk-faced, never cracked a smile, no matter how funny the jokes were in the meeting or on the set.

All three of them were brilliant comedy writers with remarkable individual styles, but today not one of them had an idea in his head.

"Somebody from ICM for you," Dorie said to Marty as she appeared in the doorway. Marty grabbed the phone. "Yeah? Yeah?" he asked. "Wheeehah!" he yelped, and put down the phone. "Charlie Roth, the God of Jokes, took the gig. He'll be here to meet with us at four. We live! The show has a shot!" Marty did a little dance of excitement all around.

"Jeez," Dave said. "Be careful what you wish. I heard the guy's a killer with the staff."

"Yeah, well, we need a killer around here to keep us on the air," Bruno said.

"Ever meet him?" David asked Lily. She shook her head,

running through a mental list of all the comedy writers she knew, the ones she'd met at the writers' summer softball games or at the Writer's Guild meetings. Charlie Roth didn't ring a bell. The God of Jokes. That one she ought to remember. "You're in for a treat," David said. It sounded ominous.

Lily looked at her watch. It was three-thirty, and she hadn't eaten all day.

"I'm going to try to find something in the commissary that's remotely edible," she said. "Back at four."

At the counter of the cafeteria, Lily realized her eyes were still throbbing from crying over Harry. She stared at the institutional food and didn't see one item that interested her.

"Eyyy, girlfriend," she heard a voice say. She turned, pleased to see Cynthia Lloyd, her friend who produced the John Terman show, which was a perfect match for Cyn, since the show was outrageous and so was she. She was a tall, stylish brunette with a loud mouth who had given birth to three children, each from a different "donor"—which was what she called her three ex-husbands. And sandwiched between the marriages there had been an admitted fling with at least one executive at every studio. "A slut for the new century," she called herself. She was always on the make.

Today she was eating a chili dog and held it up shamelessly to wave at Lily.

"Caught being a nutritional delinquent by my friend who thinks the F word is fries," she said. "Pull up some greasy food and sit down, girl."

Lily loved Cynthia's stories about John Terman and the daytime talk show. Today Cynthia hurried to the counter where Lily stood. "Here's today's contribution to the betterment of America," she said. "The heartwarming episode where John Terman helps to reunite families is entitled—and I hope you

won't steal this—are you ready? 'Hooker Moms Apologize.' "
Lily laughed and shook her head.

"And guess who had the prestigious job of keeping the hookers from shooting up at the motel this morning so they'd be
sober when they went on the air? You're looking at her, babe.
Everyone else in my class at Harvard is on Wall Street, and I
spend my life around losers and retards."

"And they say show business ain't glamorous," Lily joked,
wondering what in the hell she was going to eat. "A gallery of
processed foods designed to contaminate our digestive sys-
tems," she said. There was never anything remotely nutritious
to eat here. She'd have to start packing a lunch for herself now
that she would be packing Bryan's every morning.

"If I eat a Power Bar, can we call this a power lunch?" she
asked. But then she decided on a strawberry nonfat yogurt instead, paid the cashier, and joined Cynthia at a small table still
wet with round glass prints from the previous diners.

"Bad break about Harry Green," Cynthia said. "Who are they
going to get to replace him?"

"The guys are jazzed about somebody named Charlie Roth.
He's coming in today. Ever heard of him?"

Cynthia nodded. "Yeah. Saw his name go by on some crawl.
Can't remember which."

"The guys call him the God of Jokes. Unfortunately, it'll take
more than jokes to save this show." The yogurt was tart, and
the strawberries tasted synthetically sweet. Lily had an urge to
grab the chili dog out of Cynthia's hand and scarf it down.

"You know, I think I might have heard some stories about
this guy and grabbing ass in the office. Yeah, I think he was
the one. No harassment suit or anything like that. But he's a
lech. Better look out for your tush."

"It's taken," Lily said, flashing her heart-shaped diamond engagement ring that she knew would look even better if she ever had time to give herself a manicure.

"Well, mine's not, so if he's cute, maybe I want his baby."

Lily laughed. "Any men in your life?"

"Men in my life? Please," Cynthia said, throwing her head back and laughing her wonderful, infectious laugh. Lily laughed too. "Now we can really get down to talking about losers and retards."

Lily took a mouthful of yogurt as Cynthia looked at her closely.

"You okay? You look tired," Cynthia said with a furrowed brow.

"Housekeeper quit," Lily said.

"God. Worse than husband leaving. You get anyone new?"

"No time to interview anyone right now."

With Elvira gone, Lily had awakened at six, packed Bryan's lunch, straightened the house, tossed in a load of laundry, made Bryan's breakfast, scrambled into the shower, thrown on clothes, dropped Bryan at school, and hustled to the hospital. No wonder she looked wiped out.

Cynthia glanced at her watch. "Ooops. Have to get the hookers to the airport," she said. She grabbed her shoulder bag from the back of the chair, tossed her trash into a nearby can, and skittered toward the door of the commissary with a flirtatious wave at a good-looking cameraman she passed on her way out.

Lily finished the last of the not-so-hot yogurt and took a deep breath. God of Jokes, she thought, hear my prayer. Keep the show on the air at least until I'm safely married to Mark. Maybe we ought to forget the big wedding in December. Elope now—

this weekend—and sell my place. Bryan and I would move into Mark's pretty house, and I could quit the damn job and coast along for a while.

Sometimes she joked that she had chosen Mark because people fall in love with the person they need, and she fell for a heart specialist because most of her life she'd had a broken heart. When she told him that silly thought on their first date, he smiled a very sexy smile and said, "Not broken. Just in the lost and found, but now I'm here to claim it." How sweetly poetic, she thought, trying to remember where she'd heard that line before. When he put his hand over hers and looked into her eyes—maybe it was the red wine—she had that feeling that started in her face and chest and then rushed to her groin and made her think, Please dear God, let this be the one.

He was handsome, he was sexy, he had a real profession that wouldn't go away or fade out or become obsolete with age the way writing or acting or stand-up comedy did. Doctors could work for as long as they chose, like Jerry Michaels, Bryan's pediatrician, who was well into his sixties. When they got old, they retired and then traveled with their wives all over the world and visited the grandchildren and never had a minute when they worried about the bills. Lily had never had anything close to a calm life like that, and it was what she wanted for herself and for Bryan.

On that night of their first date, she had driven home afterward from the restaurant where they'd met. She had turned on her car radio and laughed out loud when she heard Carole King singing, "You Make Me Feel Like a Natural Woman," because she realized where the poetry had come from. "When my heart was in the lost and found, your love helped me claim it."

It wasn't until later that she realized Mark sometimes talked in song lyrics, because occasionally he had trouble thinking of words of his own. Then there were the hearts. She hadn't thought about them much, and actually found the idea endearing that every gift he gave her was shaped like a heart. Lockets, jewelry boxes, picture frames, and then the engagement ring.

"Juvenile but ingenious," her mother said when Lily told her about it. But so what? Annette, her mother, was without question the most critical human being on the planet.

"Dorky," her sister Daisy said when she saw the ring. Then she smiled and added, "But I love it!"

I love it too, Lily thought as she left the cafeteria and headed for the elevator. This was a man who took his mother out to lunch every Saturday, who'd said he would never marry until he found the perfect woman, and who had proposed to Lily on his fortieth birthday because he'd found her at last. A man who was so good to Bryan it warmed Lily's heart. She was blessed to have such a fine man in her life.

4
◇◇◇◇◇◇◇◇◇◇◇◇◇◇◇◇◇◇◇◇

The elevator doors opened, and Lily stepped on. She was about to push the button for her floor when she saw the poor man approaching. He walked with a kind of rolling motion, from side to side, and his head bobbed as he moved. He must have one of those telethon diseases, she thought, looking away, but felt compelled to look back again at his slightly twisted body and his face with the features slightly askew, like a Picasso portrait.

She managed to force a smile, but the man was too preoccupied to notice. If the damned elevator doors didn't close soon, she was going to be late, and the damned cripple was standing directly in front of the panel of buttons, so in order to push her floor number she'd have to reach across him. Unless, of course, he moved. But he wasn't budging, just standing in that small space in his faded jeans and a Hawaiian shirt, looking pitifully unsure of what to do next. Lily glanced at her watch; it was three minutes to four. The last thing she needed was to wander in late for the big meeting with the hallowed God of Jokes, who was probably up there regaling the boys right now.

Maybe she should just walk up the steps. That's what it said to do in all the health magazines she read. "Don't take the lazy way," the articles chastened. "Make yourself climb the stairs to burn off those extra calories." No. If she left the elevator now it would be too obvious to this man that she was trying to get away from him.

"What floor would you like?" she asked him in a very loud voice. He turned to her with what looked like a smile.

"Fooor."

It might be a question, Lily thought, so probably she should try again a little more distinctly. "That's what I said. Floor. What floor would you like?"

"Fooor" was all he could answer. Lily thought for a minute and then realized that maybe he wasn't saying floor. Maybe he was saying four! That was it, he wanted the fourth floor.

"Are you saying four?" she asked. He nodded. "That's where I'm going too." Lucky for him he was on the elevator with someone so sympathetic or he'd be standing there all day. "Why don't I just push the button for both of us?" she asked, moving gently past him toward the panel of numbers. But as she reached across him, the man lifted his arm and with his gnarled hand moved her arm out of the way.

"Could you hold it down, toots? I'm a cripple, I'm not deaf, and I can push the friggin' button myself," he said.

My God, all she wanted to do was help him. How annoyingly rude, Lily thought. The poor creature. "You're welcome," she said icily.

She really ought to just step off the elevator and burn the calories. Hell, three flights of stairs and she could probably cancel out that bad-tasting yogurt from the commissary. But before she could exit, the elevator doors closed, and she was trapped there until, thank heaven, they opened again on the fourth floor and she hurried down the hall to make a quick check of her makeup in the ladies' room mirror.

Her baby-fine hair looked flyaway and she knew she needed a haircut but never had the time to go to a beauty salon and get one. The new contact lenses she had ordered made her hazel eyes look turquoise today. This had better be a quickie meeting, she thought, pulling a lipstick out of her purse and pressing the maroon color across her lips. Bryan was playing in an important tennis match and she wanted to at least catch the end of it. Harry loved tennis, and he loved Bryan, so on Tuesdays he had always let her leave early.

Dorie was on the phone when Lily ran through the reception area toward the conference room. "They're all in there, and they've started," she said. Lily hurried toward the conference room and opened the door.

All of the others were seated. "Sorry," Lily said, looking right at Marty, who gave her an uncomfortable smile in return. Then she turned and felt as if she'd been kicked in the chest. The crippled man from the elevator, that mean creature, was sitting in Harry's chair. What was he doing there? Where was Charlie Roth? She felt weak. It couldn't be. The man looked amused by her astonished face and said with a twinkle in his eye, "You may not believe this ... but on my planet I'm a hunk."

The guys all laughed at that and Lily's face was hot with embarrassment. He was the God of Jokes. The realization nearly made her let out a giggle but she tried hard to contain it. She could feel that the smile on her face was one of her mother's smiles, which her sister Daisy called the "What-the-fuck-is-going-on-here grin."

With no choice she edged toward the only empty chair at the

table, the one where she always sat when Harry was well, which was just to his right. Now it was next to the God of Jokes. Nobody had told her. How could the boys not have mentioned that Charlie Roth was a serious cripple? David had said she was in for a treat, so probably they all knew. She'd strangle them for that later.

"Don't worry," Charlie said as he stood and pulled the chair out for her. "It isn't contagious. I got this way from too much oxygen in the incubator."

She felt uncomfortable, giddy, and afraid to make eye contact with the others. Certainly in this crowd of wisecrackers somebody was bound to make a joke that would offend him—or worse yet, give her a look that would make her laugh. Maybe this was a joke and the real Charlie Roth couldn't make it, so they brought this guy in from off the street to fool her. A practical joke.

"I was a playwright at Yale," he said, going back to the agenda of the meeting. His voice was backward placed and she found she had to lean in and focus to understand what he was saying. "Most of my background was in the theater. I speak eight languages. Unfortunately, nobody understands me in any of them." The guys laughed. Lily smiled. That *was* kind of funny, she had to give him that.

"I can't talk much faster than this, but that'll work out because pretty soon you'll realize you've learned how to listen slower." Funny, Lily thought. "Sometimes it can be a problem," he went on. "For example, when I watch *60 Minutes* it takes two hours."

That got another yuck from the guys, who were usually stingy with their laughter. They were getting a kick out of this man who, Lily thought, sure had an interesting way of presenting himself. He leads with the glaring fact of his disability.

Shoves it in your face so you can't turn away. Makes jokes about himself before you can even get to the jokes.

"I had to become a writer," Charlie said next. He was doing a routine to put them all at ease. "Because I couldn't get work in my chosen profession."

The men were mesmerized by him. Bruno even jumped in to give him a straight line. "What profession was that, Charlie?"

The one-word punch line was a little garbled so Lily missed it, but she knew it must be funny by the laugh that erupted from the guys. So as Charlie went on to tell the others what his plans were for the show, she wrote the words on her legal pad WHAT DID HE SAY? Then she passed it to Bruno, who passed it back with the punch line. AUCTIONEER. Hah! That was funny.

His presentation was painstakingly slow. It took a forty-five-minute explanation, only some of which Lily understood, for him to compare *Angel's Devils* to the other shows on the air. And by the time he was summarizing and getting to the part about how he was going to change things, she sneaked a peek at her watch and knew that if she didn't leave that instant, she'd be late.

Some Tuesdays she had just enough time to grab Bryan and take him for a quick dinner before she either came back to CBS or worked at home to finish a project. But at least she got to see her baby's face. How was she going to stand up now and explain her departure to the troglodyte in the middle of the show's crisis? She knew she'd have to brave it, so she stood.

"Sorry," she said, hating that her voice suddenly sounded so childlike.

"You have some kind of a medical problem?" Charlie asked. "I saw you walk into the ladies' room an hour ago." Lily felt her face flush, and she tried to push through and sound confident instead of apologetic.

"Since Tuesday's usually a light day for the show, Harry was always fine with my leaving early to pick up my son at his tennis game?" she said, and knew because of her timidity it must have sounded like a question. Charlie looked at her with no reaction. The guys were quiet. Bryan was waiting and she really had to go. She thought about turning and heading out, but she was still hoping for a nod of understanding; none was forthcoming. She couldn't add, "Is that all right with you?" because he was liable to say no, and she'd have to sit down or leave against his wishes.

The pause rang in her ears as Marty tapped a pencil uncomfortably.

"In case you've forgotten," Charlie drawled, "Harry's currently in a number of small pieces in an urn on his wife's night table. So unless you're planning to fire up a glue gun, after today the kid takes the bus. This is a war room, Mommy. Not the PTA bake sale."

The ugly, nasty gargoyle, Lily thought. Insulting Harry's memory and her in the bargain. And what could she do? She managed a nod, grabbed her notebook and purse, and hurried out the door and down the hall to the elevator. Maybe Harry was right in his pronouncement from his deathbed. It probably was time for her to look for a job somewhere else.

In the parking lot, Lily walked rapidly toward her Jeep. Auctioneer, she said in a whisper to herself, trying to pronounce it in the weird way that Charlie Roth had. The Jeep needed washing. Even from a distance she could spot how dirty it looked. But she still smiled at the vanity plate Daisy had bought her a few years ago for her birthday: HAHAHA. "Perfect for a comedy writer," was what her funky, crazy sister had said. God, that Charlie Roth was a monster, she thought. She was still smarting from the obnoxious way he'd insulted her, as if she were some fool who didn't pull her weight on the show.

She'd never thought of herself as bigoted or small-minded, but surely people like that had to overcompensate for their terrible lives by lashing out at others. Pitiful, she thought, shaking her head as she headed toward the school.

5

◇◇◇◇◇◇◇◇◇◇◇◇◇◇◇◇◇◇◇◇◇

Once, when he was five or six years old, Lily had asked Bryan, "If someone wanted you to describe your mother, what would you say?" He only gave it about ten seconds, then brightened with a face that told her he'd come up with the perfect answer.

"She's a lousy athlete."

Lily had laughed out loud. "That's it? That's the essence of me? I'm a lousy athlete?"

"Sorry, Mom."

He was right. In high school she had begged to be allowed to take the dance option so she could avoid PE. The ugly uniforms, the sweaty attempts at dull games, and living in perpetual fear that the softball, puck, volleyball, or Frisbee might come too fast and thwack her. A lousy athlete—and yet Bryan, with no father and with Lily for a mother, was a miraculously fluid and powerful tennis player.

She could see him playing with great intensity out there as she pulled into the parking lot. As she ambled toward the tennis courts, she took off her blazer in the warmth of the sunny day. She loved hearing that little grunt Bryan made before he hit the ball. Kimberly, his pretty, wild-haired girlfriend, was in the stands taking a video of the game. Bryan slammed the ball, Kim shrieked out "Yes," and Bryan moved to the net to shake the hand of his opponent, a nervous-looking blond boy with floppy hair and a fuchsia face.

By the time Lily arrived at the bleachers, Bryan was off the court and wrapping his sinewy, sweaty self around Kimberly.

"Kicked his butt," he bragged. Kim gave him a light kiss, then unwound his arms from her.

"Bry, your mother's here," she said, not sure she felt okay about Lily watching him grab her.

"Looking pretty good out there, boy," Lily said.

"You look like you've been crying. You okay?"

"Harry Green died this morning."

"Oh, jeez. Sorry, Mom." He hugged her and looked down at her face. "Who they gonna get?" Kim zipped Bryan's racquet into the case, then picked up her purse, and they walked with Lily back toward the car.

"They already got. They were all excited, saying they were bringing in the God of Jokes, so I was picturing a Neil Simon, a Larry Gelbart, a Buck Henry. So an hour or so ago a guy shows up, and they all know him, and he has one of those weird diseases like MD, CP, MS. What's it called when they move like this?" she asked, moving her hands back and forth in front of her.

"The macarena," Bryan said, and Kimberly giggled as they threw their bags in ahead of them and then climbed into Lily's car.

"Sure. You can laugh," Lily said. "I'm going to have to be funny in a room with him every day. How can I be loose when I have to worry about all those things you worry about with people like that? Trying not to stare, wondering if you're supposed to open the door for them or let them be independent, tiptoeing around what you say so it doesn't offend them. They must have been desperate to find somebody to jump into Harry's spot, because I can't imagine this man creating a real great climate for comedy."

"Is he funny?" Bryan asked.

Lily nodded. "Very funny."

"So who cares how he looks?" Bryan asked, pulling a water bottle out of his duffel bag and taking a long swig.

"Yuk," Kimberly said. "I'd never be able to hang around with someone like that. I'd be totally grossed out."

On Thursday the ghoul sent all the writers off to work independently, asking them to meet with him at the end of the day to talk about their ideas. Somehow the guys ended up together behind closed doors. Every now and then Marty's hoot of a laugh would rise or Dave's usual critique: "Piece of dog shit. Next." And when Lily heard them, she was jealous that she was left out and didn't have someone pitching with her.

Come on, brain, she thought, closing her eyes to try and call up the thousands of sitcoms she'd watched. She had seen so many of them that she knew most of their plot lines by heart. She took pride in the fact that after watching less than one minute of an episode of *Taxi,* she could identify the entire story.

"Alex bumps into his ex-wife! Jim's father dies!"

Maybe she could try a turn on one of those stories. She had noodled some ideas onto the computer screen, and now with the light coming in the window she looked at the screen and saw Charlie reflected in it. He was peering over her shoulder and reading what she had typed. "Don't like anything you have there. What else are you thinking about?"

It was a sneak attack. She wasn't supposed to be ready until the three o'clock meeting, but maybe she could extemporize.

"Well, I was going to pitch that Angel's father has to go to the hospital, and her mother moves in with her, and they're at each other's throats. But then I remembered seeing that on *Rhoda* reruns so I decided to move on."

Charlie perched on the edge of her desk and waited for her to continue. He was wearing his usual Hawaiian shirt and faded jeans, and he smelled of some cologne that she liked. And she was getting used to him. Looking into his eyes. Not afraid of his odd, crooked look anymore. "So then I was going to try the idea that Angel thinks Joey is trying to murder her, but then I remembered seeing Lucille Ball do that on an *I Love Lucy* episode, and it was so brilliant I didn't want to touch it."

"Too domestic," he said. "Get quirky."

Quirky, quirky, what could that mean? "You mean like the 'Road Not Taken' episode of *Taxi*? Or the 'Walnut' episode of *Dick Van Dyke*?"

Charlie smiled his toothy smile. "You're a regular sitcom savant, aren't you?"

Lily nodded. "I know more about the Partridge family than my own."

"Did you set out to learn all the shows on purpose? You were just a baby when *The Dick Van Dyke* show was on the air."

"I stay up late. There are reruns. There's Nick at Night. I've watched them all a million times. My insane mother is a travel agent who fell in love with travel, so she was never there, and I watched television because home meant me and my sister, usually all alone. Then for a while I was married to a man who *was* there but only in body—Bryan's father. He's a would-be producer. Wheeling and dealing and never selling anything. Or so he said every time I made the mistake of asking him why he wasn't supporting his son. The point is, television was my friend. It made me laugh, it didn't get mad at me or leave. So I am its loyal slave."

Charlie was nodding, or maybe, Lily thought, his head always made that infinitesimal motion even when the rest of him was still.

"More than you wanted to know?" she asked.

"Not at all."

"I have an idea," Lily said, changing the subject. Why had she told him all of that about her life? How stupid. He wasn't interested in the details of her life, just the number of pages she could turn out every week. Back to the show, she thought, and no more of this chummy chitchat. "We're talking quirky," she said. "Ready?"

"I'm sitting down," he said, settling into the chair by her desk.

"Angel is caught in an avalanche and is rescued by the Abominable Snowman. She thinks it was a dream, but when she gets home he starts calling her—because he's in love."

Charlie let out a giggle that was a funny cross between a squeal and a laugh. "Bring it to me when you flesh it out," he said. "And speaking of flesh," he said, looking out into the reception area at Dorie, who was dressed in a too-short skirt and a cropped sweater that left a few inches of bare midriff displayed, "you," he called out, "with too much of it showing. I have some pages in my office I want you to copy."

As Dorie got up from her desk and sauntered across the reception area toward his office, Charlie watched her with unbridled admiration. Lily put her hand on his arm and looked into his eyes with great seriousness. "If I were you I'd be careful about saying things like that around here these days. It could be perceived as sexual harassment."

"Only if it interferes with her job performance or her civil rights," he said. By now Dorie was coming out of his office waving the pages at him to be sure they were the right ones. He nodded and grinned at her. "Do I interfere with your job performance or your civil rights, you proof of a benevolent God?" he asked.

Dorie smiled at him. "You're adorable."

Lily was irritated at the interaction. She had gone to several meetings of the Women's Committee of the Writer's Guild when they had talked for hours about how to get men to understand that they couldn't ogle women in the workplace. Dorie should know better and so should this man. "Totally inappropriate," Lily said. "But you think you can get away with it because you're a—"

"Nonthreatening cripple?" Charlie interrupted, and Lily reddened. "You're right! I'm so uncoordinated I'd probably end up copping a feel of her hat!" His own joke got another laugh out of him, and he walked out of the office as Lily wondered what had possessed her to suggest that preposterous Abominable Snowman idea. She had no clue how she was ever going to make it work. She stood to close her office door so she could sit down and hammer out the story points, and just before she did Charlie was back in the doorway.

"But don't start thinking of me as some kind of mascot around here either," he said, grinning that gooney grin of his. "You yourself could fall madly in love with me."

In your dreams, she thought. "Not me," she said, holding out her left hand to show off her glistening diamond. "I'm promised."

Charlie moved closer and leaned in to look at the stone. "To a guy who gave you a diamond shaped like a heart?" He asked it in a way that was clearly mocking.

"It's shaped that way because my fiancé is a cardiologist."

Charlie grinned. "I'd hate to see what the diamond would look like if he were a urologist." His own joke cracked him up, but Lily, who wasn't amused, closed the door, then sat down to write her script.

6

"People relate to food the way they learned to at their family dinner table," Daisy told Lily as they moved along on adjacent treadmills at the Sports Club L.A. Lily was running; Daisy was strolling. "That's what this book I'm reading says. So people who have eating disorders got them from their parents and can never look at food in an objective way. For example, our mother never cooked a meal in her life."

It was true. Annette Gordon worked at Star Travel all day and at dinnertime she threw take-out food, still in the paper containers, on the table and then assailed her daughters with her own unhappiness while they ate.

"Your father and his bride are in Sarasota, Florida, where they just bought a house on the water," she'd say, picking at the food on her plate. "But me he sends checks so small they're not even worth the time I'd have to take to walk to the bank."

On some nights Daisy would wolf down the food, hoping the good taste would counterbalance the unhappy stories her mother was making her hear. On other nights she wouldn't touch a thing at the table, and when Annette had finished eating and gone upstairs—the girls were expected to clean the kitchen—Lily ran the hot water and poured the soap powder into the sink while Daisy ate all the leftovers. Lily still had very little interest in sitting down at a big meal and was picky about what she ate when she did. Which was another reason Mark was the perfect man for her, because he cooked lovely meals that were so spartan Daisy refused to come to dinner "for fear I'll starve to death while I'm at the table."

Daisy had joined Overeaters Anonymous, and every morning she checked in on the phone with her gentle-voiced sponsor and told the woman what sensible foods she planned to eat that day, and the sponsor gave her support. Once a week she went to a meeting where she admitted that she was out of control of her eating and talked with the group about her food addiction and the forces in her life that made her feel out of control. The others urged her to stay with the program and work it and complete the steps, and she said that she would. Then she would rush home and eat a banana cream pie.

"Why do you even have a pie in the house?" Lily asked her. They were in the big, sweaty, noisy room at the health club, a place Lily swore she was going to quit because she rarely had time to go there, especially now that Elvira was gone. How would she ever be able to replace her?

MTV videos blazed on overhead monitors. Lily was running and out of breath while she talked. Daisy moved as if she were window-shopping on Rodeo Drive.

"Because you never know when company could drop in and then a pie comes in handy?" she ventured.

"You never have company, so don't even try that on me. Annette brought you those gorgeous pasta bowls from Italy and you never had anyone over to show them off."

"I use them when I eat SpaghettiOs for breakfast," Daisy

said, making Lily wince. "Hey, I live alone. So I never cook. Six pasta bowls means six days of SpaghettiOs and not washing a dish."

"I don't care about the dishes, I care that you're eating that garbage."

"Don't start. I'm going to OA. I'm working on it."

Lily looked at her high-strung, chunky younger sister and knew there was truth in what her mother had said the day Lily called to tell her she'd gotten her first comedy writing job. "Well, that's a surprise. I always think of Daisy as the funny one."

Daisy was pretty damn funny but she couldn't get it together to write anything down, to have proper pictures taken to audition for acting parts, so a job that began as part-time work was her career. Selling at a large Target store in the San Fernando Valley. When you phoned her at home, her voice on the answering machine said, "Good afternoon, Target guests."

"So will you tell them about the pie at OA?" Lily asked, pushing the down arrow on the treadmill to lower the speed. She glanced at Daisy, whose face was full of pain.

"Probably not," Daisy answered glumly.

"What made you eat it?"

Daisy thought. "Mother called last week to ask me about your wedding," she said. "All she cares about is one thing."

"Let me guess," Lily said. "What everyone's wearing?" she tried, watching the numbers go down and checking to be sure she'd run for forty-five minutes.

Daisy nodded as she wrapped a towel around her neck and slowed her own treadmill so she could step off. "Most of all she's worried about what *she's* wearing, naturally. But after that comes what I'm wearing so I don't embarrass her to death in front of a bunch of people she doesn't know."

Lily clutched the railing of the treadmill. In the mirror, across

the room she could see a dark-skinned, dark-haired man, and
she felt weak. My God, she thought. That's Ernesto! But when
the man turned she saw it was one of the club's janitors picking
up a trash can, and he looked nothing like Ernesto.

"Dais, I'm scared," Lily said.

"About the wedding?"

"No, because Ernesto has been parking outside my house
every night this week. He must think I'm hiding Elvira."

"Jeez, call the police," Daisy said.

"I did. They won't do anything."

"Tell Mark. Hire a bodyguard."

"I keep hoping that once he realizes Elvira's not there he'll
go away. He has no argument with me. The times he came to
pick her up I was very nice to him. I'm so worried about poor
Elvira. She wouldn't even tell me where she was going so I
wouldn't have to lie for her."

"Yeah, Elvie in hiding. It's so sad," Daisy agreed, then put
her hand on Lily's arm. "Don't worry, he'll realize soon that
she's not coming back, and then he'll go away." Lily sighed.
Maybe it was that simple, and she was scaring herself for no
reason.

Bryan was lifting a barbell and Kimberly was spotting for
him across the room. The two sisters watched them now.

"Look at that gorgeous body, that fabulous face. And Kim
ain't bad, either," Daisy joked. "The kid is gonna be a star
someday and I can sell my story of how I changed his diaper
to *People* magazine."

"Those shoes he's wearing cost seventy bucks a pop, and I
wish he'd stop outgrowing the damn things so fast." Lily
sighed. "So I hope he becomes rich and famous and starts paying for them himself." Bryan saw his mother and his aunt
watching him and waved. "He needs a father," Lily said, wav-

ing back. "By December he'll have Mark as a stepfather and that'll be really good for him."

"Yeah, it's a little rough when the most masculine person in his life is his gay aunt," Daisy joked. "Which takes me back to the question I was going to ask. Would you mind if I wore a tuxedo in the wedding?"

"I'd think it was just fine," Lily said, putting an arm around Daisy, and they headed for the ladies' locker room.

In the shower she had that oxygenated, pumped-up feeling she always got when she finished a workout. She wasn't going to worry about Ernesto. He'd have to give up parking out there soon. And she certainly wasn't going to aggravate herself or let Daisy aggravate her with stories about their crazy mother. No. She was lucky to have this life. Supporting herself with her work, having a son who was full of life and joy and fun, and having a man who wanted to marry her and take care of her forever. Angelic Mark, her darling lover. He was comfortable and sweet in bed. Not blazing hot the way Donald used to be.

Even after Bryan was born, Donald would slide open the shower door and slip in to make love to her there, or while a baby-sitter waited for their return he would pull over and park on Mulholland Drive and drag her into the backseat. She remembered those nights he'd call her after a meeting and get her so aroused that she'd shoo Bryan off to bed and rush to the door the minute he walked in and collapse with him on the living room couch. This romance with Mark was calmer than that, and calm was good. This was adult. This was a father for Bryan, which he needed so much.

With her hair still wet she met Daisy, Bryan, and Kim in the lobby of the club. Just as they stepped out the door onto Sepulveda Boulevard, the cacophony of honking horns turned their heads, and they all stopped to watch a procession of cars

fly by that was carrying a wedding party. The first car was
soaped with the words JUST MARRIED and festooned with crepe
paper. Each of the four of them was quiet with fantasies of his
or her own. Not one of them moved until the last car passed.
Then Lily saw Kim whisper something to Bryan that made him
blush, and he threw an arm around her.

"If I get married," Lily said, "promise you won't do that to
my car."

"Promise," Bryan said, turning to take the car keys from her
and hurrying ahead to open the tailgate of the Jeep so everyone
could dump their bags in.

"Do you know you just said 'If I get married?'" Daisy asked
her, watching Lily's face carefully.

"Did I? I meant when."

"You sure?"

The kids were far enough ahead now so that Lily could tell
Daisy about what Mark had told her the night before. "He says
he can't wait until we're married so he can make me a lady of
leisure."

Daisy let out a sharp sound that was a combination sneer
and laugh. "Obviously, you never told him about the fiendish
Pencilstiltskin," she said, and Lily laughed.

"What's so funny?" Bryan asked as they got into the car.

"Pencilstiltskin," Lily said. Bryan laughed too as they all
climbed into the car.

"What does that mean?" Kim asked.

"When my mom was little, she liked to go to her room and
write stories," Bryan explained. "And Aunt Daisy wanted to
play. So my mom told her there was this freaky little man who
came in the night and told her if she didn't turn blank pieces
of paper into stories he'd do something evil."

"Not something evil," Daisy corrected him. "It was very specific what the evil was going to be. If she didn't write the stories, the little freak was taking *me* away."

Lily pulled the Jeep out onto Sepulveda Boulevard. "It scared the shit out of me," Daisy said. "I would actually push her in there and beg her to work on her stories and then I'd stay up all night peeking under my locked door waiting for him to come and check on Lily's work. She got rid of me that way a few times a week with some made-up monster who read her pages over her shoulder."

"I didn't make him up," Lily said. "Now he has a job on my show."

That made all of them laugh again.

7

At the *Angel's Devils* office the writers had been pitching out a story together all day long. It was early evening, the time when the guys liked to light cigars, so Lily would take her defensive position on the windowsill, where she opened the window as wide as possible, hoping to avoid the stinky smoke, which always lingered in her hair and in her clothes. The cigars were the reason she always wore old jeans and T-shirts to work. These days she threw them into the washing machine before she went to bed to get the thick, acrid odor of cigar smoke out.

Elvira used to do that washing for her. Elvira, whom she hadn't been able to replace. Two flaky candidates for the job had come to the house. One of them was pregnant and threw up in Lily's bathroom before the interview. The second one submitted a list of all the things she didn't do, like boys' shirts and floors and windows, and Lily sent her out the door. To hell with it, she'd do the work herself. And somehow maybe Elvira would solve her problems and come back.

Where could she be? Lily thanked heaven that Ernesto's truck hadn't been outside her building for several nights. He must have finally realized his wife was no longer there.

"Cigars are a phase," Dorie told her now as she passed

through the reception area to go to the ladies' room. "They're chic right now. Remember when the boys were into muffins and the muffin lady used to come by and they'd drop everything and rush to check out her cooler?"

"It wasn't her cooler, Dor. It was the way she leaned over the cooler," Lily answered. "And the muffins didn't make me nauseous. The smoke is killing me. The only one who doesn't light up is Charlie."

"Probably afraid he'll miss the cigar and light his nose," Dorie said and then laughed at her own joke.

All of them had taken to joking about Charlie, doing their respective imitations of him to the delight of the others. Marty's were the funniest—he sounded a little like a punch-drunk boxer. But Lily, who practiced the facial expressions in her bathroom mirror at home, had the slightly contorted face down perfectly so that when she did her imitation for Marty he would lose it.

David did the walk the best. He'd perfected that little rolling movement and would do it when Charlie left the conference room. Never when Charlie was anywhere around him, of course. That would be mean. But they were comedy writers, after all, and part of their code was that nothing was sacred.

"Hey, Lil, get back in here," Marty hollered.

Lily went reluctantly back and hopped up on the windowsill.

"Okay. If we use the credit card story, what's the blow?" Charlie asked. The end, the punch line to the story was always the hardest part of the pitch. There was a long silence.

"I think we use the blow Harry tried on us the day before he died," Marty said.

"What was it?" Charlie asked.

"Angel comes home and tells Joey she wants a divorce,"

Bruno said. "It's a two-parter and we come back next week and find out why."

"Yeah, and what did Harry say was why?" Charlie asked.

"He checked out before we asked him."

"Then getting him on the phone is out of the question," Charlie said.

"With all due respect to Harry's memory, it was a lousy blow no matter what happens in part two," Lily offered from her spot on the windowsill. Marty, Bruno, and David all had cigars going now, and the only way for her to survive was to keep the window wide open. "It's not consistent with this show. Angel and Joey's solid marriage is the foundation for all of our stories."

"I think it's funny," Marty said. "Maybe we get Joey thinking she's shtooping another guy."

"Yeah," Bruno said. "Jealous Joey is a great idea. Nicky could play jealous great." Nicky Lord, the actor who played Joey, was a former stand-up comic with exquisite timing and a rubber face. It was true he'd be funny playing jealousy, but the concept was wrong. Lily knew she'd have to fight to get them to see her point.

"It has no integrity, guys. It's smarmy."

"Have her shtoop someone elegant. Cary Grant," Marty said.

"He's dead," Bruno reminded him.

"That would make it smarmy," David said.

The guys were puffing on their cigars, and Marty was pacing the way Harry used to when he was well. Lily saw that Charlie was watching the battle lines being drawn. The men wanted Angel to have a lover, or at least for it to appear as if she did.

"She shtoops someone from another species like on that Jerry Springer show."

"She shtoops someone from another sitcom. Intersitcom shtooping."

"No," Lily said. She wasn't going to lose this one. They were having a testosterone fest and forgetting the nature of the show. "Look back, fellas. In every successful half-hour show the couples may have fought, but their marriages were rock solid. Even the supporting couples. Fred and Ethel, Ed Norton and Trixie, Blanche and Harry. They never had affairs." Lily could feel Charlie looking at her. The smoke in the room was so heavy her eyes were watering.

"The sitcom historian strikes again," Charlie said. "I like this broad. She's the one you need when you're hammering out a story. No precedent for extramarital shtooping? She's right. Let's drop it."

Charlie stood and Lily couldn't believe it when she saw him pull out a cigar from the pocket of his Hawaiian shirt. At the same time Bruno whipped a gold lighter out of his pocket and held the flame to the end of the cigar while Charlie puffed away.

"My God," Lily said. "Not you too! Stop lighting that right now! I have inhaled so much smoke this week I could be on the cover of *Cigar Aficionado.*"

David rolled his eyes as if he were thinking, This is what happens when you have broads working on a show. But so what, she thought. This was unbearable. And it had been going on for so long she could get sick from it.

"Keep talking in that shrill voice," Charlie said, "and you'll be on the cover of *Whine Connoisseur.*"

"It isn't fair," Lily said.

No one looked at her.

"I mean it," she said heatedly. "If you don't put those things out, I'm going somewhere where I can breathe."

Charlie put his cigar in the ashtray.

"I think you're going there now," he said, and in one swift move that came so quickly she wasn't prepared, he seized her and, holding her tightly around the ankles, thrust the rest of her out the window. As she shrieked in terror four stories above the parking lot, he held her out there upside down. She could see the cars below her and among them a group of people who had stopped to look as the blood rushed to her face. She could hear Marty, who must have jumped to his feet in a panic and run to the window, followed by Bruno. Who knew if this lunatic even had enough control not to drop her, head first, into the parking lot?

"Make sure she doesn't die on my car," David said, puffing away on his cigar.

"Going a little too far for the joke, guy," Marty said, hoping he wasn't going to alarm the nutcase into dropping Lily.

"Not at all," Charlie said, sounding very relaxed. "It's a comedy tradition. I heard the story about how Sid Caesar did this to Mel Brooks when they were working on *Your Show of Shows*, one day when Mel complained about the stuffy room." Then he hollered out the window to Lily, "Breathe deeply, doll, and remember what this did for Mel's career."

But Bruno and Marty leaned out the window and grabbed Lily around the waist and pulled her in. Her hair stood on end, her face was beet red, and she was filled with rage.

"Are you insane?" she screamed at Charlie. "You could have dropped me. I have a child to raise. I'm turning you in to the Writer's Guild. I'm taking out an ad in the trade papers to tell everyone you're certifiably out of your mind."

And she stormed out of the room, nauseous and humiliated. In the ladies' room mirror she looked at herself and shook her head at how horrifying she looked. This man had to go. She would do anything in her power to get rid of him. God of Jokes indeed. Shit. One of her earrings was gone. It must have fallen when the beast from forty thousand fathoms was holding her upside down. No. She wasn't going back in there. First she would go to the parking lot and see if she could retrieve her earring, and then she'd take the rest of the evening off. She'd call Mark, tell him to go get Bryan and meet her at Santo Pietro's for pizza. I hate this man. I miss Harry. What am I going to do? she thought. Then she leaned against the ladies' room wall and cried.

Three or at the most four sips of wine made her feel melty and weak in the legs, and the strangest symptom of all was the way she got inexplicably weepy. Tonight the tears were easy to explain. She had lost her mentor, she'd lost her housekeeper, she'd probably lost her job because even if she took Charlie to the Writer's Guild, what was the charge? He'd say "It was a comedy show, I was doing comedy." So her choice was to either start a big riot over his behavior or to forget it and go back in to work tomorrow as if nothing had happened.

"The guy's funny, Mom. He didn't drop you, did he?" Bryan was trying to calm her.

"He's not funny. I hate him," she said. "He's a poor, miserable man, and he's taking it out on me."

"And you're crying?" Mark asked.

They were sitting in Santo Pietro's eating their dinner and Lily still felt shaky from the day's events. There was nothing left of the large vegetarian pizza she and Mark and Bryan had shared but the end of a piece of crust, which she picked up and chewed as a tear fell on the now empty plate. "I miss Harry, and I'm probably allergic to the sulfides in red wine, and I think

I'm losing my sense of humor. One of my earrings fell off and I found it under a car in the parking lot and it was dented beyond recognition. I ought to send him a bill. The rat."

"For some reason unknown to medical science, if she has less than half a glass of wine she becomes weepy and sad," Mark said to Bryan. Then a bubbly, ringing sound interrupted his thought and he grabbed for the cell phone in the holder clipped at his waist.

"This is Dr. Freeman," he said into the phone, then frowned. "Meet you there." He put the phone back in the holder and stood. "Got to run. A transplant patient is coming by ambulance from Broad Beach. He's having some serious problems so I'm going to meet him at Cedars." He leaned across the table, picked up Lily's car keys, and handed them to Bryan.

"You with the learner's permit. I recommend you be the designated driver." He put some cash on the check where it sat in a little plastic tray, kissed Lily on the top of the head, and was gone.

"C'mon, Mom," Bryan said. "You need a good night's sleep."

"I'll probably have nightmares about being a bat," she joked. "Hanging upside down from a tree."

Bryan handled the Jeep well, and Lily was confident that he'd get them home safely even though a light rain was beginning to fall.

"I hate rain," Lily muttered. "So naturally it's raining. Dorie would probably say some spacey thing like 'Mercury is in retrograde' because so many crummy things are happening."

Bryan drove south on Beverly Glen, and just as he was about to make a wide left into the driveway, he stopped.

"Isn't that Ernesto's truck?" he asked.

"Oh God," Lily wailed. "Why doesn't he stop this?"

It was raining harder now, and Lily's headiness from the wine was gone.

"Stop what, Mom?" Bryan asked.

"He's been coming here, parking here, calling the house."

"How come you never told me?"

"I didn't want to scare you. I think he's desperate to find Elvira," Lily said, her voice sounding shaky to her ears.

"Think I should get out and tell him she's not here any-more?" Bryan asked.

"No. I have to get out and talk to him," she said, opening the passenger door of the Jeep.

"Mom, he's a beater. Elvie told us he was dangerous."

"It'll be fine. He has no quarrel with me. I'll just tell him I don't know where she is. Maybe that'll end it," Lily said as she opened the door wider and climbed out into the dark, rainy night.

The moment Ernesto spotted her getting out, he opened the door of the white pickup truck and got out too. He was slim and wiry and as they walked toward each other, despite her fear, Lily chuckled inside, thinking it felt like the showdown in *High Noon*. Tomorrow she'd tell Marty this story and they would laugh about it.

"Ernesto," she began.

"Where's Elvira?" he asked, and she saw his narrow eyes and hunched shoulders as he moved closer.

"I don't know. She didn't tell me where she was—"

"Did she go with some guy?"

"Don't be silly." In spite of the chilly night, Lily was sweat-ing.

"That's a fuckin' lie," he said, and then she heard the Jeep door close and she knew Bryan had stepped out of the car, probably because he saw Ernesto looking so menacing and he was worried about his mother. Ernesto's eyes moved to Bryan but quickly went back to Lily. He was certain that she had the answers he wanted.

"No, it's not a lie," she said, trying to keep her voice even.

"You tell me where you're hiding my wife." Even from the distance of a few yards she could smell the sour alcohol on his breath. She felt the panic in her chest and tried to think of some way she could back down and hurry inside.

Later, when she looked back on it, she realized that this was the moment in which she already knew, when she had the sickening realization that their lives were about to change inalterably.

"Mom." Bryan's voice had an hysterical edge. "He's got a gun."

Now she saw the glint of the gun in Ernesto's hand as he raised it toward her and it caught the glow of the streetlight.

"No!" she screamed as he shot and blessedly missed her.

"Mom, get out of the way," Bryan called as Ernesto spun away from Lily and aimed the gun at Bryan. Bryan turned to run, and Lily screamed from a place so deep inside her it rang through the street and resounded from the buildings. Then Bryan was lying on the ground near the Jeep, and Lily was frozen to the spot, looking first at him and then at Ernesto, who swaggered back to the truck, climbed inside, and drove away without turning on the headlights. Just the way he had on all of those nights when she should have begged the police to come. Oh God, oh God, please don't let this happen to my boy.

Somehow, Lily stumbled to the place where her son was lying. She could sense lights flipping on in the apartment buildings all around.

"I called 911," she heard someone say.

"It's that nice young boy, what a shame," someone else said.

Lily was shivering and on her knees next to Bryan, who was lying on his side, ghostly pale.

"Somebody help us! Please do something!"

"I love you, Mom," Bryan said, and she knew by the way he said it that he thought he was dying.

"I love you too," she said with as much resolve in her voice as she could summon. "And I'm not going to let anything bad happen to you."

The crowd was closing in on them, some of the people held open umbrellas over Lily and Bryan, and then the shrill scream of an ambulance mercifully cut through the rainy night. As it approached, the crowd of neighbors parted to allow it to pull near to where Bryan lay, and the two paramedics climbed out and hurried to kneel next to him. They talked to each other in cryptic language, and Lily was too numb to try and decipher what they were saying. One of them leaned over Bryan and the other went back to retrieve something from the ambulance.

"I'm his mother," Lily said. "Please tell me what—"

"We have to move him, fast," the one who returned immediately from the truck told her as a police car stopped and two policemen moved to where the paramedics were cutting off Bryan's jacket. Then Lily saw the blood, so much blood. They worked a pair of inflatable trousers onto his legs, eased him onto a gurney and into the back of the ambulance. Lily crawled in too. Bryan reached for her hand just before they pulled the doors shut and sped off into the night.

8

❖❖❖❖❖❖❖❖❖❖❖❖❖❖❖❖❖❖

Annette had a variety of smiles that she called upon for all occasions, and both Lily and Daisy could tell by the specific smile she chose exactly how she was feeling about every situation. There was her you-are-beneath-contempt smile, which she gave to people she called "worker bees," such as parking lot attendants or the would-be actresses who worked as waitresses in many L.A. restaurants. Then there was her smile for the camera when anyone took her picture, for which she threw back her head and flashed her teeth in a wide grin that she hoped detracted from the recent advent of jowls on either side of her mouth.

But the unparalleled favorite of both of her daughters was the one Daisy referred to as the you-ain't-gonna-get-me smile. It was the one she struggled to keep on her face when she faced a situation she found appalling.

"You're gay, darling girl?" she said to Daisy the day Daisy finally made herself blurt out the truth to Annette, whose lips moved into the turned-up position. "Well, that's certainly a piece of news I suspected I'd be hearing one day. And will you be bringing the young woman home? I certainly hope she's not black." And then she laughed a laugh that was supposed to mean she was just joking, but she wasn't.

Daisy swore she could hear that particular smile when she finally located Annette to tell her about Bryan.

"I told her years ago to fire that Elvira, and now it's come back to haunt her," Annette said.

"Mother," Daisy screamed into the phone, "your grandchild, maybe the only one you'll ever have, will never walk again, and you're trying to get credit for being right about firing the maid? Get in the fucking car, goddamn it, go to the airport, and come here to comfort your daughter."

"Oh, dear. I think I'd just be in the way," she said. Daisy wanted to rip the phone out of the wall.

"Make a point not to be in the way. Come to help. Clean her house, receive packages, make food. Okay, I take that part back. No food. But for once in our lives, will you fucking be there?"

"I hear what your message is, and I understand the emotion behind it," Annette said calmly.

"Don't do your imitation of Marianne Williamson! Get your ass to L.A. Now! Where are you, anyway? Where the hell is the 970 area code?"

"I'm in Telluride. I just got here. It's women's ski week."

Ah, that was the problem. It wasn't that she thought she'd get in the way in L.A. Her reluctance to come was because she'd plunked down some hefty price to stay at The Peaks in Telluride and she'd probably lose her deposit if she left for L.A. now. Without saying another word, Daisy replaced the phone on its hook and walked over to where Lily was sitting in the hospital waiting room. "Someday," Daisy said, "we'll write our mutual autobiography and call it *Without Benefit of Annette*."

"Not coming," Lily said. "What a surprise."

Mark sat on one side of her and Marty on the other. Bruno sat on the floor, and Kimberly and her mother, Robin, were on a small sofa that stood against the wall. Robin was an art teacher, blond and fresh-looking with hair pulled straight back into a ponytail. Kim looked like her father, with big, dark eyes and tons of curly black hair. At the moment she was asleep, with her head on her mother's lap.

Lily had located Mark the minute after the ambulance arrived at Cedars-Sinai hospital and Mark immediately called Roger Kramer, a spinal cord specialist. Roger had been in Bryan's room off and on all night. Two hours ago he'd told all of them that though Bryan was in spinal shock, it was evident that he would come out of this a paraplegic. Everyone was silent except Kimberly, who blurted out the naïve question, "For how long?" Nobody had the heart to reply, but her mother's tight-jawed face told her the answer, and she bit her lip and cried silently.

Dr. Kramer came down the hall now, looking for Lily. "He wants to see you," he told her.

What do I say to him? Lily felt a chill wondering how much Bryan already knew and what he was thinking. When he was a toddler and had an ear infection and the medication hadn't yet taken effect, Lily would carry him from room to room, his feverish face against her cool one, singing to some made-up tune, "It's okay, Mommy's right here. It's okay, Mommy's right here." But there was no way to say that this would be okay. In fact, maybe it never would be again. And now she had to tell him that. Tell him to forget the prom, the tennis scholarship, and God knows what he would do about sex. Lily took a deep breath and tried to create some semblance of composure as she made her way into the room.

Bryan was flat on his back, his eyes were open, and the machines were blipping, and that was the only sound in the room. But he must have heard the door open and close because before he saw her face he spoke.

"Mom?"

"I'm here, baby."

She walked close to the bed. He looked very young and pale and afraid.

"You don't have to tell me what the doctor said about me. I knew it the minute I hit the ground."

Lily leaned over him and put her face against his, and when she felt his tears on her cheek she put her arms around him as best she could.

"Mom," he asked. "How am I gonna live like this?"

Now her tears mingled with his and for a long time her sobs and his rose together from the bed. When the door opened, a round nurse with a sympathetic face was carrying a syringe and without a word she nodded a nod that meant Lily should leave.

"Back soon," Lily said, and when she opened the door to the corridor, the group of them stood waiting for her. Mark and Daisy, Marty and Bruno, Kimberly and Robin. All of them looked wrecked and exhausted as they enveloped her in a circle of a hug. Marty was crying. Tough, irreverent Marty, who hardly ever showed an emotion, fell on Lily now.

"Don't even think about work," he said. "I'll do everything for you. You're covered."

This nightmare couldn't be happening. Her baby couldn't have been cut down at this moment in his life with everything ahead of him. Kim was crying again into her mother's shirt, and Lily wondered what the girl could be thinking. What had she and Bryan done together, what hadn't they done? For an instant she thought to shake an answer out of her. To ask her if Bryan had ever experienced some normal sexuality with her since he never would again. But all she could say was what she'd been thinking all the way to the hospital in the back of the ambulance. "Dear God, it should have been me. Why wasn't it me? Why can't I take it away from my boy and have it be me?"

Marty came to work the next morning and tried to concentrate on a script he'd been rewriting, but he spent hours just staring at the same page. Bruno was late, and when he came in the two of them pitched out an idea, but Marty lost his train of thought looking out the window. He could see the studio gate below and the cars driving in. He watched people move from their cars as they walked to the soundstages, and he couldn't stop thinking about Bryan. Too fucking unimaginable.

One week ago the kid had everything. Okay, so his shithead father had left when he was little, and that had been real tough on him, but Lily had made up for that in spades. She worked her ass off to make sure he could afford to go to the right schools, and then never stopped so she could keep on paying the steep tuitions those places charged. And now he was going to be "a fucking paraplegic," Marty said out loud, shaking his head.

"I think that's an oxymoron," Bruno said quietly.

Marty didn't hear him. He was thinking about Bryan, his all-time favorite boy, lying in that hospital bed with that hot girl-friend twitching around the room, and him knowing he'd never have her. The kid's life was destroyed. Marty had four daughters all under the age of ten. All of them were in love with Bryan. When Bryan and Lily came over for an afternoon pool party, the girls would ride on his shoulders and climb all over him. Now they'd probably be afraid when they saw him. Marty hadn't even told them yet.

"Maybe we should send him over something," Dave said. "Like some flowers, or balloons . . . or legs."

"Shut up, you heartless bozos. The kid's never gonna walk again. Everybody ante up twenty bucks for a gift," Marty said, taking his wallet out of his back pocket and throwing a twenty-dollar bill on the table. Last night he had hollered at his wife, Pat, for no reason and then burst into tears.

"I guess Rollerblades are probably a mistake," Dave said dryly. Marty didn't hear him because he was out the door to Charlie's office.

"I'll go see if Quasimodo wants in," they heard him say over his shoulder.

Charlie was sitting at his desk with what looked like a frown on his face as he paged through a script. Marty stepped over the threshold to see him toss the script across the room, where it landed in a pile of others.

"There's not one script ready to go to the table next week," he said. "Where's that girl writer? Can we get her to punch up the credit card story before lunch?"

"Jeez, Charlie, I thought you heard. There was a freak accident with the maid's husband. Lily's kid was shot and the bullet severed his spinal cord."

"That's too bad," Charlie said. "Give her till *after* lunch."

Not a time for jokes, Marty thought, which for him was highly unusual. "We're each kicking in twenty bucks to send over some flowers," he said to the ugly bastard.

"Flowers are for funerals," Charlie replied, picking up his wallet and opening it to remove three one-hundred-dollar bills.

"Here's three hundred dollars. Get the kid a hooker so we can find out if he has any sensation left in his shlong."

Marty left the money, turned on his heel, and walked back into his own office, where Bruno and Dave were playing desk hockey with an unopened Reese's peanut butter cup. "A real unfeeling prick," Marty said.

"Which is kind of poetic because it brings us full circle," David said, and scored when the peanut butter cup flew into Bruno's lap.

"Ever notice how you don't talk about a subject for a really long time and then it keeps coming up?" Bruno asked.

"Or in this case, not coming up," David said, and Marty decided to go out to lunch alone.

9

◊◊◊◊◊◊◊◊◊◊◊◊◊◊◊◊◊◊◊

Bryan was sleepy most of the time, and Lily drifted in and out of the room all day checking on his breathing and his waking moods. Kimberly was always in a chair next to the bed. The first few days she had permission from her mother and the school to stay out of classes to be with Bryan. And when she did go back she promised Bryan that she would take his fervent message that he didn't want to see any of the other kids until he was ready. Now that she was back in school she had made an agreement with her mother to pick her up every day at three-fifteen and bring her to the hospital.

Two clean bullet wounds. Left scapula entrance, exit shoulder. Enter lower right back, exit at side of chest. The second bullet had barely missed his aorta. The doctor's reports ran through Lily's brain. Now he was running a fever and they didn't know why. There was nothing for her to do but pace the halls or watch daytime soaps and try to imagine what the future could possibly hold for him, or stop herself from imagining the horrors it might hold.

Bryan's plan had been to apply only to colleges with top-notch tennis teams. He loved the game. And he loved airplanes. Someday he had hoped to fly. Not as a profession but as a hobby. He had talked about it when he did the meticulous job of building those model airplanes that hung in his room at home. Both of those ideas would have to be replaced, Lily thought.

Late at night in the hospital she would let herself remember those precious moments in his life that ran by her like a slide show. His first steps as a toddler when he'd held his hand up with an open fist as if he were clutching an unseen sky hook. The Huggies swish-swishing as he moved with a grin toward Lily or Donald, who were waiting there to catch him.

The day before his sixth-grade dance when she taught him the box step, holding his skinny body in her arms. To the left, together. Forward, together. To the right, together. Step back, then together. Just make a box with your feet. The first night he stepped on her toes so many times they created a joke they always used with one another when either of them danced. To the left, ouch. Forward, ouch.

At his early tennis games, he was so fast that once she told him she thought his legs were going to turn into wheels the way the legs of cartoon characters did. Prophetic, she thought as she walked into the room to see Kim with her algebra book open in her lap, holding on to Bryan's hand and gazing at him as he slept.

"He okay?" Lily asked, not sure how she felt about the coveted chair next to the bed being occupied by the magazine-ad-pretty Kim.

"Yeah, he keeps waking for a few minutes and then dozing again. Some heavy-duty drugs they're giving him, I guess."

Every day Lily looked at Kim and wondered if the girl's continued presence was based on some trumped-up heroic loyalty that she could brag about to the kids at school. If the number of cards and letters that had already arrived was any indication of the kids' feeling for or interest in Bryan, then Kim's coveted role as the only one permitted to see him had to carry some kind of respect with it. The notes to Bryan all congratulated him on being a hero who saved his mother from the attack of a crazed assailant. The assailant who still hadn't been apprehended.

Probably, with the ferocity of emotions that were part of being a fifteen-year-old girl, Kim fancied herself as his woman and the one who should be ministering to him, so Lily was just in the way.

Bryan's eyes opened. "How long did I sleep?" Lily heard him ask Kim.

"About half an hour."

"My mom still here?'

"All day," Lily said.

"Boy, I'll bet that's exciting. When do you go back to work, Mom?"

"I don't know," Lily answered. "I'm not thinking about work."

"I mean, you just can't hang over me and monitor every breath I take. I can handle the hospital. I'm not a baby."

"Fine," she said. "I'll go take a long walk. Anything I can get you?"

There was a beat and then Bryan answered. "Gummi Bears."

Kim laughed. "Way to prove you're not a baby!"

"I'll get you Gummi Bears," Lily said.

"Hey!" Bryan's face lit up. "I must be dying. She's letting me eat junk."

"Shut up. You're not dying," Kim said and rubbed his hand lovingly. It was definitely Lily's cue to leave.

Where would she find Gummi Bears in Beverly Hills? Gummi Rolls-Royces maybe. Yes, she remembered. There was a big drugstore on Little Santa Monica and some cross street. She'd keep walking until she found it. Outside the day was so bright that she squinted, then fished in her purse for her sunglasses.

Windows filled with mannequins dressed in chic clothes didn't interest her. Once she stopped cold when she saw a white pickup truck turn the corner, but the driver was a young blond woman with a cigarette hanging out of her mouth. Ernesto was still at large. The police had an officer posted in the lobby of the hospital in case he showed up there. Most nights Lily slept in the hospital or at Mark's house, avoiding her condo completely in case Ernesto returned.

The drugstore was in the next block and she was relieved when she saw it up ahead because she was afraid to be too far from Bryan. Once she had the Gummi Bears in her purse she could turn around and go back to the hospital. She pushed the glass door open, walked down the steps, and hurried into the aisle with the CANDY sign above it. Gummi Bears? Gummi Bears? Yes. She seized a large bag of the gooey little creatures and headed for the cash register. There was a line, and she stood behind a very skinny woman in her sixties who wore jeans and a T-shirt and held a box of eyedrops.

She had been in this drugstore before, with Bryan, looking for index cards. Bryan. The steps. How would he shop in here now?

"Next," the cashier said. It was Lily's turn.

"Excuse me," she said to the young, nose-ringed salesgirl. "How would a disabled person get into this store?"

The girl looked at her as if what she had just asked was a riddle that would have a joke ending. "Um ... through the door?" she said with a look in her eyes that said she hoped she'd guessed right.

"I mean, down the steps? How would he get down the steps?" she asked, hearing the grating edge in her voice.

The girl had no idea what Lily meant by the question, and there were four other people in line behind her, one with an overflowing basket.

"I don't know," the vacant-eyed girl said, shrugging. "I guess they wouldn't."

"You guess they wouldn't," Lily said in a tone that made her sound like her mother. Annette repeated things people said in that same tone when she thought they were saying something particularly dumb. "Well, then let me make it clear to you that the law says all businesses have to accommodate people in wheelchairs."

The girl tried a smile with her shrug this time. Lily's body was stiff with rage. She put both hands on the counter and held on with white knuckles, determined not to move until she got a satisfactory reply. "I want an answer," she said, staring unblinkingly at the uncomfortable clerk. "How will a person in a wheelchair shop in this store? How will my son shop in this store?" She was crying and her tears fell on the counter and on her hands. "How," she asked to no one in particular, "will he do the simplest things?"

When there was only silence in response, she put some money on the counter to pay for the Gummi Bears, put the bag in her purse, and walked up the steps. All the way back to the hospital she looked at every store, every building, every curb and tried to imagine Bryan negotiating his entry to them in a wheelchair. Was this her new life? Screaming at people about wheelchair accessibility—something she had never thought about in her life? The only time the handicapped ever crossed her mind was when she was about to turn into a parking spot and was annoyed to see that it had the blue marker with the white stencil of a wheelchair in it.

And of course, she thought as she got off the elevator and started toward Bryan's room, she'd wondered a little bit about it after she'd met . . .

Charlie Roth. That had to be him moving toward her now with that unmistakable rolling walk of his. Why on earth would he be in the hospital? As she walked farther she could see him catch sight of her and his nod of recognition and then his steps sped up as he moved in her direction.

"What are you doing here?" she asked. The hospital days she had survived had been so long and lonely she was almost glad to see him.

"I came to tell you I'm sorry to hear about your boy," he said.

"Thank you."

He was wearing a navy Hawaiian shirt today and she realized that his eyes were navy and for an instant she wondered how he would have grown up to look if the incubator accident hadn't happened.

"I was looking for you to punch up the credit card story and Marty told me where you were." So he had come all the way from the office. That was uncharacteristically sweet of him. What a thoughtful thing to do, just to tell her he was sorry about Bryan. Maybe he would stay for a while and she would have someone to chat with while Kim was monopolizing the chair next to Bryan. Lily headed for the waiting area, chattering gratefully away at Charlie.

"You're so nice to come. My sister was here for a while but she had to go back to work, and my mother's in Colorado and Mark's in surgery. So I've been sitting here all by myself every day feeling so unsure about the future and not knowing what to do for my child."

His eyes were surprisingly kind when he looked at her. The two of them were in the waiting area now. "I understand," he said. Of course, she thought. He understands. "But just let me share that in these trying times of grief and despair, when we have so little control over circumstances, I like to shift my focus to something I can control," he said. "Service to others. Or very often it makes me feel better to throw myself into my work."

A solid piece of advice, Lily thought, but far too difficult for her to make the shift the way she'd been feeling. "But how do you do that? I feel as if I've been hit by a freight train."

Perhaps this man, after all he'd lived through in his trying existence, would have some philosophy for her. Some wisdom that might help her through this. But instead of words he pulled a rolled-up script out of his pocket and held it up. It was entitled "Charge!" It was the credit card script he wanted her to fix.

He smiled a guilty little smile and she wanted to grab the script and hit him over the head with it. Here in the midst of this mind-boggling disaster, when it was all she could do to move through the day without losing her sanity, this creature came to a hospital where her son lay loaded with pain and drugs to get her to punch up a script.

"It sure could use a woman's point of view," he said hopefully.

With her eyes never leaving his, she took the script from his hand and said, "I understand, and I know exactly what to do with it." Then, with a small flick of her wrist, she sent it sailing across the room, where it landed with a reverberating clang in a tall trash can.

"Two points," he said.

"Get out of this hospital," she said, struggling not to shriek.

"Shall I take this as a 'no' on the punch-up?" he asked.

"Get out."

As he turned and left, she marched into Bryan's room. "I brought you the . . ."

Bryan had a look on his face she'd never seen before. It was torment, and when she looked at Kimberly, she saw the same look on the girl's face. Both of them had swollen eyes. "Not now, Mom . . ." Bryan said, and Lily dropped the Gummi Bears on the bed and backed out of the room.

Standing in the corridor she thought about going for a walk, calling her mother in Telluride, going down to the cafeteria even though she wasn't hungry. There was nothing for her to do. She envied a nurse who rushed by carrying a clipboard, because she was doing something. Not just sitting and waiting and watching. Finally she sighed, stood, and walked to the tall trash can, leaned into it, shuffled through some debris, and found the credit card script. Maybe she'd just sit and look it over.

Not too bad, she thought after she'd read a few pages. She pulled a pen from her purse and scribbled a few of her thoughts in the margins. Soon she was into it. Marking speeches, cutting. Nothing funny. Maybe she'd never be funny again. But she was so involved in the notes that when she looked up and saw Mark standing over her, she gasped.

"I brought you some soup," he said, holding up a take-out carton from the cafeteria.

"Not hungry," she told him, but she took the bag and held it against her body. The heat of the soup carton felt comforting.

"The police found Ernesto this morning," Mark said. "He shot himself with the same gun." She felt nothing but hate for Ernesto and pity for Elvira, who must be hearing the news, wherever she was.

"Think I should tell Bryan?" she asked, knowing something wrenching had to be going on in the room now between Bryan and Kimberly.

"I guess that depends on what frame of mind he's in."

That was when Kim, flushed and full of emotion, came rushing out of Bryan's room and stormed past them.

"Not good," Lily said, touching Mark's arm in a way he knew meant she was going into Bryan's room without him.

Bryan was propped up in the bed, and when Lily entered the room he turned his face away.

"Mom, don't come in."

"Why not?'

"Because I don't want to talk to any—" His voice exploded into a sob as Lily moved anxiously toward the bed.

"What happened?" she asked, knowing the answer before he spoke. All along she'd been wondering how many days or weeks would pass before this moment. Bryan sniffed, and Lily took a box of tissues from the bedside table and held it for him to blow his nose, then he let her mop his miserably sad face that was contorted in sobs of agony. She waited quietly for the sobs to subside so he could tell the story.

"She said she doesn't want to be my girlfriend anymore. She said it doesn't fit in with her future plans." He closed his eyes. "She said she was doing me a favor by ending it now. Mom, I hate her, but I don't blame her."

Couldn't she have waited a few months? Why in this time of such deep despair did that unthinking girl have to do this to my child, Lily thought. She considered running out of the hospital to find Kimberly, to grab and shake her and shriek into her stupid face that this was not allowed. Not yet. Not to this boy who was so unfairly cut down.

"Oh, honey," Lily said, leaning over him. "I'm so sorry. I

know you won't believe this now, but I swear you'll be fine without her." Her hand was over his and he wrenched it away angrily.

"No I won't, Mom. At least she knew me when I was okay. Who's gonna want me now? No girl is gonna say 'Oh, cool. Can I go for a ride in your wheelchair?' Don't lie to me and say it'll be fine or some other bullshit lie. Because we both know it'll never be fine again."

Lily closed her eyes, praying for the words she could use to disagree with him, but she couldn't find them. Finally she managed to speak. "It's not true. You're still the same Bryan. Funny and smart and full of heart. Some terrific girl will see that and want to be with you."

His jaw was tense, the tears were still streaming down his cheeks, and he couldn't look at her. "Right. That's what girls are looking for. They go to parties and say to each other, 'Boy, I hope I can meet a paraplegic in a wheelchair. That's my type.' "

Lily sighed and hugged herself, feeling chilled and aching for this child.

"Remember," she asked, "how you used to love our reading time together when you were little?"

"Mmm." More of a grunt than a word.

"In your favorite book, *The Little Prince,* do you remember what the Fox said to the Little Prince?"

"Cut me a break, Mom," Bryan said, but he looked at her curiously.

"He said, 'See with your heart. What is essential is invisible to the eye.' "

"Yeah, sure," he muttered.

"Baby, when the girl for you comes along, she'll see past this into your beautiful soul."

His eyes had looked so dead all week. So devoid of anything, but for an instant they flashed with the old Bryan sense of humor. "She'll have to be a mermaid."

Both mother and son laughed a pained laugh. God, how she loved this boy. "You know, if you like really dark humor, and I know you do, that's kind of funny."

She took his hand feeling a searing in her chest, knowing this was one time, only one girl, but there would be many more who couldn't deal with this. It would be the norm that girls Bryan wanted would shy away, shine him on, leave him flat the way this one just had. And if she had been Kimberly's mother instead of Bryan's, wouldn't she have told her daughter, "You'll spend your life taking care of him. It's better to get out now." That must have been the talk Robin and Kim had last night. Lily pictured them, mother and daughter in their pajamas. "In the long run, it's the kinder thing to do," Robin must have said. "A man like that will hold you back."

10

On a Sunday in Sherman Oaks Park, the World Series of sitcom softball teams was in full swing. It was the bottom of the sixth inning and the *Angel's Devils* team of all men was being trounced by the *American Dreamers* team, which was 50 percent women. Charlie Roth, who was the coach of the *Angel's Devils* team, didn't mind that they were going to lose, because there were so many great-looking women around, and all of them were fussing over him.

Diane Bennet, the *American Dreamers* producer, was a great pitcher. Marty struck out and the inning was over just as Bruno spotted Lily walking toward the field from the parking lot. She looked weary and walked slowly, and when Bruno elbowed David to look at who was showing up at the game, David whistled to Marty and in a minute they were all walking across the park to meet her.

"They were doing some other awful procedure to him, so he sent me away, and I remembered that today was the game, so all of you would be here," she said hoarsely.

Each of them hugged her and Marty put an arm around her as they walked toward the field where by now some of the actors from *Angel's Devils* spotted her and came walking over, and so did Dorie, who was there with her new boyfriend. And Cynthia was there too, and now they all surrounded her in a self-conscious circle, not knowing what to do or say.

"Lil," Cynthia said. "I was so sad to hear about Bryan." Cynthia had sent balloons that were too big and intrusive for Bryan's room, so Lily had had the nurses take them down to the children's wing.

"Thanks for sending the balloons," Lily said as Cynthia hugged her.

Now she looked around at the others, all of them looking so helpless, and then she leaned against Cynthia and closed her eyes. Why had she come here? It was a huge mistake. "I can't really handle this," she said.

Dorie, dressed in short shorts, stepped out of the crowd. She idolized Lily and it broke her heart to see her so destroyed. She wanted to say the right words. "You poor thing," she tried. "I know how you feel." But Lily wheeled on her, her eyes burning through Dorie.

"No! You don't know how I feel. You don't know what it is to have your child's screams of misery tear into your chest. To watch him wail in outrage at the way his life's been destroyed. How it feels to screen every pair of eyes that look at him to see if they'll be phobic. To find yourself casing every building to be sure there'll be access for a wheelchair because your baby is going to spend the rest of his life in one."

Even as she spoke she knew this was out of control. It was ridiculous for her to yell at this poor girl who only meant to offer sympathy. But she was so exhausted from the all-night hospital stays, the forced optimism she tried to show to Bryan, fielding phone calls from her self-absorbed mother, trying to take in and sort out all the things the doctors were telling her she would have to do for Bryan every day. Catheterization, skin decubiti. Words she'd never imagined would be a part of her life. Concepts that had been unthinkable only a few weeks ago, before the night that served as a giant rip through the fabric of her life.

She looked around the circle at each of them, quiet, indulging her tantrum, her fit of misery. Marty stood next to her and tried to calm her. "Lil," he said. He took her arm, and she let him envelop her in his arms as she broke down.

"Marty, he was going to walk me down the aisle at my wedding. Dance with me at my wedding." Marty patted her back and held her tightly. After a while she looked over at the brokenhearted Dorie. "Believe me, you don't know how I feel. Nobody does!"

"Is there a cripple in the house?" she heard a familiar voice ask. "Why, I'm a cripple! What can we do for her son? Give him an enema. Will it help? It couldn't hurt." There he was, the beastly terror. His baseball cap was on backward and he stood there flanked by a couple of pretty young secretaries from some show or other, doing an old vaudeville routine. Lily was flabbergasted by the insult and the others shuffled uncomfortably.

"You're a lock-up case," Lily said in her most appalled voice. "My son's life has been destroyed and you're doing old vaudeville shtick? This is beyond insane." She knew she shouldn't have come here. She had known as she drove here that seeing all their pitying faces would be too difficult. But Bryan had ordered her to leave the hospital, and when she'd gotten into the car in the hospital parking lot she'd felt sorry for herself. So she'd started the car and driven north, and at Coldwater Canyon had made a right, thinking that maybe watching the friendly game of funny people would lift her spirits. She was wrong, and now that she'd made a fool of herself she'd better get back to the hospital.

"Poor Lil," she thought she heard Bruno say as she headed for the parking lot, ashamed to be poor Lil. It was an identity she'd probably carry with her forever now. Poor Lily, the mother of the boy in the wheelchair.

"You're gonna need balls for this, Mother," she heard a voice say behind her. Oh shit. Charlie was following her. The jerk. Why didn't he mind his own business? "Bigger than the kind Dick Clark drops on Times Square."

She spun and looked at him. He was holding the baseball cap and his eyes were serious. "So it looks like I'm going to have to give you lessons on the care and feeding of a crip."

"Don't you call him that," she said, mortified that he was going to apply his irreverent sense of humor to her precious child. But Charlie kept walking toward her.

"Lesson number one," he said. "Lose your fear of the words." He took her arm and she pulled away, but he stayed at her side and kept talking. "Sticks and stones may break my bones, but the fucking words don't mean shit." He actually thought he was funny. Lily wasn't going to hear another word, and she turned and hurried off, glad he was too slow to keep up. But now he was calling out to her.

"You're both going to hear them for the rest of your lives. 'Crip,' 'spaz,' 'freak,' 'geek,' 'retard,' 'gimp,' " he shouted after her until she turned back. "And those are just the warm and fuzzy ones. Along with the questions like, 'How's that poor bastard in the wheelchair gonna piss or get it up?' "

That did it. "Stay away from me," she screamed. "You're disgusting!"

"And proud of it," he said, moving toward her again. They were now halfway to the parking lot, nearing the children's play area. Filled with the kind of climbing equipment Bryan used to love to climb on as a little boy. Primary-colored tubes and slides and monkey bars, and a roundabout with bright red bars.

"There's not an ugly thing anyone can say about me that I haven't heard or said about myself already," he told her. "And you know why? Because my mother wasn't afraid to put me out there and let me hear it."

There were no children in the playground, probably because it was late in the day. Close to the dinner hour for young families. She had come to this very playground with Donald, bringing Bryan as a tiny boy. She remembered how she and Donald had been smug in the way that some new young couples are with their future lying ahead of them, and how they loved bringing their son to the park and showing him off. Then Donald left and never sent a penny or called Bryan one goddamned time.

She would turn herself inside out for that boy. And Donald, who gave new meaning to the word "deadbeat," was still living in L.A., still a would-be producer. But from the day he'd left her, walked out the front door of what was then their little Studio City house, he had never even sent his son so much as a birthday card. Mothers whose children have dead fathers are better off than mothers whose children have fathers somewhere in the neighborhood not giving a shit, she thought.

For the first few years Bryan had looked longingly, wistfully, heartbreakingly candidly at intact families they passed in the supermarket or at open school night. But somewhere during that time there was a turning point, when he no longer hoped that every one of Lily's dates might yield a surrogate father for him. In fact, he eyed the ones he met critically, including Mark, who had tried so hard to make a connection with him.

She stopped and put her hand on the railing of the roundabout, then sat on it in a heap.

"You can't take the punches for him, you can't shield him, you can't make it go away. My mother knew that," Charlie said. "By the time I was five, I was ready with every wise-ass answer to every dumbshit question anyone asked," he added, walking over to her. "My mother told me there was nothing I couldn't do, and I believed her, so I did it all." She looked at him now, more serious than she'd ever seen him. And he meant well, but she wished he'd shut up. "I rode horses, flew gliders, had a bar mitzvah for three hundred people where I made a speech about the fact that Moses was also disabled."

"Even then," Lily said quietly, "you were rewriting the Bible."

"Not at all," he said, grabbing the rail of the roundabout and running a funny little run with it to get it moving. Then, as it twirled he hopped on and the park spun around them in a blur of green. "Exodus. Chapter four, verse ten. Moses petitions God to send Aaron out instead of Mo himself." He sat next to her as they spun. "And you want to know why? Because the lead Jew had a harelip."

"Will you stop?"

"Don't believe me? How's your Bible study? Remember this? 'Please, O Lord. I have never been a man of words, either in times past or now that you have spoken to your servant. I am slow of speech and slow of tongue.' I told all of my relatives that the Jews probably could have left Egypt a lot sooner but Pharaoh thought Moses was saying, 'Let my people grow, or glow, or blow." Lily couldn't believe she was sitting there listening to him do his imitation of Moses with a harelip.

"You said that in a synagogue? Isn't it blasphemy?" she asked, wishing she could close her eyes and just make him go away.

"You're close," he said. "It's comedy. Even Rabbi Slivovitz

laughed his *tsitsis* off." He grinned, but Lily could only look at him wearily.

"I don't see the humor in that or anything else," she said. The roundabout was slowing down.

"Well, you'd better start seeing it soon," Charlie said. "Because you're going to have to come back to work this week and be hilarious."

She stood as the roundabout stopped. "There's no way on earth I could ever sit in a meeting and be funny."

"Think health benefits, babe!" he said. "Right now you need them more than anyone I know."

Maybe, she thought, that was a veiled threat. Maybe he was planning to replace her if she didn't come back to the show soon. When she stepped from the roundabout to the dirt she lost her balance and reeled dizzily for an instant. And as she tried to gain her equilibrium she heard Charlie chuckle.

"That's how I feel all the time," he said. She turned to glare at him, but he was smiling. "Give the boy my regards," he said, and headed back toward the softball game.

Watching sitcoms had saved her life all those years, Lily realized, so maybe they would help her now, she thought as she
flicked around from channel to channel on the television as she
sat slumped in a chair in the hospital waiting room. The things
the doctor had told her made her head spin. Bryan was at risk
for a clot in the legs and he had to have injections of heparin
three times a day in his stomach. He was susceptible to kidney
stones and urinary tract infections. He had no sphincter control
and a great potential for bowel accidents. How would she ever
change their home properly for him?

And there was clearly no fighting spirit kicking in. He wasn't
interested in talking about what good things the future might
hold. That hopeless, dead look remained in his eyes. That was
what filled Lily with a doubt she was trying so hard to hide
from him that the effort was exhausting her. At Mark's pretty
house in the elegant Hancock Park section of town where she
was staying on the nights that she didn't sleep in the hospital,
she would come in, undress, and then fall exhausted into bed.

Some nights Mark would come home late from the hospital,
sleep in the same bed with her, then wake up in the morning
and leave without ever seeing her awake.

Tonight on the old, wall-mounted TV in the hospital waiting room *All in the Family* was on. It was a late-night rerun, and she knew immediately which episode it was when she saw Archie and Edith Bunker sitting on the bed and heard a few lines of their dialogue. This episode was called "Too-Good Edith," and the story was about Edith having phlebitis but continuing to give a party for Archie and endangering her health. When she collapses and Archie realizes how sick she is, he's contrite and mushy and makes a sweet speech to her about their marriage.

"If the whole damn world was to go to the dogs, as long as I had you by my side everything would be okay. I ain't nothin' without you."

When Edith melted and they kissed, Lily wanted to cry for sitcom true love, but she was out of tears so she stood, clicked off the TV, and walked down the hall to Bryan's hospital room. He was sleeping peacefully, and he looked so well. If only she could find a way to raise his spirits. Tomorrow she would move her clothes and cosmetics out of Mark's house and back to her own condo.

"I'm moving back home," she had said to Mark's naked back last night, not even sure if he was awake. He was.

"Can't get you to reconsider?" he asked, sitting up. "My house is so much more accessible."

"I have to go home," she said, trying to be gentle about it.

Since Bryan had been shot she hadn't been able to make love. She was too tired, too sad, and had cried the one night Mark kissed her in a way that made her know he wanted her. She was grateful when he didn't pressure her. And then last night they had kissed and held each other and she felt her body moving into the familiar rhythm of his and she thought that maybe she would, possibly she could make love and it would relax

her. Comfort her. Quiet her. But then her mind wandered to
Bryan and the idea that he could never have this kind of inti-
macy and she went cold. She was angry at herself for being
whole and well. Mark stroked her hair.

"I want you to stay here forever," he said.

"He needs to come home to his own familiar room. He loves
that room, and I need to spend some time making that place
work for him as best I can," she said.

"This feels like a step backward for us," Mark said. "I love
coming home and finding you here, or waiting for you to come
home to me. It's why I can't wait to marry you," he said and
kissed her on the nose.

"In December," she said. "By then things will be so different.
And I agree it feels good. But right now I have to make choices
based on what's right for that boy."

"I understand," he said.

After Mark left for work in the morning, she repacked her
suitcase, put it in her car, and drove to her condo on Beverly
Glen. She pulled the car into the driveway and then stopped to
look at the spot where everything had gone bad. Just where the
Jeep was now was the spot where Bryan had stopped that night.

The spot looked unchanged. Cars were whizzing by, and a
gardener with a leaf blower two buildings over was making a
loud din. An old man was walking his Maltese and stopped so
the dog could lift its leg on the green strip of grass near the
curb. But for her and for Bryan nothing was remotely the same.

She parked and dragged the suitcase out and made her way
to the garage entrance to her unit. A ramp will have to go here,
she thought, opening the door to the kitchen. The counters were
too high, and the distance from the sink to the center island
was too narrow for Bryan to move through in a wheelchair. It
would cost a fortune to make all of the changes, she thought,

but she was determined to let him come home to this place. She would do whatever it took.

The place smelled musty, so she opened windows and made her way down the hall and stopped in the doorway of Bryan's room to look around at the accumulated memorabilia of his life. The model airplane mobiles he'd patiently glued together and proudly run to show her. The photo collage he'd created over the years made of hundreds of snapshots of him with Kim and his other friends. The dozens of tennis trophies he had lined up himself across the shelves. No, she thought, no more tears, and she was pretty sure that at this point she couldn't even call one up. She jumped when the phone rang.

"H'lo," she said.

"Hiya, sis. Just checking in," Daisy said on the other end.

Lily remembered how only a few weeks ago she had complained about the fact that Bryan was growing like a weed. Telling Daisy how she wished he'd stop wearing out his tennis shoes so quickly. Now he would never wear out another pair of shoes in his lifetime.

"Oh, Dais," Lily said, her eyes closing to shut out the collection of Bryan's things. "My baby. My poor, poor baby."

12

✧✧✧✧✧✧✧✧✧✧✧✧✧✧✧✧✧✧

"Corned beef, coleslaw, and Russian dressing," Marty said after the first bite. "Basically a heart attack on rye." He was looking lovingly at the sandwich in his hand as some of the creamy coleslaw fell out the side and dripped onto the plate. "Now this is a treat that I can never have when Lily's with us because she hollers at me if I even glance at it on the menu."

Marty, Bruno, and David sat in Art's Delicatessen having lunch.

"Any news?" Bruno asked, hitting the bottom of a Heinz ketchup bottle with the flat of his hand and aiming it toward his French fries.

"Kid's not doing great," Marty said. "I mean, his body is a lot better, but his spirits are in the toilet. It's like a death, only what died is half of his body and the other half has to carry it around."

Even in this group nobody could think of anything funny to say about that so they ate quietly until David looked up and saw Harvey Meyers approaching.

"It's a triple A," David said under his breath. "Asshole in Armani approaching."

Harvey Meyers was a network executive, and all network executives were despised by the writers. But Harvey was particularly stupid and mean.

"Hey shtickmeisters, whaddya say? Who left the cage open so you three could escape?"

His remark was too close to the truth to be amusing. Most days the writers didn't have time to leave the office and go out to lunch, and they worked as Dorie sent for take-out food. The joke they made was that she ought to just fling it in over the transom.

"Hey, Harv," Marty said. "What's a big honcho like you doing in Art's Delicatessen? Shouldn't you be someplace swanky like Le Dome?"

Harvey ignored the question. "How come Charlie Roth's not with you? Can't stand to watch him eat?" he asked, then laughed at his own joke.

"We only have a half hour," David said. "It takes him that long to open the menu."

Harvey reached down, took a French fry from Bruno's plate, and talked while he chewed on it.

"There's no doubt the guy's a geek, but he writes his ass off, so I made sure he got the job. And what cracks me up is the way he comes on to all the young secretaries. Makes me nauseous thinking about it."

The guys couldn't look at one another. They often debated about what system was in place for hiring some of the brain-dead people in those network jobs, and the three of them had wasted a lot of writing time laughing for hours about the idiotic things the "suit guys" said in meetings. This man was the lowest of them all.

"What can he be thinking?" Harvey said, taking another

French fry from Bruno's plate. "That one of the girls would actually willingly go on a date with him? Touch him? A ladies' man," he laughed.

"His poor date wouldn't know if he was having an orgasm or a seizure," David said, and that got a big, nasty laugh out of Harvey.

"Hey, Dave. Too bad your jokes aren't that funny on the show. If they were, maybe it'd get picked up for next season. As it is," he said, then moved his hand from side to side in a gesture that meant their chances were iffy. It wasn't as if they didn't know that, so what was the point of this duded-up low-life in an Italian suit rubbing their noses in it?

Harvey took another French fry, this time from David's plate, and bit into it. "This one's better," he said. "I hate ketchup." And as he took another bite, he turned and headed out the door to Ventura Boulevard. Marty looked after him with narrowed eyes.

"It's guys like him who make television such crappy, mindless garbage," he said.

It was a Saturday night, and Mark and Lily sat in the hospital cafeteria picking at dinner. Lily was eating some watery soup and Mark had a salad with Jell-O on the side.

"When I was little our maid used to make me Jell-O any time I was sick," he said. "I was five, and I'd put some on the spoon and hold it up to her and say, 'Want some?' I knew she didn't but I offered it to her so I could hear her reply, because she'd always say the same thing. "No, sah! I ain't eatin' somethin' that's more nervous than me.'" Lily smiled, and Mark put his hand over hers.

"He's despondent," she said. "No matter what I talk about

he ignores me or he rails at me. I can't do anything right for him, and I feel so helpless."

"It will take a long time," Mark said, "and we'll both try hard to think of ways to help him through it."

Lily had a bag full of things she wanted to take up to Bryan, and Mark had a few more patients to check on, so they parted at the elevator.

"See you in the morning," Mark said, and his brief, warm kiss on her cheek was comforting.

On Bryan's floor Lily hurried past the nurses' desk. Bryan didn't even look at her when she came in. He just stared straight ahead.

"I brought you some magazines and tennis videos," Lily tried.

"Take them back."

She moved closer to the bed. "Honey—"

Bryan grabbed the bag out of her hand, ripping it, and the contents spilled on the bed. One at a time he hurled the videos across the room, then he yanked off the *People* magazine cover with a picture of Leonardo DiCaprio and shredded it as his angry eyes glared at her.

"Why would you want to make me look at this stuff? To remind me of what I lost? I know what I lost," he screamed, ripping out the pages. "Sexy girls who are gonna look right through me, cars I'll never be able to drive. People running, dancing, how 'bout just standing?" He threw the magazines in all directions. "Even shitting! Who ever thought I'd miss that?"

Lily reached for his hand, but before she could take it he put it up like a traffic cop. "Stay away from me, Mom. Keep everyone else away too."

Quietly, she cleaned up the torn papers, put the videos back in the bag, and left the room. What could she do? She would have to be his whipping boy and let him take it all out on her. Eventually it would subside, settle in. But she couldn't just stand there every day second-guessing his needs and his moods.

Maybe, she thought, feeling herself trembling, I'll try working. Maybe I can come up with some idea for the show. Now she wished she had invested in a laptop computer so she could sit right there in the hospital and work, but if the offices at the studio were unlocked, she could go there and work for an hour or two.

The studio lot was quiet and a sleepy-looking guard waved her on. As she made her way through the silent office building to the elevator, she was afraid this was a mistake and that she should have stayed in the hospital, should have sat by Bryan's bed all night. She had photos of him everywhere in her cozy little office. In each of them he wore that confident, happy look she had worked so hard to put on his face. Her favorite photo was the one that sat right on her desk in a silver frame. She had taken it herself one day after a tennis tournament. Bryan still had braces on his teeth then, and his smile was big and metallic and unselfconscious. Lily picked up the picture and kissed it.

She turned on the computer and cleaned off her desktop while she waited for it to start up. There were old trade papers from weeks ago, some notes she'd made on story ideas. She knew that sometimes if she just started typing, free-associating, the ideas would come. She would sit down and begin and see what happened. She certainly didn't expect any of it to be funny, but maybe she could think of some story ideas.

"All of it is grist for the mill," Harry used to tell Lily. "That's what writers do. Someday you'll take your lowest moments, the ones you think you'll never want anyone to know about, and you'll turn them into a sitcom for several million people to watch every Wednesday night." But nothing in her life felt as if it could come close to funny.

She'd just finished typing the date on the top of the page when she heard Charlie's voice behind her. "So Angel and the Abominable Snowman kiss passionately and ride off into the sunset to live happily ever after," he said.

"No chance," she said, not looking at him. "Angel's sticking with her man. Besides—this is just a guess—don't you think a guy whose first name is Abominable would probably be hard to live with?" Now she turned to see him leaning on the door-jamb.

"Maybe the power of her love could turn his life around and pretty soon people would be calling him the Beguiling Snow-man."

Lily shook her head. "Love can't make bad things turn to good no matter how strong it is. That's what my son's girlfriend told him when she broke up with him." She'd been blaming Kim for Bryan's depression. She was furious that the girl couldn't wait, couldn't give Bryan time to get stronger before she walked out on him. "How could she hurt him so badly?" she wondered, looking around at the photos. She shouldn't have come here. She was exhausted, and she ought to stop at the hospital and see how Bryan was doing now. She clicked her computer into the shutdown mode and turned it off, then she grabbed her purse and stood.

Charlie picked up his briefcase where he'd set it on Dorie's desk, and the two of them walked slowly out of the offices and down the corridor to the elevator. In front of the building a long, white stretch limousine was waiting.

"Is this your car?" Lily asked as a very tall Hispanic man emerged from the driver's side and opened a back door for Charlie.

"One needs quicker reaction time than I have in order to successfully drive a car without fatalities. So God gave me Hugo. A chauffeur slash bodyguard—and I count on him to get me everywhere on time." He moved toward the car and then turned back to her. "When you come to understand that what happened to your son isn't a curse . . . you'll forgive that girl who left him."

"Never," Lily replied.

Charlie seemed to be thinking through what he wanted to say next. Then, with a smile in his eyes he said, "What keeps most of us from finding lasting love is the expectation we have about how it has to be, how it has to look. Some celluloid image we got from a TV commercial or a movie. And when it doesn't look that way we run, just the way your son's girlfriend did. But I promise you, Bryan will be okay."

It was a nice thing to say, and he said it in such an unequivocally gentle way that she allowed herself to stand and be engaged by his navy eyes looking into hers. "The able-bodied think they have a corner on love and passion and romance," he said. "But they're wrong. The icing may be different but the cake is the same." His words sent a surge of feeling through her that made her want to throw her arms around Charlie's neck and thank him for his optimism on Bryan's behalf. Oh God, she thought. I will pray every day of my life that what this man just told me is true. That my baby will live to know real passion in his life.

"I want Bryan to believe that so much," she said. "But his eyes look a thousand years old." She had been absent from the hospital for too long; she hadn't left a number behind with the nurses, and she was feeling guilty for even leaving at all. There was no chance that she would be able to come back to work full-time now with all that she had to help Bryan get through. He had to be well enough to go to rehab, to survive what the doctors were telling her would be the most grueling experience of his life. Surely Charlie would understand that. This Charlie. The Charlie of tonight who suddenly seemed so surprisingly thoughtful.

"I love that boy so much," she said. "I have to be there for him every day. Even if it means I have to borrow money from my mother so I can quit the show."

"Bad idea," Charlie said.

"You can handle it just fine without me," she said. "You're the God of Jokes."

"Too many jokes are what's wrong with this show," he told her. "You write stories about human folly, and that's where the real humor lies. Your stories show how vulnerable we all are. You have to stay."

"I can't," she managed. Coming back full-time wouldn't work. Until and if Bryan was able to handle this disaster, all she could do was to take care of his needs. His well-being. "I really can't," she said, and as her tears came she wasn't sure which happened first, his move toward her or hers toward him but now her face was against his silky Hawaiian shirt and his hand patted her back gently.

Daisy brought chocolate chip cookies with M&M's in them to the hospital, but Bryan wouldn't touch them so Daisy ate six of them and then left, depressed, to go to an OA meeting. Marty and Bruno brought him all of Dave Barry's books but he didn't open one of them. "A laptop computer," Mark said. "I'll get

him one so he can play computer games. And flying software,"
he said as he sat with Lily late one night in her condo. "There's
flight simulator software that's incredible. One of the docs at
the hospital has it." Lily loved him for brainstorming ideas that
could help Bryan get through this low time. When she thanked
him, he smiled sweetly and said, "You just call out my name and
you know wherever I am I'll come running."

The day Mark took the computer and the flying software to the
hospital she waited for him outside Bryan's room, deciding it
was good for him to go in without her because she was sure it
would be an important moment between them. Bryan had kept
his distance from Mark. Even on the celebratory night when
Mark gave Lily the engagement ring Mark had put an arm
around Bryan and said, "I love your mother very much, and I
want you to realize that I know I'll never be your father—"

"No problem there," Bryan said. "My father was never my
father." And then he walked away and closed the door to his
room.

In the hospital corridor now she waited hopefully. Nurses
passed and gave her a familiar wave. She knew all of their faces.
Most of them had been in and out of Bryan's room, but he
ignored them all, had no room for polite exchanges. On the way
into the hospital today Mark had told her excitedly about the
way the software re-created the instrument panel and the horizon and the virtual experience of landing an airplane in specific airports all over the world. The altruistic gleam in his eye
as he marched into the hospital room with the determination
to bring some joy to her son made her want to rain kisses all
over his face. He had splurged on a powerful little machine,
consulted with several friends to choose just the right flight
simulator software. This would be the breakthrough.

Suddenly the door flew open and a pale Mark appeared,

clutching the laptop to his chest. He looked hurt and tense, and he closed the door to Bryan's room behind him and started down the hall with Lily following close behind.

"What did he say? What happened?" she asked.

Mark stopped walking, and then in hushed tones said, "He pushed it off the table. Said he didn't want anything simulated. Only real. And that all of us were so obviously uncomfortable around him we could choke."

"I'm sorry," Lily said. "He's just so—"

"I think we ought to focus on finding a family therapist right away. These feelings of his are so loaded with issues of manhood and virility and God knows what. I mean, Lily, you and I have talked about the idea of having a child together. Wouldn't that make him terribly resentful?"

They were slipping. She was no longer the funny, airy woman with a jock son who would soon be off to college. Now there were issues and problems. There was heaviness and an uncertain future. Now she was a different package than this man had bargained for. Those were the words that ran through her mind every day when she saw Mark, and she wondered how this turn in her life was going to affect the two of them.

"Mark, please," she said. "This is so new. Let's just take it day by day. We'll learn how to deal with it." When she took his arm to walk him to the elevator, she could feel the tension in his body.

13

✦✦✦✦✦✦✦✦✦✦✦✦✦✦✦✦✦✦

Bryan moved back and forth across the tennis court with long, graceful strides, meeting the ball at just the right instant, the racket head following through to the perfect spot. He was running his panting opponent ragged. And there was Kimberly, her mane of flying hair catching the sun, those dark glasses covering her pretty eyes, as she cheered him on and— No! The tennis court and Kimberly were going away, fading and melting, and he was coming back from the dream to the fucking hospital, and another fucking doctor in a white coat with a stethoscope around his neck was leaning over him.

The medication made the world look fuzzy sometimes, usually just as he was waking, but it had never been this kind of crooked. Bryan blinked away the blurriness, but the guy's face still looked weird.

"Who are you?" he asked.

"The strange and twisted creature who works with your mother." It didn't register.

"What do you want?" Bryan asked.

"To bring you some entertainment."

Bryan wanted to go back to sleep, back to the wonderful dream where he could run, and Kimberly could watch him with that same gorgeous, adoring face. This guy was the beast, the troll, the fiend who worked with his mom. Jeez, he *was* weird. No wonder his mom couldn't stand being in the same room with him. He had a box in his arms, and he opened it at the foot of Bryan's bed.

"A bunch of movies I like to call 'cripflicks,' because each of them features a character who in some way is seriously disabled." Bryan closed his eyes. Who sent this asshole here to bust him for not being the peppy paraplegic? Probably his mom, goddamnit, he wished she'd back off.

"You gonna get out of here now, or do I have to call security?" Bryan asked. But Charlie didn't answer because he was busy rifling around in the box for something that he found and quickly concealed under his coat.

"Time to get past the self-pitying shit that's part of the new cripple blues," he said.

"Hey," Bryan said, leaning toward the night table to get the call button. "I don't want to talk to anyone, so could you just go?"

But Charlie rushed to the button first and moved it to out of Bryan's reach, then whipped a video out of the box and held it up as if he were doing an infomercial.

"*Dumbo*," he announced. Bryan put his hands over his eyes. How did this fruitcake get in here and what was it going to take to get him out? "Born unlike the others, he was not only heckled, he was jeckled. Still, he rose above the crowd, using his birth defect as an advantage."

This man is a full-out nutcase, Bryan thought. Now the goofy, crooked specimen was doing his version of Timothy Mouse talking to Dumbo the elephant. It was from the video Bryan had seen a thousand times as a toddler so he knew both the voice and the dialogue.

"Dumbo, you flew! The very things that held you down are gonna take you up," Charlie said, and he sounded the way Timothy Mouse would sound if he had cerebral palsy. Now he flopped his awkward arms like a bird and sang his version of the voice of the crows from *Dumbo*. "I saw a peanut stand, I heard a rubber band, I saw a needle that winked its eye. But I think I will have seen everything, when I see an elephant fly!"

"You are demented," Bryan shouted. "I'm calling security."

But Charlie tossed *Dumbo* back into the box and was now holding up another cartoon video. "Donald Duck," he said, as if he were about to begin a documentary. "More famous than Donald Trump! With much better taste in women. A serious speech impediment aside, he managed to have an ongoing romance with the beautiful Daisy, who was often heard asking, 'What the fuck is this piece of poultry talking about?' "

The guy was loopy, hyper, and doing his act, and Bryan was the captive audience as he held up another video. "Wrong," Bryan said. "Peter Pan wasn't disabled," knowing it was probably a mistake to interact with this crazo because he might be encouraged to keep going.

"Maybe not," Charlie said, "but his archenemy was the most murderous crip of them all." And then, in one unbelievable move, he stepped awkwardly onto the chair and did what looked like a belly flop onto the rolling bed tray, spreading his arms and legs out to either side and flailing them. "Tick tock, tick tock. The vengeful crocodile was bent on eating his other hand. But Captain Hook was slippery prey." And then he managed to slide off the table and hurry to the closet to forage inside so that now Bryan could only hear his voice.

" 'In person he was cadaverous and blackavized and his hair was dressed in long black curls, which at a distance looked like candles, and gave a singularly threatening expression to his fearsome countenance.' " Now his face peeked out of the closet. "But undoubtedly the grimmest part of him was his claw." And he emerged with a wire coat hanger up his sleeve, leaving only the hook where a hand would be. And he laughed his version of his Cyril Ritchard Captain Hook laugh.

It was funny. Bryan had to give him that. The guy was funny.

"And let's not forget," Charlie said, pulling the wire from his sleeve and another tape from the box, "Superman!"

"Not disabled," Bryan said. He couldn't believe he was actually getting into this goony game.

Charlie pulled a folded spare blanket out of the closet and now, with a funny twirl, he opened it to use as a cape, which he whirled onto his shoulders. Then he managed to climb onto the chair and grin.

"Maybe not," he said. "But what about Christopher Reeve? Since he fell off that horse, being a crip is all the rage! Besides, the man of steel can be felled by only one substance, and it was named after us!"

"It was?" Bryan asked.

"Kryp-tonite!"

That one got to Bryan. In some place he thought no longer existed, he was tickled, and he let out a giggle, and Charlie giggled with him. Then Charlie spun back to the box and held up another video. "Moving right along," he said, "to Frankenstein. One foot walked, the other foot dragged along the ground. Not unlike myself. And," he said, pulling out another, "King Kong!"

Charlie pushed the chair against the wall and Bryan couldn't control the laughter, because now Charlie was moving his arms and legs as if he were climbing up the wall and Bryan was laughing hard enough to shake the bed.

"Too vertically abundant for his lover, he carried her in his hand," he said, and then kissed his own hand. "As he climbed the Empire State Building, guns were shooting at him, but he didn't think it was unusual because he was in New York City."

"Stop!" Bryan said. The laughter made his face ache. "Oh God. Oh no!" he said as something popped and an alarm went off at the nurses' station.

Lily stepped off the elevator carrying a little basket of goodies she'd bought at Whole Foods for Bryan. A new juice drink and a granola that tasted like crumbled cookies. He'd probably sneer at first, but when he tasted it he'd have to admit it was good. She was halfway down the hall when an emergency team rushed past her. My God, she thought, somebody's in trouble.

When she saw they were going into Bryan's room, she panicked. He had sounded low when she'd called him from home, asking if he needed anything. What could have happened? She recognized the last nurse on the team who just before she moved inside gave Lily a warning look that indicated she should stay out, then closed the door behind her.

Lily put the basket down and leaned against the wall next to the door. Her whole body was pulsing with worry. She could hear the voices in Bryan's room. Bryan's voice was one of them. That was a good sign. Then—and this had to be her imagination, she thought—she heard everyone laugh, and then the door opened and she spun toward it hoping for good news.

"What in the hell are you doing here?" she asked, stunned to see Charlie Roth in the doorway of Bryan's room, wearing a white coat and a stethoscope. Maybe she was having a nightmare. "What happened to Bryan?"

"A tiny emergency," Charlie said, grinning. "He laughed his tubes out."

"What?" She was appalled. There was no reason on the planet why this man should be in her son's room. And now that the door was wide open she could hear the nurses and Bryan chatting, and Bryan was giggling that wonderful, throaty giggle Lily loved but hadn't heard since before the shooting.

"Why were you in my son's room? He doesn't even know you. How did you get in there?" she asked suspiciously.

"Disguised as a brain surgeon," he said, and chuckled.

"What do you want here?" she asked, deciding that probably it was time to officially quit the show just to get away from this man.

"To take matters into my own two gnarled hands and bring some levity to the whole thing."

That was the limit. "There *is* no levity to the whole thing," she said, proud that she wasn't shrieking in some way he'd only mock. Proud that she was controlled enough to speak in a voice appropriate for a hospital corridor. "This is a dire and painful tragedy," she said. "The pediatric psychologist told me that this boy has to take time to grieve and heal from it. So kindly take your weird sense of what's funny and stay out of our lives."

Just then the three nurses emerged from the room and all of them were smiling. One of them gave Charlie a friendly pat on the arm, then she turned to Lily and said, "You can go in now."

Lily didn't even look back at Charlie, she just moved into the room. "Honey," she said to Bryan, who was wiping his wet eyes with a tissue, "I never asked that man to come here and I promise you that—" Her words were interrupted by a peal of a giggle.

"You've gotta love this guy, Mom. He stood on a chair and did his impression of King Kong climbing the Empire State Building, and he brought me all these dopey movies." He was sitting in a more upright position than he had since he'd arrived at the hospital. Now he reached forward into a box on the bed and pulled out a video of *The Ten Commandments*.

"He brought me this one because he says—and you're gonna love this—Moses had a harelip."

Bryan was seized with a laugh attack, a big, hearty, belly laugh. And Lily was so elated and then infected by his laugh and the way hearing it made her feel hopeful for the first time in what felt like so long that she sat in the chair and laughed too.

14

Ralph and Alice Kramden had just had a rip-roaring fight and now the episode was ending and they were making up. Jackie Gleason, who had only seconds before been ranting and raving as Ralph, was now abject and chagrined as he stood before Audrey Meadows. "I love you, sweetheart. Honest I do. You're the greatest," he said, and then they kissed a big, mushy kiss. Lily had seen every rerun of *The Honeymooners,* and still the dysfunctional Kramdens always made her laugh.

She was on her sofa in the condo and Mark brought her dinner on a tray and set it on the coffee table in front of her. "Since Elvira's gone I can't find anything in the kitchen," he said, going back to get his own tray.

He is such an amazing man, she thought. Even though he hates the idea of my coming back here to live, he still shows up and cooks for me.

"This looks great," she said, spooling some pasta onto her fork and then using the remote to turn off the TV. The silence in the house was palpable. Before the shooting, a night like this would have been filled with the sound of Pearl Jam on the CD player and the raucous laughter of Bryan's friends. Now there was the same lonely silence that used to make her snap on the

TV after school when Annette was at the travel agency and Daisy built towers with Legos. Or at night when Annette went out on a date with what she called "a prospect," which meant a future father for the girls, and Daisy played with Matchbox cars while Lily watched TV.

Mark came back into the living room with his own dinner on a tray and two glasses of red wine and put one of the glasses into the waiting hand of Lily. "I love you," he said, looking into her eyes. She knew that "I love you too" was the anticipated reply, but something stopped her from getting it out.

"I know you do," she said instead as their glasses touched. The first few sips of wine sent a heavy, warm feeling through her, a pleasantly weak feeling in her shoulders and thighs. She would have to monitor herself so she wouldn't get into the sad place where alcohol sometimes took her.

"Didn't get by to see Bryan today. How was he?" Mark asked.

"He was awful in the morning," she said, remembering how he'd sounded when she'd called him that morning. "And then Charlie Roth appeared out of nowhere and brought a bunch of silly videos and must have clowned around a lot, because he made Bryan laugh his tubes out." She was smiling, but Mark looked at her with a raised eyebrow she knew was disapproving.

"Laughed his tubes out?"

"It was okay. The nurses hurried in and they had everything back in place in a few minutes."

"Are you talking about that disabled guy from your show? The one who hung you out of the window by your feet?" She nodded. "He's clearly a maniac," Mark said. "And it's okay with you that somebody like that is with Bryan when he's in this condition, getting him excited? If you ask my opinion, and

I realize you haven't, I'd suggest you keep somebody that out of control as far away from Bryan as you can."

Something in his voice was so condescendingly I'm-a-doctor-and-you're-not that it made her want to turn the glass of red wine over his head. Bryan, who had lived a nightmare, who had cried himself dry of tears, and who didn't have a smile for any cartoon or joke or meal or friend, had emitted his first hopeful signs during a visit from Charlie Roth and she couldn't let that be minimized or demeaned.

"You mean laughter hasn't been approved by the Food and Drug Administration?" she asked. "Not endorsed by the American Medical Association as a healing technique?" She heard her voice sound very tense.

Mark put his wineglass down. "Please, let's not have this same argument."

The same argument meant the way Lily often challenged the AMA party line. After spending her whole adult life sitting at computers, she believed in chiropractic adjustments to take away back problems. Mark always said with a smile on his face and a shrug, "Whatever works," but she knew he thought they were needless visits to quacks. She took a capsule full of something from the health food store called evening primrose to alleviate symptoms around the time of her periods. She sprayed lavender aromatherapy on her pillow for sleep and carried an antistress spray in her purse, which she was tempted to take out now and spray right in his face.

"Well, I'll certainly forbid laughing," she said. "How about smiling? That okay?"

He took her hand in his, and now he had that look on his face that meant, You just don't understand. "Honey," he said, and she wanted to tell him to get out and go home before he made whatever speech was about to follow. "I'll admit that state of mind is a factor in healing. I just heard a paper on it again last night. But we're beyond that here."

He moved closer to her, and she was so lonely and sad and hurting and needy that she let him put his arms around her just to feel the warmth of him near her. But she was annoyed.

"I love you for believing in the power of healing and herbal remedies," he said. "But because I love you I can't give either you or Bryan false hope. There is no cure for this condition, and the sooner you accept that this tragedy defines what his future is going to be, the sooner you'll deal with it."

No, she wanted to scream in his face. No! No! No! I won't let you say that. She imagined him with his patients, giving them this kind of pronouncement about the rest of their lives, wondering if they felt the way she did now. Or were they submissive and grateful to be in his care? She could feel his breath on her face.

"And no comedy videos or sublingual tinctures are going to change that. Believe me, I wish there was some magic too. Every doctor does, but we, more than anyone else, see every day how cruel life can be."

On Bryan's first day of rehab, an ambulance transferred him from Cedars-Sinai to Northridge Hospital in an ambulance. Lily took the tour through the rehab, facility with him as an orderly wheeled him down the hall on a gurney. They were accompanied by Dr. Dorothy Jenkins, a serious, dark-haired, dark-eyed woman about Lily's age who put a welcoming hand out to Bryan and gave him a smile of recognition that said she'd seen many like him before. They passed a boy wearing a crash helmet moving himself along in a wheelchair. The boy waved a hello to the doctor.

"That's Jerry," the doctor said. "He's brain-impaired and he's wearing the helmet because there's a piece missing from his skull and he hasn't had a plate put in yet. So he has only skin and brain and no protective barrier."

They passed a bulletin board, and the only notice that caught Lily's eye was one that said SPINAL CORD SUPPORT GROUP MEETS THURSDAYS AT THREE. Now they were at the gym, and as the doctor pushed the doors open Bryan and Lily could see the body-building equipment all accessible by wheelchair, the punching bag, the standing frame, and at the far end, a pool table.

"You'll spend a lot of time in here. You'll learn how to transfer, first from the bed to the wheelchair, eventually from the chair to the seat of a car. You'll also learn how to dress and undress yourself. You'll be sitting up for six to eight hours a day learning wheelchair endurance and balance. How to tip it, turn it, tilt it, and, of course, down the line, you'll start to play whatever sport interests you from the chair."

Bryan didn't react, and as they left to head toward his room, they passed a man in a wheelchair wearing a device that looked like a halo.

"Roger wears the halo because he had neck surgery and it keeps his neck mobilized. It's actually secured right into the bones in his skull."

"Mmm," Lily said. It felt surreal to suddenly be an insider in this world. Walking through the hall as casually as if it were an aisle in the supermarket instead of a place where victims of horrific physical problems came to learn how to cope. What an astonishing mechanism the mind had for converting concepts that were once so repellent that if she'd seen them on TV she would instantly have changed the channel. Now, not only could they not be clicked away, she was starting to become inured to it all. Conditioned.

Bryan's room at rehab was larger than the one he'd had at Cedars, and while the orderly helped him transfer from the gurney to the bed, the doctor and Lily stepped into the hall. "He has a long road ahead of him, and you and his father are going to have to step up and be ready every time he says, 'I can't handle it' or 'Get me out of here,' because you need to know up front that our rehab program is extremely grueling. We kick ass here."

"His father walked out on us nine years ago and hasn't been back since," Lily said.

"Tough," said the doctor, and abruptly turned to go into the room.

"Not unlike yourself," Lily said once she knew the doctor was out of earshot.

Charlie Roth was on his way out of the men's room at CBS when he bumped into that putz Harvey Meyers, who was on his way in.

"Heyy," Harvey said self-consciously. "How's it going, amigo?"

"Your timing is good," Charlie said. "I'm the last guy in the world you want to stand next to at a urinal."

"Funny," Harvey said. "Very funny. And you need all the funny you can get to save that show. I was telling one of my colleagues that *Angel's Devils* was so bad before Harry died that their phone number appeared mysteriously on Jack Kevorkian's beeper! Right? Funny enough to get me a job on the show?"

"You brought me in to pull it out, Harvey, and I'm going to do it," Charlie said.

Harvey flashed his white teeth. "Better do it, pal, or your next gig will be the Jerry Lewis telethon." He laughed at what he thought was a big joke. But Charlie moved away, toward the office.

"Hey, buddy," Harvey called after him, "I only say those things because I love you."

"Iago. In act three, scene three," Charlie said, turning back.

"Who?" Harvey asked.

"Oh, just a character in a drama, not a sitcom. So how could you be expected to know?" Charlie turned again. Later he'd tell the writers the question Harvey hollered after him.

"On *this* network?"

15

In week three of Bryan's rehab, the nurses and orderlies took the patients to a shopping mall in a specially outfitted van. The purpose of the outing was to teach the patients to begin to accustom themselves to the physical realities of being disabled in an able-bodied world. To begin to educate them about the thousands of obstacles that would get in their way from day to day. Bryan was dreading the trip. In the Thursday support group, the psychologist had talked it through with them, and Jason, a kid who was in a power wheelchair with a ventilator in his mouth, promised Bryan the trip would be "awesome."

"People are scared of us," he said, but Bryan didn't find any comfort in that idea. Just getting all of them down to the driveway and into the van took an hour. Bryan was one of the first ones to be loaded in, and instead of watching the sometimes painstaking journey from wheelchair to van, he watched the able-bodied people, envying the way they moved so easily in and out of their cars and to and from the hospital. He had finally perfected transferring from the bed to the wheelchair and was pretty good at getting from the wheelchair to a seat in the car. His problems came when he tried to propel the wheelchair with any speed or finesse, and all the way to the mall he worried about how he would do in a public place.

"Nobody'll even notice," Nancy, a redheaded nurse about his mother's age, had told Bryan when he'd said he was afraid.

It was a blazing hot day and the van pulled into the parking lot at the Sherman Oaks Galleria. The nurses had chosen that mall because the stores were inside and there were a few movie theaters, and the new Blues Brothers movie was playing at one of them. By the time they helped Bryan out, he was sweating and irritable.

"Okay, gang," Nancy said. "We're ready to roll!"

The cute sense of humor that was so welcome at rehab lost its appeal for Bryan as the nurse moved ahead, hoping the patients would follow her. Bryan was working hard to get the chair to do his bidding. Last night he'd stayed up very late worrying about today, staring at the TV without the sound. Now he was exhausted.

The world looked odd from the seat of a wheelchair. He was seeing things from half his adult height, as though he were five years old again. The words "freak show" sat in the front of his brain as he noticed people catching sight of the group, then very deliberately turning away. They were a bizarre parade, led by Nancy and flanked by Julio and Roman, the male orderlies. Bryan's arms ached, and he wanted to go back to the hospital. No. Back home to the condo, just to get back into his own bed and pull the blanket over his head and never again talk to another human being.

He could see Jerry at the front of the group, wearing what he joked was his dress helmet because it was multicolored and fancier than the one he wore every day. This group must be a nightmare to the able-bodied observers. Now he could see a group of girls about his age, wearing jeans and platform shoes and cropped T-shirts, moving along and giggling as they walked. One of the girls must have spotted the group from rehab because Bryan saw her stop suddenly and put her hand on her friend's arm. "Oh my God," she said. When the other girls looked to see what had stopped her in her tracks, one shrieked, "Whoa, save me!" and that made the girls fall apart.

"That is so mean," Bryan heard one of them saying. "Stop that." But the others were around the bend and out of control in the throes of shrill laughter.

Bryan could see the movie theater at the far end of the mall, but his arms were so tired from moving the chair he was sure he'd never get there. Navigating through the crowd as part of this group was too painful. Outside the theater, two boys wearing backward baseball hats were having an argument when the group passed them.

"Shut up, asshole," one said to the other. The second boy scowled and tensed.

"You shut up or I'll kick you so hard you'll look like that demento in the wheelchair."

They were inside the theater now. Some of the rehab group sat in the back row, some of them moved their wheelchairs behind the back row; Bryan transferred from his wheelchair to the theater seat. When he was folding the chair, Nancy gave him a pat on the shoulder to say, "Good work." Big, fucking deal, he wanted to scream. I got out of a chair. Three months ago my tennis pro thought I could get tennis scholarships anywhere in the country. I was going out with the hottest-looking girl in the school. When the lights in the theater went down, Bryan let himself cry.

*   *   *

Marty had stopped that morning on the way into work at Starbucks for a double espresso, so he was wired and raving in the
pitch meeting.

"Angel's uncle Louie comes to work for her and steals her
blind. No. Angel gets stopped for speeding and the cop falls in
love with her. No. Angel reads that they're looking to put a
housewife into outer space, so she signs up for the program.
Feel free to jump in here, guys."

"Major pieces of dog shit all," David offered.

"We're a little stale here this morning," Charlie said. "It's a
gorgeous day. Let's go for a stroll. Maybe we'll get ideas." After
he was out of the room, David turned to the others.

"I hope he doesn't say, 'Walk this way,'" and he imitated
Charlie's walk.

"Not funny," Lily said.

Out on Ventura Boulevard, the group moved together, staying at Charlie's pace. They stopped to peer into store windows,
and David lit a cigar.

"An alien disguised as Joey comes to Angel's bedroom one
night. But she gets suspicious when the alien actually stays
awake for sex," Marty said, still so hyper that he punctuated
every few steps with a little skip.

"The old 'alien stops by for shtooping' plot," Charlie said
dryly. "Haven't heard that one since *My Favorite Martian*."

They were passing Crown Books, and Lily spotted a window
full of children's books.

"Hey! What if Ali wants to join a father/daughter book club,
but Joey has to admit he doesn't know how to read? I like this.
It gets us into the issue of literacy, and we could make an important statement."

"Pass," Marty said. "The only important statement I care

about is the one I get from the bank. We start doing that 'important' shit and we're all out of work."

"Yeah," Bruno said, "Hold the issues. This is comedy."

"Wrong," Lily said irritably, "*Maude* ran for six years, and they got comedy out of abortion. *Murphy Brown* ran for seven years, and they got comedy out of breast cancer. *Ellen* did a story on . . ."

"I rest my case," Marty said. "The minute that lesbo started doing that dyke shit she went right into the crapper."

Lily winced. How could someone she loved as much as Marty, who could be so sensitive about so many things, be so stupid? "Marty, the show needs to—"

"Hold it," Charlie interrupted. "Before we say no to the literacy story, let's think it through and see if it works."

Lily smiled a tight smile at the boys, and Marty pulled a cigar out of his pocket, which he pointed at Charlie as he asked Lily, "Are you shtooping him?"

"She's not that lucky," Charlie answered, and that seemed to ease everyone's mood.

By the time they arrived at the office an hour later, they had broken the back of the literacy story and were already into writing the dialogue. Dorie watched them stream through the door, still pitching, with Marty in the lead.

"So Angel says to the English teacher, 'Don't mind my husband. Deep inside him there's a very nice person.' And the English teacher says—

"Only if he recently ate one." Lily finished Marty's thought.

"Funny," Charlie said as they fell into their usual spots at the conference table and Lily hopped up on the windowsill.

"The end of act one has to be when she realizes that all these years, Joey's been faking. Acting as if he can read," Lily said as Dorie peeked into the room and looked right at her.

"Bryan's on the phone," she said, "and he sounds real upset."

"I'll just grab it here," Lily said, picking up a phone and holding her other ear so she could hear Bryan's voice, but for a long time all that came from the other end of the line were Bryan's choked sobs.

"They made us go to a mall," he said, trying to gain control. "We were the fucking freak show. People laughed at us. I want to come home now. Come and get me, Mom. I can't stay in this ward for weirdos anymore. I fell out of my chair and people in the mall were laughing."

The world went gray. The worst was happening. The reality of what he'd become had kicked in. And while it did, she had been walking down the street cracking jokes instead of being there to oversee his care. If she had been there, she would have told them it was far too early for Bryan to be exposed to a bunch of insensitive jerks in the mall. And why did they have to take them in a group? Couldn't they take patients one at a time? Bryan in his wheelchair was so attractive he never would have caused the revulsion the others did.

"Hang on, baby. I'm on my way out there right now." She would storm in and raise hell with those people. Warn them not to lump her son into a group. In fact, she'd tell them they were not to do anything with him unless they asked her first. This was a child who refused to let any of his high school friends visit him at the hospital or rehab. He was terrified of being ridiculed, reviled, and humiliated. All of the things they had let him be today.

She moved back to the windowsill to grab her purse.

"You leave this room and you're out of a job," Charlie said. Lily turned toward Charlie in disbelief.

"You can't fire me for going to take care of my child. Those people made him go to a mall where he was stared at and laughed at. He was humiliated, and he fell out of the wheelchair." There was no way in the world he was going to stop her from going out there and screaming the place down if she had to. Charlie was actually smiling. The idiot was smiling.

"Isn't it lucky," he said.

"Isn't what lucky?" she shouted.

"Now he has that experience in his emotional quiver. He's learned in one day how certain stupid people will always behave, and he can go on. Getting the rhythm of the chair will come. Soon he'll fall into the music of it."

Lily was incensed. All he cared about was the show and her staying in this room to write the damn jokes while her child was in the hands of incompetents.

"The music of the wheelchair?" she said, hot with anger. "What are you? The Phantom of the Cripples?"

As if to make his point more emphatic, Charlie stood. "You start a pattern of rescuing him now and you'll both regret it for the rest of your lives. Learn to replace 'Oh my God' with 'Isn't that lucky.' "

" 'Lucky' doesn't apply here," she said, angry at herself for wasting one more second engaged in this conversation when Bryan was waiting and in such emotional turmoil.

"The hell it doesn't," Charlie said, and she saw a fire in his eyes she'd never seen there before. "Isn't it lucky that now he understands that people's reactions don't make him who he is? Isn't it lucky that he's finding out who inhabits his body, because the body is only a container for the soul? Isn't it lucky for him that you have an employer who will fire you if you leave this room? Now kindly stop pissing and moaning and let the boy get through this on his own. Just sit the fuck down and work on the literacy story."

Lily looked around the room at the guys. All of them were frozen in their seats, very uncomfortable and stiff, waiting to see how she'd react. Then she looked at Charlie and he met her gaze unflinchingly, and she saw his life flash before her eyes. She was hit with a whirlwind of images of all that he must have seen and suffered and overcome, and she knew that what he was saying was true. Start fighting the battles for Bryan now and he would never learn to do it on his own.

Slowly she walked back to the windowsill, hoisted herself back up, and picked up her notebook and pen.

"Well, okay," Marty said, his giddy voice breaking the silence. "Let's write some big, funny jokes now."

An hour later in her own office again with the literacy story in her head ready to put into the computer, she closed the door and called Bryan. He was sullen when he picked up the phone. "You in the car?" he asked.

"I'm in the office."

"Mom, when are you coming to get me?" he shouted into the phone.

"I'm not coming to get you. I've reconsidered and decided that you have to stay the course on this one. They know what they're doing, and all of it will prepare you for the future."

"No," he said, "I'm out of this place. I'll get out somehow, but I'm not one of *them* and I won't stay."

"You will, and you'll take every drop of what they have to offer. I'll call you tomorrow," she said, hanging up the phone and looking heavenward, hoping for strength.

Burning with rage, Bryan propelled the chair faster than any of them had ever seen him move it, roaring down the hall toward the gym. And seeing his own miserable face in the mirror as the automatic door opened made him angrier.

"Fuck! Shit! Goddamn her! Goddamn this place! I hate this

fucking place!" he screamed and drove the front of the wheelchair into a wall and then away and then rammed the back of
it into the wall, screaming, "No! No! No!" He'd been at it that
way for several minutes when he saw Nancy the nurse in the
mirror.

"Don't try to stop me!" he screamed. "I hate this place. I hate
my life. I hate my mother. And don't tell me I can't do this."

"I won't tell you anything," the serious-faced nurse said, and
from behind her back she pulled a helmet. "Just wear this." She
held it out to Bryan, who knocked it angrily out of her hand
and continued to try to destroy the chair until he stopped out
of exhaustion and cried. After a long time, Nancy came into the
gym and wheeled him to his room.

16

Lily had a few last-minute changes to make on a script, but she was resolved that by 10:00 A.M. without question she would drive out to Northridge to see how Bryan had survived the ordeal and the night. Yes. She'd run into the office, put the changes into her computer, pop out a disk, then run up to Santo Pietro's to get a pizza and take it out to the rehab center for Bryan's lunch.

"The end," she typed. It was her polish on a script of David's, and she was thrilled to be finished. Hooray! She popped out the floppy disk, dropped it on Dorie's desk and said, "Lose my number, Dor. I'm out of here." And then she was gone, into the corridor and on the elevator, practicing the way she would behave with Bryan. Loving but firm. Sure of her position that the rehab people knew what they were doing. She took her car keys out of her purse and was about to insert one into the car door when she saw Charlie in the passenger seat, holding a copy of *Variety* up in front of his face as if that could conceal him.

"I don't know why you're sitting there, but kindly get out of my car," she said, annoyed. Charlie lowered the paper, and she saw the devilish gleam in his eye.

"It's such a long ride," he said, "I knew you'd want company."

"Well, you were wrong," she said. "Get out."

"The kid likes me," Charlie said. "He'll be glad to see me."

Lily sighed and slid into the driver's seat. Bryan did like him. And maybe seeing him would keep it all a little lighter. Bryan was probably furious at her, but he might not be so quick to get all over her about her failure to show up yesterday if Charlie were with her. She started the car. Neither of them said a word all the way to the pizza place. Charlie was either very interested in the articles in *Variety* or pretending to be. The first words he said were when she stopped the car to get out at Santo Pietro's.

"No pepperoni for me. It gives me heartburn."

When she came out and slid the large pizza box into the backseat, he had moved on to working on a script and was making notes on it here and there and dog-earing pages. Lily looked at the clock, quiet as she pulled onto the 405 freeway heading north, thinking that if there wasn't too much traffic, she'd probably get to Northridge just before they served the food Bryan had been describing with disgust to her all week.

"Mind if I ask you something really important?" Charlie asked. Her thoughts were on Bryan, so she didn't reply. "Don't you think," he continued, "that when they get to the bowling alley Angel should admit that she can't face turning thirty-five?" The traffic was slowing, so Lily could turn to look at his face.

"Pardon?"

"I think it's a nice character moment for her."

"Good-bye, Charlie," Lily said, and she veered out of her lane into the next right lane and the next one until the car was on the shoulder of the road. Slamming the car into park, she turned to him. "Get out of my car," she said, "before I come over there and drag you out." Cars were whizzing by, and she knew this was insane behavior, but she was feverish with anger.

"You don't have a shred of interest in my son," she said. "You just want to squeeze every second's worth of work out of me that you can. But I won't let you, so you can just walk."

Charlie's eyes were wide and he burst into that cackling laughter of his. "You have spunk," he said through the laugh. "I hate spunk." She'd heard that line before.

"Ed Asner to Mary Tyler Moore in the pilot episode," she snapped.

Charlie held up a gnarled hand on which two of his fingers were curled down. "Gimme three," he said, and laughed again.

"Get out," she said angrily.

Charlie continued to laugh. "My God," he said, "Even Ebenezer Scrooge was nicer to Tiny Tim. Let me come along and I swear I'll behave. I'll tell jokes. How did the cripple cross the road? Very slowly," he said, laughing that laugh again, and Lily grudgingly released the emergency brake and eased the Jeep back into the hurried freeway traffic.

Bryan was sitting in the wheelchair next to the bed, laughing with one of the nurses as if nothing had happened the day before. Lily figured that even if he was angry at her, he'd forgive her once he smelled the pizza.

"I've got good news, and I've got bad news," she said. "I brought pizza . . ." And as Charlie entered the room, she added, "And him." Bryan's eyes brightened considerably at the sight of Charlie.

"Hey! A dude who walks funny!" he said.

"But not as funny as you do." They shook hands as Lily placed the pizza box on the rolling bed tray, opened it, and wheeled the pizza over to Bryan, who looked at it wistfully.

"Too bad I can't eat this," he said, sighing and inhaling the pungent scent of the oregano rising from what was now a luke-warm pizza. "I'm going downstairs for a cystoscope. They think I might have kidney stones."

Lily looked worried, but Charlie grinned. "Isn't that lucky?" he asked, turning to her. "While he's having the test, you and I can spend some time rewriting the bowling story."

Why had she let this clown come here with her? What she needed was some quiet alone time with Bryan to rehash yesterday.

"I was nuts to let you come here with me. Back off," she said.

"Mom," Bryan said, "chill. I'm glad he's here."

Charlie shrugged and smiled at Lily. "Misery acquaints a man with strange bedfellows. *The Tempest*. Act one, scene two," he said.

Big deal, so he could quote Shakespeare. She wasn't going to do any work for the show now. She was here to focus all of her attention on Bryan. "I'm not working on any bowling story," she snapped.

"You're right," he said. "We ought to talk about the Christmas show."

"I," she announced, "am here to be with Bryan. I'm going to do whatever he chooses, and I'm sure that won't be for me to sit and work with you while he has some invasive test."

A nurse appeared in the doorway and nodded at Bryan. "Time to go down, kiddo," she said. Lily moved forward with Bryan, and when they got to the door he said, "Uh, Mom, do you think that maybe Charlie could sit with me while I have the test and keep me laughing so I won't think about it?"

"Oh, sure," Lily said, trying to look as if she didn't care.

Bryan nodded, and Lily looked at Charlie, who reached into his pocket and pulled out the script in question.

"Needs new dialogue right from the top," he said, handing the pages to her just before he, the nurse, and Bryan left the room.

She was angry when she first sat in the chair in Bryan's room, but after she read a few pages she had some ideas about how to fix the dialogue in the scene when they first arrived at the bowling alley. Funny things about the fact that Angel's thirty-fifth birthday was being held in the same place as her sixteenth. And soon she was caught up in the story, scratching out old lines and jokes and writing in new ones. She was so into it that she actually didn't think about Bryan for a few minutes.

Bryan was lying on the table in the sterile little procedure room, and Charlie sat on a nearby chair. When the woman in the white coat walked in, it took them both a minute to realize that she was the doctor. She was a knockout, a tall redhead with a body that made Charlie let out a low "whoa." She looked as if she were playing a doctor on one of those hospital TV shows.

"I'm Dr. Blake," she said, "and what I'm going to do this morning is insert a tube into your urethra."

"Almost makes you glad you're a paraplegic, don't it, boy," Charlie joked as the serious doctor ignored him and went on.

"The tube will enable me to look around in your urinary tract to see if I can locate any stones."

"I saw the Stones at the Forum last year. Keith Richards looked like they brought him back from the dead," Charlie said, moving his chair closer. Bryan held on to his arm while the doctor worked on him.

"Jagger," Charlie was rambling, "is still very cool. When we go back upstairs I'll do my version of 'Honky-Tonk Woman' for you. I'd do it now but I don't want to risk inflaming the doctor's desire and ruining your tests." That made the doctor laugh an outraged laugh.

"I'll be back in a minute, you two," she said. "Don't get into any trouble while I'm gone." When she left, Charlie watched her go.

"She's wild about me already," he said, nudging Bryan like one kid to another at a fraternity party. "Because the secret of making a woman fall in love with you is making her laugh. A guy with a sense of humor can always get a girl into bed."

"Great," Bryan said. "But you forgot to mention what I'll do with her once I get her there."

Charlie looked at the door, then leaned in confidentially. "Oh, kiddo," he said, "so many things even my filthy mind boggles at the list. And in good time you'll figure them all out. I swear."

Bryan was embarrassed. Lily sometimes used to try to talk with him about sex, usually to warn him to stay safe and be thoughtful. "Women will love you," Charlie said now, and Bryan felt himself blush, "because they'll know you bring something special to the party. And you certainly aren't led by your dick."

Bryan laughed. This guy might be off-the-wall but he was the only person in his life, including Lily, who never minced words or looked at him funny or sighed or averted his eyes when Bryan was in the room. "Are you kidding?" Bryan answered. "I can't even find my dick." That was when the doctor walked back in.

"Unfortunately for you, *she* can," Charlie said, and the two friends laughed.

17

◊◊◊◊◊◊◊◊◊◊◊◊◊◊◊◊◊◊◊◊◊

Lily's literacy story was about to be read at the table, and Lily had a stomachache. It wasn't the usual *Angel's Devils* fare and she thought the goons from the network might have strong objections to the serious underpinnings of the story. But after the cast began to read the pages to the assembled production staff, even that sloth Harvey Meyers seemed to be nodding with approval and laughing at her jokes. At the end of the first act in the part of the story when Angel is out of town and can't read the ritual good-night story to her daughter, and the child asks Joey to substitute for mom, he agrees. But as he's unfolding the Peter Pan story, the little girl realizes he's improvising and not really reading. In fact, she points out that he's holding the book upside down.

"End of act one," the stage manager read.

"Strong," Harvey Meyers said out loud. When everyone agreed, Lily took her first deep breath in days. At the close of the show, when Joey agrees to get a reading teacher, Chris Barlowe, the actress who played Angel, was crying.

"I had an uncle like that," she said.

"People are gonna love this," Harvey Meyers said as he and two other guys in suits stood. Harvey walked over to Charlie and gave him a hearty pat on the back. "Getting good work out of these writers, Charlie m'boy," he said. "Keep turning out shows like this one and who knows?" Then he winked flirtatiously at Lily, and the three men marched out of the soundstage.

"Let's eat," Marty said, and the boys followed him off the set toward the offices.

Charlie was talking to the director, and Lily waited for him.

"Thanks for believing in this idea," she said.

"Thanks for saving my ass," he said. "You took an idea that could have come off as a polemic and made it palatable by making it funny. I like that in a woman."

"Bryan's sixteenth birthday is this weekend," she said. "We're inviting some friends to rehab and I know he'd love it if you came."

"Will the heart-shaped fiancé be there?" he asked. She nodded. "I wouldn't miss it," he said. When she turned to go to meet the guys for lunch, she could feel him watching her.

The offices were empty. The guys had left without her, so instead of going to lunch she sat in her office worrying about her wedding to Mark. December wasn't that far away and she hadn't planned a damn thing yet. She knew there were zillions of details that would need her attention in order to make the wedding what Mark wanted it to be. Caterers, florists, musicians. All of it a colossal waste of money in light of Bryan's needs. Maybe she should get out a legal pad and make some sort of preliminary list of people to call to get the ball rolling. But after twenty minutes all she had written on the pad were the words LILY AND MARK'S WEDDING, followed by a big question mark. So instead she made a list of things she needed for Bryan's birthday party.

*   *   *

"All right, who has a match?" Daisy asked, and Bruno, Marty, and David all pulled cigarette lighters from their pockets. They were assembled in Bryan's room at rehab for his birthday party, and Bryan was in such a good mood he had even let Lily invite his friend Arthur and his friend Joel from the tenth grade.

"Sixteen candles," Daisy said. "And one for good measure and one for good luck and one to—"

"Don't say grow taller," Bryan joked. No one laughed but Charlie.

They were all wearing pointy paper party hats that were secured to their heads by thin elastic bands. Only Mark had abstained from wearing the hat.

"Okay, while we're singing," Daisy said, grabbing a nurse who had peeked in to see why there was so much noise coming out of this room, "you take a picture!" She handed the camera to the nurse. "Everyone gather round the birthday boy. Mark, put on a hat," she said, thrusting one on him. Mark smiled a tolerant smile and put the hat in his pocket. But he did move into the group around the bed, and as they all lined up and smiled for the camera he noticed Lily put a friendly arm around Charlie's shoulder.

"Happy birthday to you!" The group stood closely together and as they sang Lily was struck with a thought that for some inexplicable reason hadn't occurred to her until this moment. If the bullet had entered Bryan's chest a quarter of an inch to the left, it might have pierced his heart and she would have lost him. "Happy birthday, dear Bryan. Happy birthday to you."

"Make a wish," Charlie said.

"Well, since I can't wish it were six months ago, I think I'll go for Cindy Crawford," Bryan said, and blew out the candles in one breath.

"You open the presents while I cut the cake and try not to eat most of it," Daisy said to Bryan.

Charlie moved the stack of presents to the bottom of the bed and took the first one, which was an envelope, and Bryan held it to his head as if he were a psychic. "Let's see," he said. "Definitely not a gift certificate for tap shoes."

"Spoken like the son of a comedy writer," Bruno said.

Now *Bryan's* doing it, Lily marveled to herself. That behavior he'd learned from Charlie. He's catching on to that "I'll poke fun at me before you get there" humor, making it clear that there was no need to walk on eggshells about his condition because he never would do that himself.

"Gift certificate to the Wherehouse from Marty and Bruno. Thanks, guys."

The next gift was a long box Bryan tore into, and he fished around for the contents. It was two long handles unidentifiable as anything he'd ever seen before even after he'd turned them over and moved them around.

"They're from me," Charlie said. "They're portable hand controls that can be used on any car so you can drive it. I know you had a date at the DMV to take your test and you're going to keep it. I'll make sure you get your license right on schedule."

Of course driving would be the first thing on Bryan's mind when he turned sixteen. Lily was embarrassed that it was Charlie who'd thought of it first, but more than that she didn't like the way he assumed it was all right to make decisions for Bryan like the one he had just made and announced without asking her.

"One more picture," Daisy shouted. "Mark, you party pooper. Put on the friggin' hat. Don't worry, we're not selling the photos to the *Heart Doctor's Gazette*. Nobody's gonna know."

"I don't think so," Mark said. Lily gave Daisy a look that told her to stop bothering him.

After the photos Lily collected a pile of the wrapping paper. Charlie helped, and they walked out into the hall to find a trash can.

"Great party," he said.

"Thanks for coming," she said, then sighed. She knew she had to confront him. "Listen, I know your intentions are good, but I have to tell you something before this goes any further. I don't want him to rush into driving. He can barely pilot the wheelchair, and driving lessons will just be one more kind of pressure for him. So even though it's a nice thought, let's just not mention it anymore. He'll be so busy trying to adjust that he won't even notice."

"You're wrong," Charlie said, and Lily felt a rush of anger.

"Maybe I am, but in this case I get to decide. So listen carefully. No driving lessons. No driving lessons. When the day comes that I start feeling he's in some shape to handle it, I'll take him to a driving teacher to learn. But in the meantime, repeat after me—"

"No driving lessons," Charlie said. Surprisingly, there was no joke to follow.

When Hugo dropped him off in Malibu, Charlie was still wearing the party hat and carrying a balloon. Maybe that was why when he walked into the house, the baby in the high chair stopped whining, looked at him, and laughed.

"Glad you're home, honeybunch," Natalie said. "We're starving. She's been wondering where you were."

Natalie looked gorgeous, and she was in the exact spot where he loved seeing her the most, in front of the stove. Nobody cooked like this amazing broad. God, how he loved her.

"Hello, my angel," Charlie said to baby Francie, and she put her hands up to him to be taken out of the chair. Charlie leaned over her, gave her a big kiss, and extracted her as she made happy cooing sounds.

"The hat does wonders for you, sugar," Natalie said. "Leave it on. I'll take a video of the two of you with the balloon."

"No more videos," Charlie said. "You're obsessed with that new camera."

"Oh, come on," Natalie said, picking up the camera and aiming it at Charlie and the baby.

"Do you have any idea how much I love you?" Charlie asked the happy Francie.

"Not even approaching how much she loves you," Natalie said.

"Go out on the deck where the light's better, and let me get you two together out there. Then you can play with her while I set the table. Dinner'll be ready in ten minutes."

Charlie kitchy-cooed the baby and walked out on the deck, where his brother-in-law Frank sat on a chaise longue talking on the cordless phone. Frank wiggled his fingers at Charlie and Francie, and Natalie got a shot of all three of them. Charlie loved Frank and had since the day his sister Natalie had married him. The tall, handsome, financial whiz had a business management company, and his investments had made Charlie and many of his other clients very wealthy.

"I know," Frank said to the baby, "your uncle Charlie is your favorite."

Natalie shot Charlie walking down to the beach holding Francie on his hip. The baby waved to her mother over Charlie's shoulder with a little pudgy hand as Charlie took each step one at a time, holding on to the banister. When they got to the sand, he put the sweet little girl down and she looked around with a face shining with the joy of her freedom and then she took off with her jiggling run, racing toward the water with Charlie toddling behind.

"Here comes the sea monster," he shouted, and Francie looked over her shoulder, smiled an open-mouthed smile, and kept running until Charlie caught up with her and scooped her into his arms. Francie let out a sound that was somewhere between a scream and a hysterical giggle as he twirled her in a circle. They tore up and down the beach, and their laughter rose above the sound of the crashing waves. While she clutched his index finger, they chased the receding water into the sea and ran screaming from it as it chased them back.

They patted a poodle and a golden retriever that passed them, and then they dropped to the ground at the borderline between the wet sand and the dry sand and dug a big deep hole. Charlie was tired. He wanted to go inside and have a drink. He was thinking about Bryan. The kid was fantastic. Crabby and annoyed at the world, just like him. The kid was so much smarter than most people.

It was obvious Bryan liked Charlie too. Didn't care about the inane bullshit that adults laid on everything. Charlie sighed now remembering how it felt at the birthday party when for one of the early group pictures Lily had actually put her arm around his shoulders. Of course it was just to pose for a picture, but she had gotten close and touched him. Maybe there was something to it. He sighed, watching a sailboat in the distance. He could smell the garlic chicken Natalie was cooking all the way down here. "C'mon, Francie girl," he said. "it's time for you and Uncle Charlie to head back up to the house."

Francie was squishing her toes in the wet sand and loving it, so the idea of going into the house didn't interest her. "C'mon," he said. When she ignored him again, Charlie bent to pick her up and, while she protested and wiggled, he put her back on his hip and walked up the beach toward the steps.

"We'll come back out after dinner," he told her. At the bottom of the staircase, he stopped to look back at the ocean. Isn't it lucky, he thought, that I have the wherewithal to live a life like this? A beautiful home and a family who come to visit me and want to be with me. And a relationship with this baby who hasn't yet figured out that everybody doesn't have an uncle who's trapped in a mangled body. Dear God, he thought, don't ever let her look at me and feel afraid.

"Up we go, Francie pants," he said. He was holding her on his left hip and again he took the steps one at a time. Step up with the right foot, join it with the left. Step up with the right foot, join it with the left, but on the fifth step his right foot faltered and his left flew up underneath him and his balance was shaky. Helplessly he felt himself going backward but he couldn't grab hold of the banister.

Toppling, flying, feeling the wooden steps on his back and on the back of his head, grabbing for Francie to block her fall and finally landing on the hard sand below with a powerful thud. Francie was screaming as Frank and Natalie flew down the steps. Frank seized the screaming baby from where she lay on Charlie's chest, flailing and terrified, and Natalie fell on Charlie, touching his face, his head, brushing the sand out of his hair.

"Shall I call an ambulance?" she asked him.

"No ambulance," he managed to say. "Baby okay?"

He looked forlornly up at Frank, big and blocking the setting sun. Francie was in his arms, whimpering.

"She's fine," Frank assured him. "I saw you go, and she fell on top of you."

Frank turned and took the baby up the steps while Natalie sat on the sand next to her brother. The sun was moving lower in the sky and the water was a bright teal green. A man Charlie's age, with a toned and tan body, ran down the beach with his German shepherd on a leash. Charlie looked after them with pained eyes.

"Glad you didn't get *that* moment on video," he said.

"Chars," Natalie said. "All these years you've taken care of me. Paid my college tuition, for God's sake. Now it's my turn to take care of you and help you make the move out of this house. I know you love it, and it's very sexy, but it has too many steps for you, and it's too far away from town. Let me find you a broker and I'll help you look for a place closer in that's more in keeping with what you need."

Charlie was stone-faced. He was hurt from the fall and imagining what could have happened to Francie if he'd come down at a different angle. And he hated himself, his awkward, irresponsible self for being so selfish and endangering her.

"I made your favorite garlic chicken and Mom's roasted potatoes."

Still he didn't look at her.

"It isn't the fall that's hurting you is it, my darling brother?" She knew her sibling so well. She had grown up watching his relentless fight for normalcy and the day-to-day battles he'd fought to be in the mainstream. And from his struggle had come the off-the-wall sense of humor, which had yielded a spectacular success that had made him rich. Rich enough to pay for her four years at Columbia and for her wedding to Frank.

There had been setbacks for him, temporary illnesses related to the cerebral palsy, but none of them could squelch the power of his spirit. She and Frank had speculated more than once about what Charlie might have become if the circumstances around his infancy had been different. Too smart to be president. But maybe Robin Williams.

Charlie brushed the sand from his legs and stood.

"Want to tell me about the birthday party?" Natalie asked, putting her arm around his shoulders.

"Greatest boy on the planet turned sixteen today," he said.

Natalie was sure there was more to the story but she knew not to push, so she moved Charlie along to the steps and took them slowly with him on their way to dinner.

18

◇◇◇◇◇◇◇◇◇◇◇◇◇◇◇◇◇◇◇

The meeting was supposed to start at ten and Charlie was just finishing a phone call in his office when Marty came up from the commissary holding the *New York Times*. "We're in the *Times*, you guys," he said, laying the Arts and Leisure section on the conference table as the others gathered to look.

On an inside page of the *New York Times* was a photo of the cast of *Angel's Devils*, and the headline ANGEL'S WRESTLES WITH ISSUES. "Oh shit," Marty said. "We're dead meat. I told you we should have laid off the issues. Listen up." Lily's heart sank. She had been the one to push the idea of dealing with issues, and now it had backfired. Now the show would never get a pickup and it would be her literacy idea that broke the camel's back.

She was already wondering if she should sell her condo as Marty read out loud with his eyebrows raised, *"Angel's Devils* pulls itself out of the depths at last with a touching and funny story in which Joey, the macho husband of Angel, confesses to his family that he can't read. A sure Emmy candidate, this episode changes the tune and the tone of the sagging sitcom. Whoa, Lil! Gimme five there, buddy."

Lily picked up the paper and reread the review slowly. It

was praising her writing and the turn the show had taken because of her nagging.

"Yeah, well, if we're such hot shit, how come we don't have a script for next week?" David asked.

"I had an idea," Charlie said, coming in. "Why don't we do an anniversary story that flashes back to Angel and Joey's wedding, and all the reasons they fell in love?" The guys were all silent and Lily looked up from the newspaper. That was an odd idea coming from him. It wasn't a hard joke ha-ha story or quirky and off-the-wall the way Charlie liked them.

"Sounds cute," she said.

"A little soft for your style, Charlie." Marty said. "Want Lil to take a pass at it?"

"Nope. I think I'll try it myself," Charlie said and turned to go. Lily caught Marty's shrug, and she raised her eyebrows in return.

"Oh and my sister just called," Charlie said, turning back. "On Sunday you're all invited to her house for a barbecue. You really should come if you want to see me flip burgers, some of which might actually land on the grill."

"Christ. First he comes up with a romantic story, and now he wants to hang around with us," David said after Charlie left the conference room. "Did somebody slip something into his coffee?"

When Lily arrived at rehab on Sunday morning, Bryan wasn't in his room or in the gym so she stopped at the nurses' station. Delia, a round black woman and Lily's favorite nurse, was on the phone, but she held the receiver against her large chest and said, "Bryan's been outside on the tennis court for hours."

Lily found her way out to the courts and stopped a few yards away when in the distance she heard a familiar sound she thought she'd never hear again. It was that little grunt of effort Bryan made just as he slammed the ball across the net. Plop. The ball landed, then there was another grunt and a thwack. Bryan hit it hard. And again.

Getting close to the court now, she watched the ball machine spitting the balls out while Bryan with his increasingly powerful arms rolled the streamlined chair rapidly from one side to the other. And it was his same masterful stroke that was placing the balls back on the other side just where he wanted them. It was damned impressive.

"Agggh, crud!" he yelled as he missed a ball and the machine sent another one whizzing by him too. But then he was back in the rhythm again, gliding across the court this way and that.

Lily moved closer and stood on the sidelines, her face shining with joy at the way he'd adapted his stroke to playing from the chair. Mastering a new version of his favorite sport.

"Hey, lady, get out of my shot," she heard Charlie say, and when she turned she saw him sitting on the bleachers behind her, holding a video camera.

"Shouldn't you be cooking away for the party?" she joked. She had come to pick Bryan up and take him to the barbecue at Charlie's sister's house.

The machine was out of balls, and Bryan took a deep breath as it clicked off.

"Why don't we all go to the party together, Mom?" Bryan asked. "You can pick up your car later."

Lily looked at Charlie. "Couldn't have said it better myself," he said, placing a familiar hand on the handle of the wheelchair. "Hugo's waiting out front."

In the cool backseat of the limo, Lily's back relaxed against the black leather upholstery. She could hear soft jazz coming from one of the speakers. Charlie and Bryan were running the video on the small screen connected to the video camera.

"I borrowed my sister's video camera so I could show Bryan how good he looks out there," Charlie said.

"Should have borrowed her tripod," Bryan said. "Looks like these were shot by Stevie Wonder." That made them both laugh.

"It does kind of rock from side to side the way he and I do," Charlie admitted.

Lily felt something loosening in her back that had been too tightly wound there for months. Now it was opening the way it did in the deep relaxation exercises she did in those yoga classes that she and Daisy loved and always swore they'd go back to but never had time for. It was a sense that all of the horrible fears that woke her in the middle of the night, the pictures in her mind of a pitiful future for Bryan and for her, were unfounded. Somehow she felt an understanding that normalcy was relative and that it was possible that Bryan would find some version of it. Slowly, to be sure, but he would find it.

Charlie's sister's home was on Rockingham in Brentwood. It was a very grand two-story white Mediterranean house with a red tile roof. Inside there were ceilings with hand-painted beams. And in the foyer there was a large, dark table with dozens of framed photos spread across it. Charlie left the video camera on a chair next to the table and opened a glass door so he and Bryan could hurry down to the pool.

Lily stopped to take a long look at pictures of Charlie's parents, a handsome couple, of Charlie and his sisters and brothers as children on a beach, of Charlie in his prayer shawl at his bar mitzvah, of the proud parents and the siblings standing next to Charlie, in a cap and gown, at his graduation.

"I'm Natalie Gold, Charlie's sister." Lily looked up to see the woman from the photos. She was holding a pretty baby girl. "And this is Francie. She's Charlie's niece." The baby was pink-cheeked, with a mop of gold curls, and Lily melted when she looked at her.

"Lily Benjamin."

Natalie smiled as if the name had some meaning for her. "My brother's crazy about your son," she said. Francie put her head sleepily on her mother's chest.

"Charlie's been more than helpful these last months," Lily said.

"He loves kids," Natalie said. "Especially this one who is just about to go down for her nap." She kissed the baby on the top of her curly head, and Lily felt a wave of baby envy, remembering how she had loved it when Bryan was that age and how good it felt walking around and holding a snuggly little one in her arms.

"We do this barbecue for Charlie every year because he loves to entertain and it's far too hard for him to do it on his own. So my husband and I tell him to invite all of the writers on whatever show he's doing, and I cook too much food, and we have a party. Looks like most of them are already out at the pool. Enjoy."

The lawn on the way down the hill to the rectangular turquoise pool was bordered everywhere with multicolored impatiens. Lily took off her shoes and scrunched her toes into the newly mowed grass. Last night she had told Mark on the phone that she had to go to Charlie's sister's party because all the writers would be there, and since Charlie had gone out of his way to be nice to Bryan, she owed it to him. And Bryan and Charlie did have a kind of friendship going so she really couldn't insult the man. But why did she feel as if she'd been overexplaining it to Mark, as if she were covering up the truth?

And the truth was that she was eager to see Charlie at play, and meet his sister and her husband, and get some sense about his family. After all, she thought, if you're working so closely with someone, it's good to know as much about him as possible.

She could see the others in a circle at the far end of the pool. Marty and his wife, Pat—or "Marty in drag," as Bruno called her, because she and Marty were so much alike: short, pudgy bodies and big personalities. Pat was a nursery school teacher and talked to everyone in a voice that sounded as if she were talking to three-year-olds. Bruno's wife was Lolly, a former Las Vegas showgirl who always looked made-up enough to walk onstage; and David's wife was Greta, a tall, leggy blond with a long mane of hair who was endlessly bickering with David, who loved the battles. Lily was crazy about all of the wives.

Everyone in the circle was already in bathing suits and they were playing some game that made them erupt now and then in big, raucous laughs. Lily stopped at the pretty stucco hut that was a cabana bathroom and stepped into the cool, tiled-floor room to change into her suit. It seemed like years since she had worn a bathing suit, and if it wasn't the old gang out there she'd probably be reluctant to put one on now.

Even Mark hadn't seen her in a bathing suit in the last few years. Naked, yes. Bathing suit, no. There was something about squeezing herself into a scanty little costume the fashion industry deemed "beach attire" that she didn't like. Especially because every suit on the rack seemed perverse, with padded breast enhancers and "tummy control" panels.

Maybe, she thought as she removed her shorts and T-shirt, she never wanted to pull on one of those suits in front of Mark because he was in such perfect physical condition and looked so good in everything he tried on. She was always afraid he expected her to look taut and lean, too. And she tried. Before the shooting she had forced herself to go to the gym on weeknights and Sunday mornings. But her work took so much time and energy that when she actually had moments of her own, she collapsed instead to read and sleep. And now with Bryan's care requiring so much time, she didn't have any spare hours to work out.

The suit she stepped into now was a very old black tank and it made her look a little bulgy in the rear, but no one in this crowd would care. Well, maybe, she thought, she'd just slip a T-shirt over it. Another peal of laughter rose from the group as Lily stepped out into the sun. It was a scorching day and the surface of the pool rippled in response to a light breeze that brought an instant of relief.

"Okay. My turn," she heard Charlie shout.

"You got it," Pat said. "Here it is."

Lily arrived in time to see Charlie open a rolled-up strip of paper and read it to himself. There were bowls of chips and chip dip on a low table in the middle of the group, and while Charlie thought about whatever was written on the paper, Marty grabbed a handful of chips and chomped on them noisily.

"What category is it?" Bryan asked.

Charades, Lily thought. Great, I'm good at it.

Lolly waved a little wave to Lily, but the others were all focused on Charlie, who put the piece of paper down on the table and announced, "Okay, I'm ready. It's a film."

Then, as he moved his hands up to his mouth in thought, Marty shouted, "*All Quiet on the Western Front.*"

Charlie turned to Marty in mock affront. "I haven't done anything yet."

That got an enormous laugh from everyone, especially Bryan.

"Think that's funny?" Charlie asked. "Well, you're going in the pool," and he grabbed the handles of the wheelchair, turning it to face the pool, rushing it forward and tilting it so that the laughing and shrieking Bryan flew out of it into the water.

All of them watched in horror as he plunged to the bottom, and no one uttered a sound while they waited for him to rise to the top. Lily was afraid that being thrown in that way in front of everyone might have been humiliating to him, that he might be mortified at his inability to fight back. She'd know the instant she saw his eyes. A giant bubble came to the surface followed by Bryan's shiny hair and then his face with eyes that were filled with happy surprise.

"This is awesome," he said. "I should have done this before. I feel weightless."

"You do?" Pat said. "Then that's for me." She stood and pulled down the flouncy little skirt on her bathing suit then dove headfirst into the pool.

"Me too," Marty said, and he ran toward the water doing a belly smacker of a dive that got everyone wet. Now everyone was ripping off T-shirts and cover-ups, including Charlie, who held his nose and jumped into the deep end. When Lily realized she was the only holdout she pulled the T-shirt up over her head and slid her warm body into the cool water.

Charlie and Marty and Bryan were playing a very noisy game of tag and Lily swam laps underwater, opening her eyes to see the others float past her.

She never did have much of a stroke, but underwater it didn't matter, she could just push away the water to propel herself, dive lower to move along the bottom. Someone else was moving along the bottom. Shimmying toward her in an otterlike move.

Who was it? The bubbles and the shimmering sunlit water made it unclear. Then she realized it was Charlie's face looking at her, but the flickering image created by the changing light and the water's movement made his face, for only an instant, look perfect. Surely the way it would have looked if the incubator accident hadn't occurred.

Lily rushed to the top and swam to the steps, climbed out of the pool, and wrapped a towel around herself. A familiar bleating sound made her turn to her purse and take out her ringing cell phone. "Hello?"

"Hi, sweetheart," Mark said. "Bored to death yet?"

"Uh . . . well, actually, it's not so bad," she told him, shaking off the water in her hair.

"*There's* high praise," he joked.

Lily was watching the group in the pool. They'd obviously decided to have a chicken fight. Marty was holding Bryan on his shoulders and Bruno was holding David. Lolly and Pat were cheering them on and Charlie was whispering chicken-fighting techniques to Bryan.

"I mean, Bryan's having a great time," she told Mark.

"I'm glad," Mark said. "And you'll be home . . . when?"

"Don't know," Lily replied.

"In time for me to fix you dinner?"

"Um . . . I don't think so. We just got here."

"Call me if you change your mind," Mark said. "Love you." And he hung up.

Lily felt odd about the exchange, but she wasn't sure why. Then it occurred to her that the feeling was guilt. Mark had expected some conspiratorial whispered exchange in which she would tell him, in secret code if necessary, how miserable she was at this party without him. And instead she was feeling great and having a fine time. She could see Natalie on her way down from the house, carrying the video camera and aiming it at the pool, laughing as she shot the battle of the chicken fighters.

After a while she came and sat next to Lily. "My brother loves these parties so much I almost can't wait for the summer so we can have them for him." Natalie opened a cooler that sat next to her chair, took out a diet Coke, and handed one to Lily. They sipped quietly as they watched the group at play.

"When Charlie was born and then the terrible accident happened in the hospital, my mother was terrified that bringing him up in our household would destroy the rest of us because as a baby and a little boy he required so much care and attention. But it turned out to be the exact opposite. He was always the glue that held us all together and made our family special, as in 'the ones with the weird kid.' And because of who he was he gave us a standard, someone we had to strive to be like because hell, if he could get through it, we should certainly be able to. Not to mention as a kid he was filled with joy and humor."

Lily looked at Natalie and wondered why she was making this speech and if she made it to everyone or if there was some reason for it.

"If that's hard to believe, rest assured it's only in his adult life that he's become a shit. Probably because he realizes, the way we all do at this age, that this life is finite and most likely he will have lived his out without ever becoming a father."

The screams of laughter rose from the pool and both women looked out to see Bryan toppling David into the water to cheers from everyone.

"He could be, you know," Natalie went on. "What he has is not genetic."

Charlie was cheering Bryan on and congratulating him, and

Marty was jumping up and down so Bryan rose and fell into the water, laughing.

"Imagine," Lily said, looking at Charlie. "A child with his spirit."

"Too bad that ring probably means you're engaged," Natalie said, leaning in to look at Lily's left hand. "Wow! To a guy who gave you a ring shaped like a heart."

"He's a cardiologist," Lily told her. "That's why it's shaped like a heart."

"Thank God he's not a urologist," Natalie said, and laughed. Lily looked surprised.

"Charlie did the same joke when I first met him," she said.

"Hah!" Natalie said, nodding. "That's our family. In our house there were no holds barred, nothing we couldn't joke about, nothing that wasn't funny. My mother's philosophy was, 'If you give your child a sense of humor, you give him a special way to look at the world that will never fail him.' "

Lily pulled a squeeze bottle of sunscreen out of her purse, squished some into her hand, and smeared it on her legs. Isn't it amazing what the unconditional love of family can do? she thought. And that's why Charlie's inner child of the past is whole and well, and mine's a bloody pulp.

That night Hugo dropped Lily and Bryan at the hospital in Northridge and Lily walked up to the room alongside Bryan's wheelchair to say good night. "Two more weeks here, Mom, and then I come home," he said, transferring from the chair into his bed. Neither of them wanted to talk about his return to school and how soon he'd feel well enough to face a disabled life in a world where only months ago he had been a star athlete.

Teenagers could be mean, and there was nothing she'd be

able to do to soften the pain. Bryan needed something to boost his confidence that was his own, the way tennis had been for him since he was ten. Something unrelated to the disability, but she couldn't imagine what that would be. "You can take your time about going back," she assured him. "The teachers all offered to send work home, even to come to the house and work with you until you're ready to go back."

His face was sunburned from the hours in the pool and his cheeks were rosy and glowing, but the light mood she'd seen in him all day was gone.

"Honey, you don't see what everyone else does about the progress you've made," she said. "The way you've come back so incredibly from the most horrendous disaster. You're heroic and resilient and strong, and all of your friends will see that."

"Two more weeks" was all he could say. Lily didn't feel eager for the two weeks to pass.

19

◇◇◇◇◇◇◇◇◇◇◇◇◇◇◇◇◇◇◇

On the set of *Angel's Devils* this week, they were shooting Charlie's show. One of the scenes was a flashback to the day Angel and Joey were married. All of the writers were on the set for the dress rehearsal. When Lily looked at Chris Barlowe as Angel, dressed in the white lace off-the-shoulder bride's dress, she thought that an expensive frou-frou dress one never wears again was another way for the fashion industry to make fools out of women.

In this episode Angel's mother was a peach, the sitcom funny, platitude-spouting, lovable mom. Angel and Joey were sitcom blissfully in love, and Lily found herself wondering if there were any real people on earth who felt that way about each other. She had been aroused by Donald, in the deranged, reckless way of a needy girl who had never been touched before. In fact, when she met him she hadn't been touched too much outside of a one-week affair with a sexy motorcycle maniac who departed so swiftly she'd always suspected that Annette paid him off.

Now she was engaged to marry Mark. She felt safe with him but it wasn't what she'd imagined love could be with that elusive soul mate. The way it was in mushy song lyrics. "When I fall in love, it will be forever. Or I'll never fall in love." So many things about her relationship with Mark were right, seemed right, had to be right. Besides, being gigglingly hysterical about romance was out of the question for a thirty-eight-year-old woman with a sixteen-year-old son. Being heart-thumping wild about someone seemed absurd.

When Chris walked onto the set in the dress and twirled around, an "oooh" went up from the crew. At the same time, Nicky Lord, the actor who played Joey, was complaining because they had to girdle in his paunchy middle to make him look like a thinner, younger Joey.

"People," Peter Baldwin, the handsome white-haired director, called out to the jabbering extras, "bridal party and guests, take your places; bridesmaids, get ready to walk down the aisle when you hear the music. Families on both sides, get ready to turn and look when you hear the music."

The actresses playing the bridesmaids were in long lavender dresses, and Lily thought about Daisy and the commotion that was going to happen when it came time for her to confront Annette about her wardrobe as maid of honor.

The music began. It was Vivaldi's *Four Seasons*. I will never be able to pull off something like this, Lily thought as the bridesmaids walked down the aisle toward the actor playing the minister. When Chris, as Angel, appeared in the doorway, Lily felt a sob rise in her throat. This is a dress rehearsal of a made-up story about fictional characters, she told herself. And even more absurd is that it was written by the least sentimental man on earth, so get a grip, will you?

The rehearsal went smoothly, and the usually blasé crew laughed at all of the jokes. And in the scene where Joey's aging Italian mother was giving him advice about women, Lily noticed that one of the bulkier guys on the crew was sniffling into a handkerchief.

"Where's the gimp?" Lily heard Bruno ask Marty.

"Left a message that he doesn't like to be around when his work is being staged, so he isn't coming in all day," Marty explained.

There was a three-hour break between the dress rehearsal and the taping, so Lily went up to the office to call Bryan and get some work done, but when she got to her desk there was a fax sitting on it in Bryan's handwriting: MOM. MEET ME HERE AT THIS SPOT IF YOU CAN GET AWAY TODAY AT FOUR O'CLOCK FOR A BIG SURPRISE. LOVE, BRY. Underneath the message was a hand-drawn map to somewhere in Van Nuys with the words MAKE A RIGHT HERE. And an arrow and then PARK HERE and an X.

Van Nuys on a summer day was not the place anybody wanted to be. Lily couldn't think of a reason Bryan would be there. Maybe the rehab group was having a good-bye party for him at Chuck E. Cheese, but why didn't he say that in the note? Charlie's absence from work today was a definite advantage if she wanted to leave. Her work could wait, there was nothing pressing. Maybe she'd follow the map just for fun and show up for him.

"Hey, Dor," she said on her way out, "I'm going out to meet Bryan for a while. If Charlie comes in, tell him I'll be back in time for the taping."

It was just four o'clock when she realized the place the arrow on the map was indicating was the Van Nuys airport. Bryan hadn't said what he'd be doing here, maybe they had a flight simulator and they were letting him try it. Maybe the group was having his party here because they knew how much he loved airplanes. As Lily got out of the Jeep, the scorching Valley heat engulfed her. Probably Bryan was in one of those air-conditioned buildings, she prayed. But then there was no mistaking what she saw ahead of her on the tarmac.

The limo. Charlie's goddamned limo. And there was Hugo, tall and dark, leaning against it. So whatever the surprise was, it obviously had something to do with Charlie. He was here planning something behind her back with Bryan and that was the real reason he wasn't on the set that day to watch his show's rehearsal.

She didn't try to get Hugo's attention, she just moved toward the buildings hoping to find some cool air or at least a cold drink. She watched a teeny little prop plane as it came in for a landing. Who'd go up in those flimsy little numbers, she wondered, and then her stomach lurched when the realization fell over her that the pilot of that plane, the person she had just spotted through the window, was Bryan.

Inside the Cessna the teacher was congratulating Bryan on the smooth landing, and Charlie was in the tiny backseat singing at the top of his lungs.

"I saw a peanut stand, I heard a rubber band, I saw a needle that winked its eye. But I think I will have seen everything when I see an elephant fly."

"There's my mom," Bryan said as he taxied the plane down the tarmac.

"Ooooh," Charlie said. "I recognize that expression on her face, and she's as mad as a snake."

"Think so?" Bryan asked, much too preoccupied with braking the plane to notice.

"Same look she had on her face the day I held her out the window."

Bryan turned off the engine and the teacher shook his hand. "Well done, pal. You should keep these lessons going as often as you can. Wheelchair aviators have a club that meets out here, and I expect they'd be real pleased to have you on their roster."

Bryan couldn't keep the proud grin from his face. "Thanks. I'll check it out."

"Not so many more lessons and pretty soon we'll send you up there all by yourself."

Charlie took out his wallet and handed the teacher cash for the lesson, and Bryan opened the door to see Lily standing a few yards from the plane.

"Mom! Charlie bought me flying lessons. The planes have hand controls and pretty soon I can get my license and fly!"

Lily fought back the anger, the outrage that was struggling to get out of her chest and wanted her to run to Charlie and pummel him for not getting her approval on something as dangerous as flying. For not thinking about how he was putting her only child in that little tuna can of an airplane. For thinking it was all right to co-opt the parenting of this child without her consent.

"That's wonderful, honey," she said.

Bryan had unfolded the wheelchair and now transferred onto it and lowered the ramp so that he and the wheelchair were on the tarmac. Charlie was climbing out the other side of the plane.

"You said no driving," he said to Lily with a triumphant twinkle in his eye. "You never mentioned flying."

"That isn't funny. You have to stop shoving yourself into my child's life and going over my head to provide him with something as dangerous as flying lessons." The flying teacher was writing a receipt for Charlie, which he handed him, then slipped away with a look that said he didn't want to be anywhere near the argument that was about to happen.

"Listen carefully," Lily said to Charlie. "I decide what's best for this boy and not you. Do you understand?"

"Good work, Bryan," Charlie said, and then turned to walk to his car, where Hugo opened the back door for him. He climbed inside.

"Jeez, Mom," Bryan said. "Thanks for messing up the best day of my life."

Lily looked at him and guilt spilled through her. "The best day of your life?"

"I was gonna go to school and tell those boys who are learning to drive that I'm learning to fly."

Lily watched the limo glide off the tarmac and out into traffic and she felt stung. Charlie was making her look like the ogre in her own child's life. She had to make it clear to Bryan that she wouldn't allow that. She took a deep breath and tried to sound even. "He has to learn to consult me when he's doing things for you. Has to, Bryan. I hate that he's making me the outsider in my child's life. I hate that all of a sudden he's closer to you than I am." A small private jet was taking off, and both mother and sun watched its swift climb into the brown-with-pollution sky.

"No, you don't, Mom," Bryan said seriously. "What you hate is that you think he's incredibly brilliant and funny and cool, but you can't walk your talk. Can you? You can't see through his disabled body to his soul."

Lily felt as if someone had dropped a piano on her. The weight of what Bryan said was crushing. Maybe he was right and all along the feelings of jealousy she was having were not because Charlie was with Bryan and she wasn't, but were because Bryan was with Charlie and she wasn't. Maybe the man she loved was the crazy, funny maniac inside that damaged body. Good God.

No, it was impossible. She was in love with Mark. She was getting married within the year, if she ever found the time to get on the phone and plan the damned wedding.

"I'll take you back to the hospital," she said, following behind the wheelchair so he couldn't see her very confused expression.

20

◇◇◇◇◇◇◇◇◇◇◇◇◇◇◇◇◇◇

The "cute" carpenter, which was how Cynthia Lloyd described the workman she recommended to make Lily's condo wheelchair-accessible, was also an actor. So after he finished the job on Thursday morning, he had to run off and audition for a commercial. It looked to Lily as if he'd done all of the work and it was okay. The place wasn't perfect, but it was certainly functional until she and Bryan had a better idea about what their future would hold. The floor spaces were clearer, thresholds were removed, everything had been changed to specifications given to Lily by the doctors at the rehab hospital.

Closet bars were lowered and a seat and a grab bar had been put into the shower in Bryan's bathroom. Two of the doors had been converted to pocket doors because a standard door took up too much space in the room. Lily walked through the house, room by room, trying to imagine Bryan's return and how he would navigate, wondering what she'd forgotten. She was late for work, so she called Dorie and told her to make excuses to Charlie.

Since their confrontation at the Van Nuys airport he had been cool to her. No teasing, no jokes, a perfunctory "that's funny" when she came up with an idea that worked. Today he was in his office with the door closed when Lily arrived. She was reading one of Marty's scripts when she heard a woman's voice ask Dorie, "Is this where I find Charlie Roth?"

"In there," she heard Dorie say.

Lily's curiosity was stirred, and she stood and opened the door to her office to see all of the guys positioned in the doorways of their cubicles looking at the woman, who was a gorgeous blonde dressed in a great-looking designer suit. The woman turned to smile at the boys, and it was a drop-dead killer smile. Then she turned the knob to Charlie's office and after a second they all heard him say, "Hey, babe. Lay a kiss on me!"

Lily raised her eyebrows, the boys exchanged an envious look. Lily sat down at her desk, but now she couldn't follow Marty's story. Every now and then a laugh rose from Charlie's office and it rattled her. She left her door open and a few minutes later she saw Charlie and the blonde emerge.

"Back in a few weeks," Charlie said to Dorie and the guys. Lily was irked. Why hadn't he introduced any of them to his lunch date? How rude. It wasn't as if she was some young chicky he'd be embarrassed to be with. This was a beautiful, adult woman who took his arm as they made a very grand exit. Who cares? Lily thought. I hate him anyway.

Charlie had looked so pleased with himself, and it was clear by the way the guys looked after them as they left that they envied him. She tried not to watch the clock while she ate a sandwich that she'd made for herself at home. When she realized she'd put too much mayonnaise on it so that it was soggy, she felt like crying. Charlie and that woman had left at twelve, for heaven's sake, and here it was two forty-five. None of the writers would dream of taking such a long lunch, and now here they came. She could hear them giggling up the hall in that way that people do who have had a few glasses of wine with lunch.

All of the guys were back in their doorways, and Charlie looked around at them and said, "Oh, my goodness, Marilee, I forgot to introduce you to my boys. These are my boys. And Lily in there . . . she's a girl."

"Thanks for noticing," Lily muttered. She walked to the door of her office just to get another look at the beautiful Marilee, and as soon as she did she felt shabby in her jeans and Earth Day T-shirt, but she managed to call up one of her mother's best so-lovely-to-meet-you smiles. Then she closed the door. But when she sat down she could still hear the guys talking too loudly and Marty sounding hyper for a while. Finally their silence told her that the lovely Marilee was gone.

"Daisy's on the phone," Dorie opened the door and shouted in to Lily.

Lily was happy to have a reason to stop working. Marty's script was impossible to fix.

"When's Bryan's big homecoming?" Daisy asked.

"Tonight. I pick him up at six, and then we're going to have some dinner and take it really easy and let him move around the condo and tell us what's missing." Now she realized that Dorie hadn't closed the door when she'd delivered the message and that Charlie was standing in the doorway. Lily wasn't sure why her heart thumped when she saw him.

"I'll bring the salad," he said. Lily held the receiver to her chest.

"You're not invited," she said.

He grinned and closed the door.

"Who was that?" Daisy asked.

"Charlie. He's insane. I can't wait until the season's over so I can look for a job on some other show," Lily said.

"Bryan told me you really took him apart at the airport. How come you don't just fall to your knees and pray to the guy? He's the best thing that ever happened to Bryan."

"No, Dais. He's out of line."

"This was a kid who six weeks ago thought he had no life left and now he's trusting the man, laughing his ass off, flying a plane, for Christ's sake, and you're such a self-absorbed pain in the ass, you think that unless you're the one doing those things for Bryan, they don't count. I recommend that you go kiss the guy's crooked little everything and admit that not only does your kid love him but that you have the all-time crush on him."

"You're crazy. I'm engaged."

"Both of those statements happen to be true," Daisy said. "Nevertheless, you dig the guy. You should see your face when his name comes up."

"You're delirious," Lily said, and hung up the phone. She worked until five-thirty, and after she packed up her things she tiptoed by Charlie's open door. His back was turned to her as he slowly pecked away at the computer keyboard.

"What'd you do to the house?" Bryan asked as Lily waited in the ONE CAR PER GREEN LIGHT ramp to get on the freeway.

"I had a carpenter come in and make things easier for you to reach," she said, trying to make it sound as if it had been a breeze. The carpentry bill was sixteen thousand dollars and there was still more to do. Mark had offered to pay the bill for her, but she felt better about asking her mother for a loan.

"I'd rather be lending it for college," Annette said on the

phone after she'd agreed to send a check. "Tell him I'll be there in two weeks to see him." She had gone from skiing in Telluride to a music festival in Aspen, and was now at home in Connecticut getting ready for her trip to Hawaii, so she'd be passing through L.A.

"Who's gonna be there?" Bryan asked.

"Just Mark." Lily wondered if there would be some rush of emotion for Bryan when he first saw the building, but he didn't even turn to look at the spot where the shooting had happened. In the garage in the wheelchair, he moved toward the ramp the carpenter had built and rolled the chair up it easily toward the door to the kitchen.

"Somebody left something out here, Mom," Bryan said, and Lily followed behind to see a rectangular shape wrapped in aluminum foil on the floor in front of the door. She picked it up and opened the door and followed Bryan into the kitchen. As he looked around at the changes, she opened the foil.

"It's enchiladas," she said, looking into a long Pyrex baking dish.

Bryan rolled the wheelchair close to the counter and looked into the dish. "It's Elvira's enchiladas," he said.

"She must be back," Lily said, grabbing the phone and dialing Elvira's old phone number, the one she'd had in the apartment in East Los Angeles. Maybe she was back from wherever she had gone to hide. But after two rings a recording told her the number had been disconnected.

"She wanted me to have her cooking," Bryan said. "She's around somewhere, Mom."

"Welcome, welcome," they heard Mark's voice call from the living room.

"She wants us to know she still cares about us," Lily said,

taking Bryan's hand. "Maybe one of these days she'll let us see her," she said hopefully as Mark marched into the kitchen.

"Just been watching some golf," he said. He was carrying a clipboard, which he held up. "To keep track of what needs to be done," he explained uncomfortably, and Lily thought then that she had never seen him look so unsure of how to behave.

"Hey, Mark," Bryan said by way of greeting. He put his hand out for Mark to shake, but Mark wasn't sure how to approach the wheelchair so he reached for Bryan from too far away and they barely touched fingertips.

"Well, why don't we go from room to room and see what you think about all the big changes your mom made."

"Not so big." Lily hurried to correct him. She wanted to downplay the expense and effort so Bryan wouldn't worry. Besides, this was just Mark's way of hammering his point home again. Every time she mentioned the dust the carpenter was making or anything about how different certain rooms in the house looked now, he jumped in with the idea that it was a waste of her money to redo the condo. Less than a year and they would be married and she and Bryan would be moving into his house or, better still, a brand-new house.

"Going to see my room first," Bryan said, and Lily knew with certainty that this had been the right thing to do. She watched him stop in the doorway of his room to look around at his trophies and airplanes, then wheel himself inside. "No way I'm not having a door," he said.

"You have a pocket door now." She showed him how to release the new door the carpenter had installed by creating a space inside the wall. "And here's the lock," she said, showing him the simple latch that would assure his privacy.

"Cool." He wheeled over to his closet door to look at the

photo collage he'd pieced together over the years. Earlier that week it had occurred to Lily to rip up all of the Kimberly photos before he got home, but she knew that was out of line. Maybe he'd want to keep them up there in the hope that Kimberly would come back.

He didn't move from the closet door for what seemed like a long time, and from where Lily stood she couldn't see his face. She opened the door to his bathroom, hoping curiosity would pull him away from the images in the collage, but he didn't budge, and when he finally turned to head toward the bathroom he had wet tracks making a trail down his cheeks to his chin.

"Thanks for keeping things close to the way they were, Mom," he said, looking into the bathroom.

The doorbell rang. Daisy, Lily thought. Stopping in to give Bryan a homecoming hug.

"I'll get it," she called out to Mark, who had wisely retreated to the kitchen, where he would be putting the finishing touches on dinner.

"No, I'll get it," Bryan said, moving the chair into the living room and opening the door.

Charlie was standing in the doorway holding an unusual-looking object.

"Just a welcome-home penis pump," he explained. Bryan blushed and cracked a smile. "Every household needs one," Charlie said. He moved inside as Bryan backed the chair up, and Lily and Mark stood wordlessly behind him.

"Uh . . . Charlie, you remember my fiancé, Mark Freeman?" Lily asked. All she could think was that there wasn't enough chicken, so Charlie better not think he was staying for dinner.

"Of course," Mark said. "Great to see you again." Lily was sure he would have preferred to shut the door in Charlie's face. "Glad to see you too. Here, hold the penis pump while I bring in some other things from my car," Charlie said, thrusting the gizmo toward Mark, who put his hands up as if to say, "Don't get that thing near me." That made Charlie laugh a scoffing snort of a laugh. "What's the problem?" he asked. "I didn't ask you to hold the penis. And even if I did ... what's the big deal? You're a doctor!"

Without even looking, Lily could feel Mark stiffen next to her. Every day she worked next to people whose stock in trade was their inventive, quirky minds and their uncensored mouths that spewed outrageous ideas. Mark's world was one of sterilized precision blades, no margin for error, and thoughtful, documented statements backed up by data and studies and research. She wondered what he could be thinking about this creature in the doorway. Charlie didn't seem to care what anybody thought about him ever and tonight was no exception. Now he looked into the living room and pointed.

"That rug's no good. The pile's too high for the wheels. And it looks like you forgot to put in a ramp for that step up into the dining room."

"No problem, no problem," Mark said. "I'll just move the coffee table, and Lily and I can take the rug right down to storage."

Lily leaned over the coffee table, and as Mark picked up one end she picked up the other, and they moved it against the wall. Then they went back to roll up the rug.

"How're you doing with the chair?" she heard Charlie ask Bryan.

"Lousy," Bryan said.

"Got a boom box?"

"In my room."

The rug was rolled now and Mark lifted his end of it; Lily crouched to pick up her end, and then they hoisted it onto their shoulders and moved to the door in the kitchen. Lily knew there would be room in the big wood locker above her parking spot, so they slowly made their way down into the cool garage. "I forgot the damn key," Lily said as they laid the rug on the garage floor. "Be right back." But as she turned, he caught her wrist in his hand.

"Lily," he said, and she saw some unidentifiable look on his face. Was it hurt—or jealousy? He was worried about something, and he pulled her close to him. His blue oxford shirt smelled so fresh and his arms were so strong when he wrapped them around her that she tried to let herself relax in the moment. The sweet man she loved wanted to hold her. More than hold her. He was filled with that eager tension he had in his body when he wanted to make love. Almost as if he wanted to unroll the rug and have sex on it in the garage, right now.

He kissed her hard, then placed softer little kisses all around her mouth, and it felt good and right and awakened her body for the first time in months. "I love you so much," he said into her hair. "Don't do anything more to this place. Let's move the wedding date up."

She loved it that he wanted her so much. This divine man adored her and sometimes she couldn't imagine why. But this would be the worst time in the world to rush into a wedding. Bryan needed time. She needed time.

"Oh, Mark. He's crazy about his room here. He used to call it his lair and I know he's not ready to give it up. Too much has changed in his life already for me to force anything else on him this minute. Let's just keep things the way they were and have the wedding in December as planned."

"It's going to be such a long road for him. I worry for you."

She had both of her arms around his waist and she hugged him and put her face in his chest.

"I worry for me too," she said, and kissed him a quick kiss. "Let me run upstairs and grab the key, and I'll be right down."

Halfway up the steps she could hear the loud music. Probably the entire building could hear it. It was some bluesy, rock 'n' roll tune she couldn't name until she opened the door. Then she remembered. It was from that dopey *Blues Brothers*, a film Bryan used to rent at least once a month. Lily walked into the kitchen and opened the drawer where she kept the keys and found the one for the locker, but instead of going back down to the garage she took a peek into the living room.

With no rug and the coffee table moved aside there was a big surface of hardwood floor exposed, and Bryan was manipulating the wheelchair around it in a way that looked as if he and the chair were dancing to the music. From the hall tree near the front door he had removed one of Lily's hats, and with it he was wearing the sunglasses she always kept on the front table as a spare. Charlie had on his own sunglasses, and now the two of them were spinning and sliding and hooting as they whirled. Neither of them had any idea she was standing there as they rocked their bodies to the music. Lily was swaying from side to side to the music too, and she couldn't resist moving into the room with them. They both grinned when they saw her.

"We're on a mission from God," Bryan shouted. It was his favorite line from the movie, and Lily grabbed an *Angel's Devils* baseball hat from the hall tree because it was the easiest to reach.

It felt so good to be moving to that music. In high school and college she had loved to dance—not the sappy slow dances but the rock 'n' roll, free-spirited, sexy, shimmying kind. Now she moved her feet in circles around Charlie and Bryan, who cheered her on. Boogying, swiveling, she didn't know how much time had passed or that she was still holding the locker key in her hand until she saw Mark standing in the doorway.

"Wait!" Charlie shouted suddenly to Bryan. "Maybe you don't need a ramp up to the dining room. Maybe you can just pop a wheelie."

Lily was flustered and sweaty from the dancing and thought that surely she must look like a jerk to Mark as she pulled off the hat and shook out her hair. Bryan moved the chair to the far end of the living room then propelled it toward the kitchen, getting faster and faster, tipping it back just in time to hurl it into the dining room to the cheers of Charlie and Lily, who hurried to him with shouts of congratulations.

"As soon as I get the rug put away we can eat," Mark said quietly, but nobody heard him

21

❖❖❖❖❖❖❖❖❖❖❖❖❖❖❖❖❖❖❖

Neiman Marcus in Beverly Hills was brightly lit, sparkling with color, and dotted everywhere with mannequins squashed into dresses no human could possibly wear if she were going to breathe at the same time. Daisy and Lily were rifling through racks in the couture department, dressed in jeans and T-shirts.

"Mother would be physically ill if she were here to see us shopping in these outfits," Daisy said.

"Fortunately," Lily said, holding up a gold-beaded strapless, "the biggest part of mother's charm is that she's never here, so we don't have to worry about that." Lily hung the gold gown back on the rack and shifted the hangers along so she could look at the next dress and the next. "Am I wrong or are these clothes freaky-looking, overpriced, and insulting? Maybe it's just that having a disaster in your life slaps your priorities into place, but look at this." She held up a red taffeta gown with purple piping and long, pleated sleeves. "Five thousand dollars. I could put a lift on the front of the building for that so Bryan wouldn't have to use that steep ramp to get in."

"But you'd have to go naked to the Heart Ball," Daisy said.

"Forget it," Lily said, taking her sister's arm and steering her toward the second-floor coffee shop. "I'm not going. I'll just tell Mark I'm not ready to go out in big crowds of people who will cluck their tongues and say 'Pity about your son,' or 'You're so brave.' I just don't feel like it. I know he's the chairman of the damn thing, but I think I'll call him tomorrow and say, 'Honey, why don't you take your mother to the Heart Ball?' "

"Tell him you'd never be caught dead at any event named after two body parts," Daisy said as they stepped into the line waiting to get into the tiny coffee shop. Lily watched the chic and wannabe-chic women marching by, toting their shopping bags, and she thought it was a good thing department stores were open on Sundays or she'd never get any shopping done. Not that she'd bought a single thing, but it felt so good to be away from the house and hanging out with Daisy.

Bryan seemed glad to get her out of his hair. He was watching tennis on TV and even made a few phone calls to some school friends, inviting them over. Things had been calm for the last few days. She had gone into the office and had actually been funny in a few of the meetings.

The cashier showed them to a small table that a waiter was clearing and the two sisters sat across from each other looking at menus.

"Shit," Daisy said. "They've got that dainty little Beverly Hills food here and I need a cheeseburger."

"You don't *need* a cheeseburger."

"Today I do," Daisy said, looking at her watch. Lily read her worried look.

"I forgot," Lily said, looking at her own watch and feeling some of the same anxiety Daisy was feeling. Their mother, An- nette, was arriving at five o'clock.

"She hates me," Daisy said.

"She does not," Lily said, raising her hand to get the attention of a waiter.

"Wrong," Daisy said. "I embarrass her ass off. I'm a fat, butch dyke who works at a Target store in the San Fernando Valley. If she ever deigned to set foot in a place like that, I'd be one of the worker bees she'd run over with her shopping cart."

Lily wished she could produce a credible rebuttal, but they both knew she couldn't.

"I mean, how could she ever get who I am? She's a woman who xeroxes her jewelry." That memory set them off, remembering the day Annette proudly came home from her office at the travel agency with a shopping bag of her jewelry and a ream of paper, each sheet containing a xeroxed image of a piece of her jewelry. "It will help me create a file so I can decide what goes with what. That way I can keep track of the new pieces I might need," she had told them.

"Two Chinese chicken salads with the dressing on the side," Lily said to the waiter before Daisy could order for herself.

Annette was stopping in L.A. for two days on her way to Hawaii, where she was planning a tryst with a man at the Hana Maui Hotel.

"Dais, listen. I'm a skinny, successful writer in the most competitive business in the world, engaged to the most appropriate catch in the solar system. Any other mother alive would look at me and say, 'There's a daughter I'd like to have.' And Annette niggles and pokes and picks and sneers at what I wear and what I say and how my house looks. That's the nature of the beast. Our only hope is that she's mellowed with age."

As soon as she spotted her mother at the airport curb dressed in an Armani pants suit and surrounded by five large, black Tumi suitcases, Lily knew there had been no mellowing. When

Annette saw Lily pulling up, she picked up the smallest bag, opened the passenger door, and put that one on the floor. Then she moved into the Jeep and sat down, leaving Lily to put the four large cases in the back.

"Hello, Mother," Lily said, leaning into the car to offer a perfunctory hug.

"I brought swatches," Annette greeted her. "And darling pictures of dresses for the bridal party. Naturally, allowing for your sister's size. Is she still gargantuan?" Lily was lifting the first of her mother's heavy suitcases into the car when she heard that.

"Mother," she announced, shoving the suitcase in and coming around to the passenger door where Annette sat with the window open, "if you're going to hurt her feelings, you can leave for Hawaii now. We're a very fragile group looking for tender, loving care, which you may not have in your repertoire. And if you don't, don't come home with me."

"You look great," Annette said, but her eyes were watching a good-looking sixtyish man as he hailed the Hertz shuttle.

"Thanks, Mother," Lily said, lifting the next suitcase and carrying it to the back of the Jeep.

"I was rehearsing what I was going to say to your sister. 'You look wonderful, Daisy.' I hope my nose doesn't grow."

Lily picked up the third bag with a grunt. "White lies, Mother. They're okay, and she needs to hear them from you."

"You look great," Annette rehearsed again.

Lily pulled the Jeep onto the freeway, and, within yards, the traffic ahead had slowed and soon she was at a dead stop.

"Los Angeles," Annette said, sighing. "I never could connect with this place. It's so unattractive, and there's such an uneven jumble of people and styles here. How unfortunate that both of my children chose this city when there are so many good ones all over the world."

"Hard to get a sitcom writing job in Rome," Lily said.

"But sitcoms aren't real writing anyway, are they?" Annette noted. "F. Scott Fitzgerald would never have taken a TV job."

"As it happened, he took a screenwriting job, Mother, and he couldn't handle it. That's because it takes a hardened-by-life type like me to be able to survive the cutthroat world of Hollywood."

Annette laughed. "When did life ever harden you?" she asked, pulling down the visor and looking at herself in the mirror. "You lived in the best neighborhood in the sweetest house. Okay, so your father walked out, but wasn't I always both parents to both of you?"

The traffic was starting to creep forward.

"Yes, Mother."

"White lie?" Annette asked, pulling out a lipstick from a small, faux leopard skin cosmetics bag in her purse.

"What do you think?" Lily asked. She was wishing she had given Bryan a few more months to adjust before she let her mother come barging back into their lives, however briefly.

"I can't wait to meet Mark," Annette said. "Tell me all about the wedding plans." She was moving to what she was sure was a safe topic.

"I haven't exactly had time to make any of the plans between all that's happened to Bryan and my work, but I will soon, I promise."

"Do you have any idea how far in advance the good caterers and florists are booked?" Annette asked.

"It can't be helped. When I'm ready, I'll do it," Lily said, feeling a stomachache coming on.

"You're not considering backing out?" Annette turned to look at her.

"Don't be silly," Lily said. "I'd never deprive you of wearing whatever it is I'm sure you've already bought."

"A Donna Karan, on sale. It's a drop-dead knockout."

Lily, who had been happy in her condo since the day she'd moved in, noticed today, as she pulled up with Annette in the car, that the exterior of the building needed a paint job. She began to worry that the interior wouldn't be up to Annette's standards.

Bryan and Daisy were out in front playing badminton and laughing. "Oh my God," Annette said, and Lily wasn't sure if her dismay was for seeing Bryan in a wheelchair for the first time or for the number of pounds Daisy had put on since the last time she'd seen her.

Lily tapped on the horn and Bryan and Daisy looked up. Each of them made what Lily knew was an effort to smile. She pulled into the driveway and stopped, and Annette got out of the car and looked at her grandson, her eyes filling with tears, but before she could say a word, Daisy was on the attack.

"Hold down the angst, Mother. We're all way past that point."

Annette took a breath and composed herself. A performance, Lily thought. Her whole life is a performance. "You're right," Annette said, moving awkwardly toward Bryan. "You still look handsome to me," she said, and Bryan turned the wheelchair to the side so she could present him with a stiff, perfumed hug.

"And God knows," Daisy said, "that *is* what counts."

"When do I get to see the bridal dress?" Annette asked, not rising to Daisy's bait.

"Haven't got one yet," Lily said.

"I brought swatches and photos for the bridesmaids," Annette announced, turning to Daisy, who had probably rehearsed her reply for weeks.

"I'm wearing a black tux."

"Perfect," Annette spat. "You'll look like Pavarotti."

"That's it," Daisy said, throwing down the badminton racquet she'd been choking. "I'm leaving."

"Whoa! Aunt Dais," Bryan said, laughing. "A personal best. Gram didn't even get inside the house and the fight's already started. I'm proud of you."

Annette's neck was longer and stiffer now. It was her battle posture and her daughters knew it well. "I'm the mother of the bride, an honor we all know I won't be having again, so I'm sure you don't blame me for wanting the wedding to be perfect."

Lily knew a scene was about to occur and she wondered, short of preventing it, if she could move it inside and away from the sidewalk.

"Dais," she tried, but Daisy's eyes were red with rage.

"I've got a hot flash for you, Mother," Daisy said.

"I'm sure she can have one of those on her own," Lily joked, but her mother and her sister were locked in combat and neither of them cared what she had to say.

"For once in our lives this isn't about your distorted point of view." Daisy's nostrils flared. "Until you understand that fucking Martha Stewart is the devil incarnate, challenging us that unless our lives look a certain way we're doomed, you aren't my mother!"

"I can live with that!" Annette said, and Lily heard Bryan emit an outraged giggle at the exchange. Or maybe it was because he saw the limo pull up. Dear God. It was Charlie's limo. And the impish look on Bryan's face told her he had invited him. When the back door of the limo opened, Lily watched Annette's expression turn from expectation to revulsion. Lily was about to introduce Charlie when Daisy jumped in.

"Mother, this is Mark," Daisy said. Annette's face was bloodless.

"No it isn't, Gram," Bryan said, trying not to laugh at Daisy's shot at a joke. "Mark's in New York and I invited my friend Charlie Roth for dinner. Charlie, meet Grandma."

Annette produced a prefab smile Daisy would have characterized as what-the-fuck-is-going-on-here? "Nice to meet you," she said loudly, offering a tentative hand to Charlie, who didn't take it but threw his arms around her neck instead, which made her stiffen and wince.

"Any grandma of Bryan's is a grandma of mine," he said, and Lily was relieved that he released his hold so quickly or Annette might have started screaming. She looked him over, unable to figure out who on earth he could be.

"I like your Hawaiian shirt," she said, this time not only talking loudly but stretching her lips around each word in case he had to read them.

"He's not deaf, Mother," Lily said.

"I changed my mind, " Daisy said, enjoying everyone's discomfort. "For this, I'm staying."

Bryan handed Charlie a badminton racquet and another one to Daisy.

"Let's go inside," Lily said as she ushered Annette toward the front door. She prayed that Bryan and Daisy hadn't made too much of a mess while she was gone. She had started the dinner early that morning before she and Daisy had gone to Neiman Marcus. It was Mark's recipe for chicken chili, and all she had to do was heat it up and toss the salad.

She rifled through a drawer looking for the salad tools as Annette took a bottle of Crystal Geyser out of the refrigerator, found herself a glass, and poured a cold drink.

"I can't seem to find anything in my kitchen now that Elvira's gone," Lily said, knowing that she sounded too apologetic, but she saw her mother's critical eye looking all around the kitchen.

Knowing Annette, it was only a matter of time before she made some comment about the fact that the kitchen wasn't sparkling the way she liked kitchens to be.

"She was no bargain when she worked here," Annette commented. "She should have told you that husband of hers was violent. I blame this all on her and her lack of judgment."

"She did tell me, Mother. None of us thought it would come to this."

Annette was leaning on the sink, looking out the kitchen window and watching the badminton game between Charlie, Bryan, and Daisy. "Looks like the Special Olympics out there," she said. Lily was so appalled she dropped the plate she was holding and oily salad spilled to the floor.

"Mother, my God."

"Don't be offended. Two of them *are* crippled, aren't they? And your sister is an emotional cripple, so she fits right in."

Lily pulled a length of paper towel from the roll under the sink and picked up the lettuce and tomato from the kitchen floor. "You are so cruel, Mother. I don't know why I ever asked you to come here. I must have been clinging to the foolish fantasy that maybe the day would come when you'd try to nurture me and Daisy a little bit instead of insulting us all the time. But I give up. Why don't you just leave now and make it easy on all of us?"

"You and I were doing fine until your sister thought it was cute to play that awful trick on me."

"What awful trick?"

"Pretending a man like that was Mark. I nearly fainted."

"Why? Why would you faint?" Lily asked, her voice rising in anger. "That man has a successful career, a brilliant talent, a sense of humor unlike any other, and your grandson adores him."

Annette looked away from the group outside and peered

closely at her daughter's confused face. She was trying to identify the expression. Was Lily defending the cripple because
since the boy's accident she'd become the poster mother for the
disabled? Or was there more to it? Annette was reminded of
the time when Lily was in the tenth grade and a tattooed biker
who wore a red bandanna to cover his hair was crazy about
Lily and no amount of warning was enough to get her to tell
him to go away.

Annette had begged her, cajoled and punished, and always
Lily had the same flushed-cheek look that she now wore. It took
the biker moving away to Sebastapol to end that little crush.
But surely she couldn't be having romantic feelings for this man
who somehow was driven around in a limousine. Lily was engaged to be married, for heaven's sake. And yet there was
something about the way her cheeks looked now that made
Annette worry.

"Honey," she said as Lily wiped the floor with a damp paper
towel, "I would pray that you wouldn't try to prove anything
now that you're so close to this crisis. You get involved with a
man like that and you'll spend your life having people stare at
you and wondering what in the hell someone as pretty as you
could be doing with a person like him."

Lily's stomach ached, and her heart hurt, and she wished that
she hadn't come from the body of this narrow-minded woman.
"Is that what some mother is going to tell her daughter about
Bryan?" she asked.

"Bryan isn't afflicted like that pitiful creature," Annette said,
and then she did an ugly imitation of Charlie. "Any grandma
of Bryan's is a grandma of mine," she said, and Lily realized
that all of those books and jokes that deal with how we inevi-
tably become our mothers as we age were probably true. After
all, it wasn't long ago that she had thought of Charlie as pitiful

too. What else *would* she think after years and years of being raised by this woman?

"Thank God, at least Bryan looks normalish," Annette said. Lily held tight to the center island in fear of what Annette would say next. "You're much too smart to make your life a marketing campaign for the disabled just to prove something to him. Marry that doctor fast and get knocked up before you're too old to give him some kids."

"Mother," Lily said, not knowing now if she hated or pitied her. Annette's dark brown roots were showing under a bad blond color. The collagen injections in the lines from her nose to her mouth had created an odd bumpiness there, the eye job she'd had ten years ago was null and void, and the once xe-roxed jewelry now looked overdone and silly. "Daisy said it all, but I'll say it again, because I know from all these years that you never really hear what either of us says. When we were kids, on those rare days when you managed to find yourself at home, you convinced us that the way things looked and what people thought of us was what mattered. And it was a hide-ously wrong lesson, one which I reject totally. Those things don't matter to me one bit!"

Annette sighed and shook her head at the idea that she could be so misunderstood. She busied herself by pulling some cloth napkins from one drawer and some place mats from another and turning toward the dining room to set the table.

"Mother!" Lily snapped. "Will you kindly use the napkins that match the place mats!"

When Lily called the others in for dinner, they were laughing and sweaty and arguing good-naturedly about who was the best badminton player and laughing about the birdie getting lost in a tree and Daisy's brave climb to save it. They were as ragtag and silly as a group of six-year-olds, and Lily watched her mother watching them. She seated Annette on the far end of the table, putting herself on one side of her and Bryan on the other.

She saw Annette's disapproving eyebrow rise as Daisy reached for the bread, slathered butter on it, then shoved the piece hungrily into her mouth as she said, "Starving."

"Let's get back to the wedding plans," Charlie said, and Lily nearly dropped her fork. "I think we should all rethink what we're wearing. I personally favor a pink peau de soie tea length for me." All of them looked at him. "A cross-dressing cripple," he laughed. "Wouldn't that be an ugly hybrid? Even Geraldo hasn't had that one on yet." The joke made Annette smile uncomfortably.

"The truth is," he said as Daisy took another piece of bread from the basket, "when it comes to what one wears I always keep in mind what Thoreau said on that subject, 'Beware of enterprises that require new clothes.' I actually live by that philosophy and the proof is that the jeans I'm currently wearing still have my name tag in them from summer camp."

Annette smiled almost warmly at that, and Lily saw the look in her eyes change from disdain to tolerance. "Your humor is ingratiating, Mr. Roth," she said. "I'm very glad someone so inspirational is in my grandson's life."

"Translation," Daisy said, " 'Keep your palsied paws off my daughter Lily.' "

"Daisy!" Lily said, certain that Annette, who was just beginning to look as if she was relaxing, would now spring at Daisy's throat with a stinging reply. Instead, Annette looked wearily at Daisy and pursed her lips as if deciding what to say. Bryan was rubbing a piece of bread around his plate to soak up some of the sauce that was left there. He was so used to Daisy's out-of-line behavior he didn't look up.

Charlie didn't crack a smile. Lily was about to apologize to him for Daisy's remark when Annette spoke, in a voice that actually sounded contrite. "Daisy," she said, "Mr. Roth makes a good point about the clothes, and I'm sorry. I was wrong to care about what you plan to wear in the wedding. Naturally you should wear whatever makes you comfortable."

Daisy looked at her plate and stuck the prongs of her fork into the small pile of remaining chili. "You must be reading that off a TelePrompTer, Mother. Or maybe Lil wrote it for you when I was outside but I'm not going to—"

"Accept," Lily said sharply.

Daisy was silent for a long moment. "I accept," she said finally.

This time the quiet in the room was a peaceful quiet.

"Pass the bread and butter," Annette said, and Daisy did.

22

On Tuesday morning after Lily dropped Annette at the airport, she was surprised by the sadness she felt when they parted. For the first time in her life, she felt sorry to see Annette go. "You will hang in and handle all of it with great aplomb," Annette had said, hugging her at the airport curb while a porter struggled to lift her bags onto a dolly. And Lily, smelling her mother's familiar Tuberose perfume, had wanted to hug her forever and cry into her shoulder and make up for all the missed hugs over the years.

The day before, they had taken a drive out to the beach, and when they passed through what Lily thought was Charlie's neighborhood in Malibu, she pointed it out to her mother. After they'd driven a few miles in silence, Annette looked out the window as she talked.

"I made a mistake when I married your father," she said. "He was the same type as your first husband, responsible only to himself. But I loved who he was on paper. A lawyer, meaning he'd have money. From a good family, meaning he'd have money. I forgot to notice one thing. That he didn't have any idea who I was or what I wanted to do or be. It didn't matter to him as long as I enhanced him. When I decided to open the travel agency, which I did all with my own money that I'd been saving, that was the beginning of the end.

"He knew by the way I loved my work, planning the tours, organizing the corporate travel, finding the undiscovered hideaways for my clients, that I wasn't going to be satisfied just being there looking pretty and being Mrs. Him and Mommy to two girls who were in school all day. It never occurred to him that the business gave me so much. Just being out there having people praise me for how efficient and talented and creative I was. Not once did that cross his mind. All he knew was that if I wasn't at the bar association dinners in a knockout dress, I was a dud."

Lily replayed the monologue over and over in her head that night at the dinner table with Mark and Bryan. They were talking about what to do for the coming Fourth of July weekend.

"Charlie's family has a box at the Hollywood Bowl, and he invited us all," Bryan said. "The music's for old people, but the fireworks afterward are cool."

Mark shrugged and looked at Lily. "Sounds okay to me."

The third of July was a Friday, and Lily pulled into the parking lot at CBS to see Cynthia Lloyd getting into her Range Rover, which was full of balloons. Lily hopped out of the Jeep, and when Cynthia spotted her she waved.

"Rushing off to the day camp," Cynthia said, backing out of her parking spot. "There's a preholiday party at noon. So I'm leaving 'Mother and Daughter Phone Sex Teams' to fend for themselves while I head out to the Valley with balloons and cupcakes."

She waved again and rolled up the window and then stopped, suddenly remembering something. She rolled the window down again on the passenger side. "Hey, I can't believe I almost forgot to tell you this," she called out. "Diane Bennet, the executive producer of *American Dreamers*, is one of the moms at the camp. I saw her at the pickup yesterday and she was asking me about you. She said somebody sent her a few of your scripts and she went bananas over them. She'd like to steal you away from *Angel's* and make you a producer on her show."

Lily was surprised. She even thought for a second that Cynthia might be kidding. *American Dreamers* was a show about a group of women friends who start a small business together. It was a wonderful show with thoughtful stories and special characters. Lily had fantasized more than once about what it would be like to work on a show like that. "I love *American Dreamers*, but I've never produced anything. Why would she want me?"

One of the balloons bobbed its way out the window and Cynthia reached over to tuck it back in. "Because there are only a handful of people who can write really strong stories and you're one of them. So I guess shows like that figure they make you a producer and you have a vested interest and stick around."

"Cyn, you know what it takes just to eke out enough time to be with your kids every day. A producer has to oversee everybody else's scripts, so I'd never get home. I couldn't do it."

"It's the number one show in the country. At least take a meeting and hear what they have in mind," Cynthia said.

Lily didn't even want to fantasize about that kind of job because of the work load she knew would be part of the deal. "I can't," she said. "Bryan needs me now more than he ever did."

Cynthia shrugged sympathetically, waved, and drove off.

In the office Lily tried not to think about *American Dreamers*. Not to call up what it said in an article she'd read a few weeks back in the *L.A. Times* about the writing staff and how smart and vibrant they all were. And if Cynthia was right about what Diane Bennet had said, she could be their producer. In the writers' meeting that morning everyone seemed particularly grumpy. Every idea Lily offered was shot down and not in the collegial way the guys sometimes had of doing it, but with some hint of rancor.

"What if Angel starts to resent the idea that she's the breadwinner and that Joey is spending more time with the kids than she is?" Lily tried.

"Authentic portion of canine excrement," David said, stifling a yawn.

"No it isn't, Dave. That's a real tear with working mothers. I think there's a story there." She wasn't doing very well at hiding her annoyance.

"You're right, but it's a dull story," Bruno said. "I like Marty's idea about a sex shop opening next door to Angel's bakery."

Lily sighed and made a silent vow to keep her mouth shut for the rest of the meeting. Charlie didn't like anyone's ideas today, and by seven o'clock, after a soggy take-out lunch and too many munchies that Dorie brought in to keep them going, they hadn't come up with one story that was halfway decent. Lily had been in the meeting in body but her mind was far away, thinking of great stories for *American Dreamers*.

"Let's go home," Charlie said finally. "We're running out of steam."

The guys stood and David stretched. "Nice weekend," Marty said to Lily as the others were off down the hall and out of the building. Lily would go into her office, turn off the computer, hurry home, and bring a pizza to Bryan, then take a hot bath and get to sleep early. Tomorrow night she and Mark and Bryan would join Charlie's family for a picnic at the Hollywood Bowl, and she'd try not to think about work for a few days.

"Someone sent Diane Bennet your scripts," Cynthia had told her. It was hard to believe her agent, Arnie, had decided to do something aggressive behind her back. But maybe now that her literacy show had been so well reviewed he was interested in advancing her career. No, no work thoughts, she decided, walking out of the conference room and into her own tiny space. Good-bye, she thought, clicking the shut-down option. ARE YOU SURE YOU WANT TO SHUT DOWN THE COMPUTER? Yes. She wanted to shut down her brain.

"Lil?"

It was Charlie. "Yes?"

She stuck her head out the door. All of the others were gone. "I just got a call from Hugo," he said, "and he's deathly ill and can't pick me up. Any chance you could drive me home?"

Malibu. Yechh, on the third of July the traffic would be a mess. She wanted to say no.

"I can always take a cab," he said as she stood in the doorway wishing she could think of a good reason why she couldn't drive him.

"Sure, come on," she said, deciding that seeing the ocean would feel good. She'd drive along the Coast Highway with the windows open, and maybe the salt air would relieve some of the sadness she was feeling since her mother's departure, or maybe all the way back to her arrival. While Charlie gathered his papers into his briefcase, she called Bryan.

"Hey, Mom," Bryan said in a voice that told her friends were around, "is it okay if I order out for a pizza? Art and Jerry are here and we're watching *Space Jam*."

"Sure, honey. You have money?"

"Yep."

"Is it okay with you if I get back a little late? I have to drive Charlie out to Malibu because Hugo's sick."

She heard a smile in his voice when he said, "Heck, yeah."

"I like your new script," Charlie announced as she pulled onto the Ventura Freeway, heading for Malibu Canyon. "I love the ending where his luggage lands on top of hers. I thought it was sexy. I never saw luggage mating before."

Lily smiled. "I have to admit, I stole that from my favorite movie of all time. *And Now My Love.* Ever see it?"

He nodded. "I know why you liked that movie. The lovers don't even meet until the last few seconds of the film so we never have to see them deal in life's ugly realities."

"What's your favorite movie?" she asked, glad suddenly that she was doing this. It felt good to have Charlie all to herself for a while.

"*The Devil at Four O'clock,*" he said.

"I don't remember that one."

"It's about an escaped convict who falls in love with a blind girl who's in charge of a leper colony that's located on top of a volcano. Every time I watch it I think, 'You know, my troubles aren't so bad.'"

Lily laughed. She was right about the freeway traffic, it was moving along very slowly, but she didn't really mind because now they were talking about the old sitcoms and their memories of them. Then the very old ones Lily had seen in retrospectives and reruns. "Gracie Allen is my favorite," she said. "She was the forerunner to every TV comedienne. That amazing delivery she had was so uncluttered with mannerisms. It was just out there and perfectly straight-faced against George Burns. Don't you think?" she asked.

"I do," he agreed.

"Every time I get to see another episode of the two of them, I watch it very carefully. It teaches me about timing and how effortless good comedy should look. I even listen to tapes of their old radio shows just to hear the banter and what the rhythm is like." Comedy and how it worked, there was a subject she could talk about for hours. "There's a very cute one where she says to him, 'Ya know, George, you ought to be in pictures.'" She was doing her best Gracie Allen imitation, which she'd only done until now for Bryan and Daisy, who both thought it was pretty good. "'You have everything any leading man has. I'll prove it to you.' And George says—"

Before she could finish the sentence, Charlie finished it for her, holding a pen in his hand as if it were a cigar. "'Charles Boyer,'" he said in his version of George Burns. Lily was surprised. It was an old, obscure routine.

"'Charles Boyer?'" she asked, and this time she tried harder to make her Gracie voice sound more authentic, and she liked the way it came out. "'What's he got?'"

"'What's he got? How about those eyes?'" Charlie said, looking at the pen the way George Burns always looked down at his cigar. It was George Burns all right. A little slower than the great comic spoke, but the sound and the attitude were right.

"'You have just as many,'" Lily said as Gracie. She and Charlie both laughed. Amazing, she thought, that he knew that same old routine.

"I liked the way you used your pen as a cigar," she said. The traffic was moving along now. "Smells a lot better than the one you were smoking that day you threw me out the window."

"I didn't throw you out, I held you out," he said. "Which reminds me," he added, reaching forward into his briefcase and pulling out a box. "This is for you. I've had it for weeks and kept it in my briefcase because . . . I don't know why."

Lily looked at the dainty little box, and it seemed out of place in Charlie's hand. "It is not shaped like any organ of the body, internal or otherwise," he said.

"Very funny. What is it?"

She was tempted to take the next freeway exit, stop the car, and tear into the box. "You open it for me," she said.

"Are you kidding? Ever see me try to undo a knot? It'll wait." The box lay on the seat next to her until Charlie showed her where to make a U-turn so she could pull up right outside his Pacific Coast Highway house. From the road all she could see were three satellite dishes on the roof.

"Is this your house or CNN?" She laughed.

"I have DirecTV, EchoStar, and Primestar," he told her.

"Why?"

"Have to know what's happening if you're going to be funny about it," he said, turning to open the car door, but then he turned back. "The truth is, it keeps me occupied when I wake up at four in the morning with no one to talk to." Then he put his hand on the door handle. "Thanks for the ride," he said. "You can open that box when you get home."

"Not a chance," she said, turning off the engine and picking up the box. "Not that I want to sound ungrateful or anything, but you got a gift for me . . . why?"

"Self-explanatory," he said.

She opened the box, which held a pair of earrings identical to the ones she had lost that day hanging out the window. She couldn't imagine how he'd remembered. There wasn't a man on the staff of the show who could have told him what her earrings looked like. Maybe Dorie had helped him. Whatever the method of finding them, she couldn't believe the gentleness of the gesture. And she laughed when she thought about how she had hated him that day. The day of the shooting. The day she had told Bryan and Mark at dinner that nothing could get worse than working with Charlie Roth.

"This is so thoughtful of you," she said. "It almost makes up for what a jerk you were that day. Not completely, but close."

"Well, you have to admit I got your attention," he said. "Put them on."

She pulled the rearview mirror toward herself and slid the earrings on to her ears.

"They're exactly like the old ones. Thank you so much. You really didn't have to."

"I had to." He smiled. "Damn good-looking. And the earrings ain't bad either."

Tonight he was bringing home a pile of scripts and a full briefcase and she had parked several yards from his house on Pacific Coast Highway. "Why don't I help you?" she asked.

"Thanks," he said, and she picked up the scripts and followed him down the road to his house.

As soon as he unlocked the gate and she saw the gorgeous brick courtyard filled with overflowing flower boxes she fell in love with the house. Glass and used brick and giant windows everywhere, overlooking a deck that faced the rushing ocean. The kitchen windows were open and the wet, kelpy scent filled the house. The sun was a huge orange ball hovering over the glowing water.

"Can I offer you anything?" he asked. "Champagne? A sunset?"

"No thanks," she said, wishing she could stay just until the sun disappeared. The sea air was intoxicating, and she remembered how much she loved it out in Malibu. Many times she had promised herself that one summer she'd rent a house at the beach for a few weeks. It would feel so good, so summery, to sit and have a drink out here. No. It was irresponsible to leave Bryan and his friends at home without an adult. "Bryan's waiting for me," she said, shaking her head.

"I understand," he said.

"Maybe I'll see how he's doing." She put Charlie's scripts down on a counter and picked up a cordless phone. There was a giant TV screen in the living room where she imagined him sitting at four in the morning watching all the shows he must be able to access because of those saucers on his roof. The house was immaculate. If she stayed she might be able to find out if the person who cleaned for him had an extra day to clean for her. She walked out on the deck with the cordless phone. Now the ocean was teal and orange.

"Bry?"

"Mom."

"Are you okay?"

"Yeah. Why?" He sounded impatient. "We're in the middle of watching a video. What's up?"

"Just thought I might stay out here for a little bit and—"

"Go for it, Mom," he said, and hung up.

When she turned back to tell Charlie she'd stay for one drink, he was standing behind her holding two glasses of champagne, one in each hand. His had a straw in it. He touched his glass to hers. "Let's drink to your getting a job on *American Dreamers*," he said. She couldn't hide her astonishment. "Diane Bennet used to be my secretary," he said, smiling. "We talk all the time. I told her to watch your episodes and read your scripts.

She wants to steal you. I think you're crazy if you don't go in and see what she has in mind."

Lily took a swig of the champagne. "Trying to get rid of me so you and the guys can smoke your cigars in peace."

He looked out at the horizon and took a sip of the champagne and was silent.

"I'm sorry," she said after a moment. "I appreciate that you were doing me a favor, but I can't handle a new job and new people and all the responsibility of having to work on all the other writers' scripts all the time. I need to be with Bryan. And besides, pretty soon I'll be getting married, and Mark wouldn't want me to work all those hours."

Charlie shrugged, and Lily took another sip of her champagne, and they leaned on the rail of the deck, standing close to each other as the sun melted into the water. Her legs felt achy the way they always got from just a little alcohol.

"I guess too that after what's happened I feel better about being with people who already know about my situation," she said.

Charlie sighed. "I wonder if my mother thought of her life with me as a situation."

"Your sister told me what your mother thought. That you were the one who brought them together, made them special, gave them character."

He laughed. "That's her stock speech," he said. "She could give that one at luncheons."

"Sounded sincere to me."

"Was she trying to get you to date me?"

Lily smiled. "I think she would have if she hadn't noticed that I'm engaged."

"She must have been distraught when she saw the heart-shaped diamond," Charlie said.

"She made the same joke you did. About the urologist."

He laughed. "It's in the genes. My mother and my dad never stopped laughing and joking. She'd say to him, 'Fred, when one of us dies, I'm moving to Miami.' "

Lily smiled. The sun was gone now, and the sky was orange and navy and maroon. Lily knew it was time for her to go.

"When you marry the heart doc," he said quietly, "promise you won't let him retire you. Because next to your love for that boy I know you're wild about your work. You're a natural storyteller. So never let the little demon who forces you to write go away."

That was too much. Pencilstiltskin. Nobody could have told him about that. "How do you know about that?" she asked.

"Because I'm tuned in to you. I know who you are. I see through your façade to your sunny, funny, quirky self and I don't want you to give that self up, because she's more exquisite than that whacko mother ever told you. And by the way, I'm nuts about your crazy sister too."

Lily's eyes filled with tears. She had to get out of here now.

"I'd better get home," she said, and in her haste to get to the living room in what she realized was now a very woozy state, she nearly walked into the glass door.

"You okay to drive?" Charlie asked. "I can have Hugo take you."

"I thought you said Hugo was deathly ill," she said, feeling weepy and annoyed at herself for drinking even that one little measly glass of champagne when she knew what it would do to her.

"Oh, right," Charlie said. "I did tell you that, didn't I?" And then he winked.

Now the tears came spilling out onto her cheeks, and her lower lip trembled, and then popped out in a sad pout as she wept.

"What is it?" Charlie asked her.

I am really a jerk, she thought. This man has befriended my son, recommended me for the best job in the television business, even bought me a pair of my favorite earrings for God's sake, and I have been nothing but a raving bitch to him since the first day we met. Well, she couldn't say all that. He'd laugh at her. "Sometimes when I have wine I get a little weepy, that's all," she said, knowing she was definitely in no condition to drive all the way home now.

"I recommend a few more sips, because then I start to look like a much younger Paul Newman," he said, laughing.

I owe this man a big-time apology, she thought, and she moved toward him, trying to get the nerve to blurt out what she was thinking. "You have been so wonderful to my son, and I'm such a disgusting bigot. When you first came to work on the show, I made fun of you. I did imitations behind your back."

As soon as she said those words she was sorry. She wanted to be aloof, to seem together to him, not admit to being the juvenile goon she really had been during those first weeks he was on the show. So oblivious to his feelings, so thoughtless.

"I'd kill to see them," he said.

"No, you'd be horrified."

"Ahh, go on," he coaxed. Lily, realizing she was still holding the champagne glass, drained it. "Please," Charlie said. "It'll assuage your guilt. Clear your conscience."

She forced the tears back down and tried to remember what the lines were that she sometimes did in Charlie's voice. The ones that always cracked Marty and Bruno up. "Okay," she said, putting the glass on a table, "here it is." Then she narrowed her eyes and contorted her face to make it look like his and spoke in some version of his voice, "I can't talk much faster than this, but that'll work out because pretty soon you'll realize you've learned how to listen slower."

"You sound like Marlon Brando in *The Godfather*," he said, laughing as he directed her. "I don't talk that fast. You have to slow it down a little."

"Everyone's a critic," Lily joked, then went back into her Charlie mien and this time she spoke more slowly. "Sometimes it can be a problem. For example, when I watch *60 Minutes* . . . it takes two hours."

"Brilliant." Charlie was applauding and laughing and Lily laughed too with relief that he thought it was funny. But then, as she turned back toward the house, the sky and the ground switched places and she felt queasy and dizzy. Her head was throbbing, and she had to sit down.

"I have an awful headache," she said. "I don't think I can drive. Or maybe even walk."

"Maybe you ought to lie down," Charlie suggested, following her into the living room, where she looked around at the furniture deciding where to collapse. She chose the white sofa that faced the deck.

"I think I'll be okay if I just sit for a minute," she said. She put her head against the arm of the sofa, then closed her eyes groggily and said, "Just for five minutes." And as Charlie watched, she fell asleep.

Then he went into the kitchen and poured himself another glass of champagne and sat on the deck drinking it. The night was black and full of stars, but for hours he never took his eyes from Lily.

Mark sat in a chair next to Howard Banks's bed, holding his patient's hand and looking into his exhausted eyes. There was no doubt in his mind that Howard wouldn't make it through the night. Ellen Banks stood near the bedroom door, and when her husband closed his eyes and Mark stood she opened the door and walked him out into the hall.

"Thanks for coming all the way out here, Doctor. He just couldn't go back into the hospital one more time."

"I'm sure being here with all of you is better for him," Mark said. He could see the Banks adult children assembled in the front room of the family's pretty Broad Beach house. All of them were wearing solemn faces. He knew when he had gotten the call at 2:00 A.M. that sending an ambulance out there to bring Howard in was a mistake. He was sure he could give the dying man something that would keep him comfortable in his last hours, so he dressed and made the long ride along the dark stretch of Coast Highway.

Now at dawn he drove along, looking out at the ocean, thinking about Lily and wondering what he could do to get them back to the solid footing they'd once had. He missed her, missed her in his bed. There had to be a way he could prove to her that his commitment to their future was strong enough to handle Bryan's struggle. That was all she cared about now. In fact, there couldn't be anyone better in her life than someone who understood the jargon she'd have to decipher in the world of medicine. He would take care of her, maybe they'd even have a child together, and within a few short years Bryan would be out on his own.

She loved him, he knew, but she was confused and still raw from the tragedy and it would take the kind of patience he had to persuade her to let Bryan find his own way through the ordeal. Now he was passing the Malibu Colony and the shopping center and he thought that maybe instead of going home he'd go into the office and go over some paperwork. It was a holiday and nobody would be there. He could probably get a lot done.

It was a beautiful morning, and he thought about how much Lily loved the beach. Maybe after they were married they'd buy a place out here and use it in the summer, he thought, and then was dumbstruck by what he saw as he passed through Carbon Beach. There was no mistaking the white Jeep Cherokee with the license plate HAHAHA. It was in front of that used-brick Cape Cod house. The one with three satellite dishes on the roof.

There was no other car on the road so he slowed down, trying to get a better look at the house, but from the road the gate obscured it now. What on earth would Lily be doing out here at this hour? He didn't want to think about the possibilities. Instead of driving up Sunset to head for his office in Brentwood, Mark stayed on the freeway and drove home.

Lily heard a crashing sound. She opened her eyes and looked at her watch. It was six-thirty in the morning and she realized to her dismay that the crashing sound was the ocean against the shore and that she had spent the night at Charlie Roth's house. Why hadn't he wakened her and sent her home? She tried to think back to what had happened last night, and reached down to find an afghan covering her that hadn't been there the night before when she put her head on the arm of the sofa. The champagne had given her what Mark called liquid courage to do her horrifyingly awful imitation of Charlie. That was all she wanted to remember.

She stood, sure that Bryan was probably worried sick. Or

with any luck he had fallen asleep and didn't even know she wasn't home now. That's what she had to do, creep out of here and get home before Bryan woke up. Not let him see her come in the way she looked now, staring in Charlie's powder room mirror, at her frowzy hair and smeared makeup and wrinkled clothes.

The house looked even prettier at this hour than it had at sunset. The ocean was gray and the morning sky was filled with white clouds and the light that poured into the room was bright white. My God, she had slept in this man's house. What if someone saw her now as she was leaving? No, nobody would know. She would leave right this second, she thought, and she made her way to the front door, grabbing the knob and pulling it. The instant she did, a clanging bell pounded its warning that a door was opening. The deafening alarm system was activated. She had tripped it, and didn't know how to disarm it, and now it would wake up all the neighbors. Flustered and mortified, she looked around for a control panel, for an off switch, for something to stop the din, when she saw Charlie in a white terry-cloth bathrobe at the top of the steps.

Laughing, he made his way down, opened a closet near the front door, pushed a few buttons that stopped the ringing, then turned to look at the chagrined Lily. "Was it good for you?" he asked. Then he chuckled and turned to go upstairs and back to sleep.

She was out the door, unable to get to her car fast enough. So many people in the business had houses out here, and she certainly didn't want any of them to see her at this hour, looking like this, coming out of here. Good God, she couldn't wait to get home and into the shower. What if Bryan's friends saw her tiptoeing in? At the red light at Sunset, she stopped and pulled her rearview mirror toward her to look at her bedrag-

gled face, and she saw a flush in her cheeks she hadn't seen
there in years.

Safe in her own garage, she took a deep breath, climbed out
of the car, and walked up the ramp to her kitchen door. She
put the key in the lock slowly, turned it carefully, and smiled
to herself, thinking that she hadn't tiptoed in this way since she
was a teenager. In the quiet of her kitchen, she had a craving
for a hot cup of coffee and she put her purse down on the
counter and opened the freezer, where she kept the beans. She
jumped when she heard Bryan's voice behind her. He was in
his pajamas, looking up at her from the wheelchair.

"Guess you two had a lot to talk about," he said. He was
grinning.

"Hate to squelch your romantic fantasy, but I had a glass of
champagne and passed out," Lily said.

"Sounds pretty romantic to me," Bryan said.

"And the part that really made him fall for me was when he
woke from a sound sleep to the sound of me tripping the alarm
and had to troop down at six-thirty to let me out," she said.

"Can't take you anywhere." Bryan laughed. "What's for
breakfast?"

"What's your pleasure?"

"Remember those eggs you used to make me when I was
little that you put in a cup with strips of toast sticking out of
it?"

Lily pulled a carton of eggs out of the fridge and held them
up. "You got 'em," she said. By the time she had the toast in
the toaster, Bryan's friends Art and Jerry were awake too, and
the four of them sat at the table together munching cereal and
teasing Bryan about the dainty five-minute egg-in-the-cup that
he loved. Lily sat with her elbow on the table and her face in
her hand watching Bryan joking with his friends and rolling his

way around the kitchen to help clean up, and a cloud of worry seemed to be slowly lifting. Maybe on Monday when the work week started again she would call Diane Bennet and at least entertain the idea of a new job. Meanwhile, she realized, today was the Fourth of July.

23

Summer nights at the Hollywood Bowl are electric. Groups of people carrying baskets of food and blankets are full of cheer and anticipation for a night of musical entertainment at the amphitheater under the stars. And the best of all the summer nights is the Fourth of July, when at the end of the show the Los Angeles Philharmonic plays the *1812 Overture* and the night sky is filled with a stunning show of fireworks.

Tonight Bryan was in the lead, charging through the grounds, weaving his chair expertly in and out of the crowds, while Lily and Mark advanced slowly behind, sometimes losing sight of him. Charlie had left a message on Lily's machine saying that his sister was bringing a picnic for all of them, but Mark was too well brought up to arrive empty-handed, so he carried a cooler containing a few bottles from his wine cellar.

"None for you," he told Lily as she watched him pull the cooler out of the backseat of his car. "Bryan and I can't handle the tears that go with it."

She looked so beautiful tonight, all in white with her straight black hair loose around her shoulders, Mark thought. Surely everything he was worrying about couldn't be true. All day he had struggled to find reasons and excuses for why her car had been out in Malibu this morning.

He knew he should confront her, simply tell her that he'd been to the beach to see a patient and how coincidental that he had seen her car, and then watch her face to see what it revealed. Or listen to some plausible explanation. But something stopped him from mentioning it.

Now, as they moved inside the gate, Bryan tooled toward the box, where Mark could see Charlie standing on a chair, waving to Bryan to show him the way.

"Heyyyy," Charlie called out as they approached the front row box. He greeted them with the enthusiasm of a child. Marty and his wife, Pat, were already seated and Natalie and Frank were pulling Tupperware containers out of the picnic basket. Mark opened the cooler, and Lily watched as Natalie and Frank fussed over the labels and the vintages and compared wine notes with Mark as Charlie gave her a sly smile.

"Got home safely?" he asked quietly, and she nodded and looked away, not sure why she was feeling uncomfortable. Nothing sexy had happened.

"Hope we're not late," Lily said.

"Don't be silly, we just got here ourselves. The traffic in Malibu was bumper to bumper and Hugo had the day off, so we had to drive all the way out to pick up Charlie."

"And every lousy driver was on the road. And just as I'm making the U-turn to his house somebody was stopping to point at the satellite dishes on the roof, and I nearly rammed into him. Not that I blame them. It looks like an alien invasion."

Charlie laughed. "You don't think so when you come over to watch some sporting event you can't get at your house," he said.

Mark looked at Lily, who seemed flushed and deliberately busying herself with the picnic food. The house with the satellite dishes was Charlie's. Her car had been outside Charlie's house at dawn, which had to mean she'd spent the night there. What on earth could that mean? Was she romantically involved with this man? Surely that wasn't even a possibility.

Bryan transferred out of his wheelchair into a chair in the box, folded the chair with ease, and set it outside the box on the aisle, since the box was too crowded to hold it. Everyone was digging into the chicken when a very tall, nervous-looking usher in a red jacket stopped and looked into their box with an expression on her face that said somebody had done something wrong.

"Okay, whose chair is this?" she asked, pointing to the wheelchair.

Bryan spun around. "Mine," he said.

"Yeah, well I'm gonna take it away for safekeeping," she said, and she started to walk away carrying the folded wheelchair.

"No," Bryan and Lily said at the same time. "He needs to—" Lily was about to move past Bryan to tell the usher to kindly leave the chair there, but Charlie grabbed her arm and, making sure Bryan didn't see him, put a finger to his lips to tell her not to speak for the boy. When she nodded and stepped back, Bryan piped up.

"That chair is my legs," he said.

"Well, if everyone's rushing out of here in an emergency, they're gonna trip over this thing," the usher said brusquely.

"If everyone's rushing out of here in an emergency, what happens to me?" Bryan asked and the usher frowned.

"We'll bring it to you," she said.

"You mean, in the middle of an earthquake or a fire I'm supposed to count on you, a perfect stranger, to remember to save my life, which is what it amounts to, since nobody in this group is strong enough to carry me out of here?"

People in neighboring boxes were picking up on the conversation and leaning in to hear what the kid was saying to the scowling, annoyed usher.

"Hey, look," she said loudly. "I'm just trying to do the right thing for everybody, and you're just thinking of yourself."

"Go get me your boss," Bryan said.

"What do you mean?" she asked, flustered.

"I think he'll agree that you and I have a lot in common," he said calmly, and Lily glanced at Mark, who looked uncomfortable.

"Oh yeah?" the usher said. "What does *that* mean?"

"That you don't have a leg to stand on either."

Some of the people in the adjacent boxes snickered. Lily held her breath.

The usher, who could tell by the elbowing of the people listening in that she was now the laughingstock of the first few rows of boxes, said in a hurt and martyred voice, "Fine. Keep it there." Then she turned, and as she walked away, Bryan got a standing ovation from at least a dozen people in other boxes. As they cheered him and he nodded happily in reply, Lily leaned in and whispered to Charlie, "He got that snarky little attitude from you." Charlie grinned.

It was one sentence and Mark didn't even hear the words, but there was something so clearly intimate about her body language that as Mark watched the interaction his fears were confirmed, and he knew without question that he was in for a battle.

*   *   *

It was obvious that Diane Bennet really had read every one of Lily's scripts instead of giving them to a reader. She remembered jokes and story turns Lily had nearly forgotten herself. She was Lily's age and had been spoon-fed on television. There was clearly an affinity between them. "Look," she said, "I know you're the one for this show, not only because of what I've read and seen, but because crazy Charlie Roth, who never has anything nice to say about anybody, raves over the way you think and the work you put out."

"Thank you," Lily said.

"Thank *him*," Diane replied. "We have a lot of controversial story lines coming up because we have a character who's HIV-positive. We think we can get humor out of the stupid things people do around that. The phobias, the lousy comments. You know what I mean?"

"I know exactly what you mean," Lily said. The night before she had watched an episode of *American Dreamers*, knowing that she had this meeting today and wanting to be prepared. If there was such a thing as sitcoms for people who were thinkers, *American Dreamers* was it. Impressive, lively, smart and edgy.

"I'd be lying to you if I didn't say that we work so hard we hardly ever leave this place, but the staff is strong and smart and the shows we turn out are worth it. Kind of like the literacy show you wrote for *Angel's*, which I personally loved."

"Thank you," Lily said.

Diane stood and put out her hand. "Think it over," she said. "We really want you. Everyone here admires your work so much."

As they walked down the hall of the well-kept bungalow on the Fox lot, Diane stopped at a corner office with French doors that opened onto a patio covered with bougainvillea. "This was Tracy Cavendish's office," she said, stepping into the room and gesturing for Lily to follow. "She wrote and is producing a feature so she had to leave. This would be your space, and Pam out there would be your assistant if that's okay with you."

Lily sighed at the perfection of the way it all seemed.

"Listen," she said, knowing she'd hate herself later for being so honest. "A few months ago my son was—"

"I know," Diane said, "and I'm sorry."

"So I feel as if I should be taking on less right now instead of more," she added, and she hoped she didn't sound as if she were whining about it.

"I'm a mother myself," Diane said. "And for me it's been a struggle to juggle home and work with just the normal everyday problems. So if you decide to say no, I won't take it personally."

Lily walked down the hall and took the steps to the lobby instead of waiting for the elevator. By the time she reached the parking lot she had made her decision. It was a no. She was away from home too much now. Bryan was certainly showing signs of independence, but there was still so much that he needed from her. Attention, time, and thought. Besides, Mark would balk at her doing a show that took so much of her time. Tomorrow, when she got to her office she'd sit down at her desk, call Diane Bennet, and thank her for having the confidence in her, but no, she really couldn't take that wonderful, prestigious job on the number one show in the country for a million reasons.

24

Mark wanted to talk. It was easy to see he was upset and when he began to go on about what was on his mind it sounded too much as if he'd rehearsed the words over and over, making sure he got them exactly right. But then he always was a little stiff. Very earnestly and carefully he stated his case.

"I drove through Malibu at dawn last week and saw the Cherokee on the Coast Highway. It's taken me this long to realize I can't just pretend I didn't see it or that it didn't happen because if this means what I fear it might, I need to go on with my life. So don't stop me . . ."

He took a deep breath and paused, summoning up the wherewithal to go on. "You and I both know that if you make a choice to spend your life with a man because you think he's going to be a role model for your sixteen-year-old son and two years later your son goes off to college, you're still there with the man. So the wise thing to do is to choose the man who's going to be able to provide you with all of the things you said you wanted out of life—riding horses together on the beach, skiing in Switzerland, and, most of all, having at least one more child, maybe a few. That's why I'm here to beg you to think about what you're doing."

Charlie nodded at the end of what was obviously a carefully planned speech. He couldn't help thinking how silly Mark looked in his Italian suit standing on the beach, the breeze blowing his dark hair away from his face. Probably he came here straight from the hospital. Frank and Natalie were in their bathing suits over near the house. Francie had been digging in the sand for hours, and now as Frank fired up a barbecue, Francie made sand cookies with a cookie cutter and Natalie captured it all with the video camera.

"Please let her go." Mark looked pleadingly into Charlie's eyes.

"I never knew I was holding her," Charlie said, wondering for an instant if Mark had been drinking, but there was no scent of alcohol. No other indication except this painful monologue.

"She's under your spell because she thinks Bryan needs her to be with you."

Charlie closed his eyes and forced himself not to reply to that insult. He knew he should send the son of a bitch away now, before he said anything else that stupid.

"Let's go inside," he said instead, and made his way slowly up the steps from the beach to the deck with Mark following. The sun had burned his shoulders and he felt the sting as he wiped his sandy feet and stepped into the cool living room. "Something cold to drink?" he asked, but Mark shook his head.

The sun went behind a cloud, and Charlie grabbed a flannel shirt of his that was hanging on the back of a chair and put it on. "What can I do for you?" he asked. Mark took a deep breath, as if he were about to tell him, when Natalie rushed in carrying the video camera and Francie.

"Excuse us. We have a potty emergency," she said, setting the camera on the coffee table and hurrying upstairs.

"Go on," Charlie said.

"I came here to say that I think Lily Benjamin in her idealistic way believes that by loving you, she can prove to Bryan that someday a wonderful woman will love him too. And I understand that. You're an extraordinary man, and your accomplishments against all odds have been remarkable. I can't tell you how much I admire you. That said, you and I both know that's not a good enough reason for her to give up what she could have with me. She is still in a siege mind-set based on the shooting, and she isn't thinking straight."

There was nothing to do but listen to him. What did this putz think? That Charlie was going to sit down with him and bond, swapping Lily stories? Mark was downcast and ashen as he went on.

"I've dropped all pretense and pride to come here and fight for her because I love her so much. And I know she loves me too, but her terror for Bryan's future is getting in the way. You're a hero to Lily and Bryan right now. An example of how to be, and I'm glad they have you, but I think Lily's mind is clouded."

"That's because I'm Lamont Cranston," Charlie said. "No, wait, he only had the power to cloud *men's* minds."

Mark didn't get the joke, and Charlie was too tired to explain it. He knew he ought to just tell him to fuck off, but the prospect of listening to someone like this rant on about how Charlie was his big romantic rival was more than a little appealing, even though the asshole was insulting him at the same time. Both men sat quietly for a long time, looking out at the waves coming close to the deck. The same deck where Charlie had sat that night and watched Lily sleep on this very sofa where a beaten Mark now sat slumped.

How ironic that Charlie would have given everything to be this man that night, the man who was here begging him to back off as if he were actually some threatening force, a serious contender for the hand of Lily. Lily, who was so frayed at the edges, so unsure, and so endearingly good-hearted and funny that she was worth fighting for. And Mark was right. Lily's life's goal was to put that boy on the right path. Which, of course, made Charlie the absolutely perfect man for her because he knew how to get the kid there. Wasn't he doing it already? Didn't he get Bryan to let go of the self-pity long enough to learn to fly?

"What about the fact that I love her too?" Charlie said, surprised to hear the words coming out of his mouth. "More than I ever thought I could." It was not an admission he'd made even to himself up until that moment and he could hardly believe he was admitting it now, spilling it out to this near stranger, his rival.

And it was true, he did love her and that boy, loved them both. The way they were with each other and with him. They understood his jokes and saw through his anger and made him laugh right back. If he had any balls he'd tell this schmuck to get out of here, then get on the phone and call Lily to tell her how ridiculous this jerk was, and propose to her himself.

So what if she only loved him because he was a good role model? God, he hated when people called him that. Whatever the reason he should seize it, go for it. Strike while the iron lung was hot, he joked to his addled brain. What can I do? What should I say to this man? That I'll back off? That I'll dowdy down my act, not be available, not be the wise old cripple who's been through it himself so he knows the disabled ropes? Not that he'd been actively pursuing her. Well, maybe just a little bit. All right, he admitted to himself, some of his reason for helping the kid was about getting to be around Lily, but maybe it was time to stop doing that too.

The ocean was pounding loudly and rhythmically against the

deck. Clearly what Mark was telling him was true. If that same woman didn't have a disabled child, she would never have paid an instant's attention to him short of pity. She only focused on him because he had what she needed at this moment. And that was as bad a reason to have a relationship as skiing in Switzerland.

The best choice, his mother always said to him and his siblings, is the one that blesses the most people. What would bless Lily and Bryan more? Charlie pursuing her, all the while knowing she would probably never really want him? His retreating from Lily and Bryan's lives as quickly as he could was the choice that would ultimately make the most sense.

He saw her dealing with both his infirmities and Bryan's, always slowing her pace, always scaling back the size and speed of the adventure to accommodate not one disabled man but two. He imagined that spirit of hers capped down because of him. It was clear she loved the boy unconditionally and would take care of his needs forever without a complaint if she had to. But if Charlie let her know how he felt, courted her, wooed her, and won her over, eventually she would have to resent it.

The heart doctor was right. Charlie had been seducing Lily with his strongest suit, his link to Bryan, and he could tell by the gratitude he saw smeared on her pretty face each time the boy responded to him that if he played his cards ever so carefully he could get to her. But as Nixon so aptly put it on the Watergate tapes, "That would be wrong."

She needed to get back to where she was before Charlie limped into her life. And Bryan needed that too. To have this very straight-ahead man in a secure and respected profession become a family with them. That was the direction in which they'd been moving until that terrible night, and doing what was right meant letting the three of them continue on that path. Stepping aside.

"Everything you said is right," Charlie sighed and allowed himself to tell Mark. "And I'm going to back off."

In the morning before she left for work Lily called Diane Bennet. "I'm so flattered by your offer, so grateful for the time you spent reading my work, but I don't think the job is right for me at this time in Bryan's life."

Diane was quiet for a moment. Then she said, "I won't take this as a definite no. Please think about it for a little while longer."

Driving to work, Lily thought about Harry and all of his admonishments to her to get a classier writing job. But that was before the shooting. Harry would understand why she couldn't make the move now. At CBS, while she waited for the elevator, she looked at the black-and-white photos that lined the hallway. Group shots of the casts of the current CBS sitcoms. Lily stopped at the one of the cast of *Angel's Devils*. She felt sentimental about all of the familiar faces and the years she'd spent working with those people. More sentimental about the writers. Marty and Bruno were like brothers to her.

Dorie was on the phone and everyone's office door was closed as Lily turned the knob to open hers. She reeled at the sight of the boxes on the desk, the unplugged lamp, the computer packed in a box next to the printer in a box.

"What is this? Who did this?" she said to the air, appalled.

"The God of Jokes," Dorie answered, hanging up the phone. "Hey, congratulations on the new job!"

"What new job? I'm not taking a new job."

Charlie's office door opened. "Yes, you are," he said. "Because you're fired."

"You can't fire me!" she screamed. "I'll call the union. I need the health care, what are you thinking?"

"I'm thinking you can call facilities and they'll help you load that stuff in your car so you can drive it over to Fox."

"I don't want to work at Fox. I'm calling the Writer's Guild." She marched into her office and grabbed the phone, which was unplugged. "As soon as I get home. I'll call from my car. I'll go there now and report this."

"Leave the lightbulb," Charlie said over his shoulder. "It belongs to CBS." He walked back into his office and closed the door.

"No," Lily said to no one because Dorie was back on the phone and gave her a little shrug of "oh well," and if Marty and Bruno and David were around they were too afraid to come out from behind their doors.

She left the building without taking anything and got into her car. By the time she had turned onto Ventura Boulevard she was crying quietly. Not for the job, to hell with the job, but for all the mornings when she'd put her work first and rushed out of the house to be on time for a meeting, so that Elvira was the one who drove Bryan to school, packed him a lunch, kissed him good-bye. She was weeping now for all the nights she got home late from work and went into her baby's room to kiss his sleeping face, hurting that the pre-bedtime story time he'd remember hearing had been in Elvira's lap and not hers.

When she stopped at the light at Holmby Park, where children climbed on play equipment and young mothers and uniformed nannies sat chatting, she thought about all the park days she had missed, all of the times she'd been so exhausted on the weekends that she'd set up the Legos at the foot of her bed, put Bryan in front of them, and slept away most of the day.

The Saturday morning she forgot to wake him for a soccer game, the time he had spilled the tray bearing her Mother's Day breakfast in bed and she snapped at him, as if he weren't heartbroken and embarrassed enough. She had been a terrible parent and how awful for Bryan that she was the only one he had. Never, never, never would she take that job, and Charlie the interfering skunk would hear from the Writer's Guild before this day was out.

Of course, she thought as she traveled south on Beverly Glen, if she took the new job she'd be earning double what she was earning now, and she would be able to get Bryan his own car, one with built-in hand controls. Not have to ask her mother or Mark for a loan. In fact, she'd be able to pay her mother back for the loan to redo the condo, and she could even pay for the wedding herself since that was traditionally what a bride was supposed to do. She reached into her purse and fished out some Kleenex, blew her nose, and mopped her eyes.

At Beverly Glen and Santa Monica she stopped at the light and watched a pretty young mother crossing the street with a baby in a backpack and a toddler boy holding her hand, chatting away to the little boy. I want that job, she admitted to herself. If there was some way I knew I could take it and Bryan would be okay, I would call them and accept. But there isn't, is there? Oh God, she thought. I need help, a sign. Something to tell me how to behave and how I can handle this dilemma.

And when she pulled around the corner to her condo she saw Elvira sitting on the low wall that surrounded the two-story building. Lily slammed on the brakes, didn't even turn off the engine, just pulled the emergency brake and threw the door open to jump out and run to her. They held each other tightly, and Lily felt the small woman's body shaking with emotion.

"It's all my fault," Elvira said into Lily's shoulder.

"No it isn't, Elvira, I never thought that," Lily said, and it was true. It had never crossed her mind that Elvira had any responsibility for Ernesto's behavior.

"My sister saw it in the paper and when she told me about it, I came back. One day I left Bryan's favorite enchiladas for him, but I didn't stay to see him because I thought you would be so angry at me. I want to see my boy, but I worried that he would look at me and think it was because of me. Today I stayed out here to wait for you because I thought maybe you wouldn't want me to see him."

"No one blames you," Lily said, looking at Elvira's face, which seemed years older than it had only a few months ago.

"I knew Ernesto was a bad man, but I didn't think he would hurt a child," she said. "Maybe he was jealous because he knew how much I love that boy."

"Bryan loves you too."

"Do you think I could come back?" Elvira's eyes were pleading. "Even though I brought the curse on him, I want to make it up to him and to you. I'll come and take care of him and make his favorite foods and be here for him."

"Let's go inside," Lily said, realizing she'd left her engine running and turning toward her car. "He's been trying to catch up on all the months of school he missed. He's starting a summer program next week, so he's been studying a lot," Lily said as Elvira followed. After she parked, Lily opened the kitchen door and the two women walked in. Elvira looked around at all of the changes as Lily called out, "Bry, someone's here to see you."

"There in a minute," Bryan answered, and after a quiet moment they heard him wheeling down the hall.

"No way!" he said, grinning and wheeling into the room, his face filled with raw emotion. Elvira couldn't contain hers and fell on him with kisses and tears and Bryan looked over at Lily happily.

"Jeez, Mom," he joked. "Guess we don't need you around here anymore."

Lily felt a blanket of relief fall over her. "I think this qualifies as a miracle," she said out loud.

Within days the house was immaculate and Elvira's singing filled every corner. Bryan loved having his buddy back, and they played endless games and squealed with laughter and Lily wasn't jealous about any of it. Just pleased that the house was clean and the food was cooked. When she made the decision that she would take the job, Bryan was the first one she told. "Cool" was all he said. Then she called Mark. "Meet me for lunch?" she asked.

"You have time to meet for lunch?" he said, delighted.

"I do because I left my job," she said.

"You did?" he said. "Hooray!"

"Well, don't cheer too fast. We need to talk."

They decided to meet at Campagnola on Westwood Boulevard. Lily arrived first, and she ordered a San Pellegrino, watched the door for a while, then studied the way the light bounced off the facets of her diamond ring, which she polished with the cloth napkin. Mark looked so handsome when he walked in the door. Lily watched as four women at a table near the entrance all looked up from their conversation to check him out.

Eat your hearts out, Lily thought. He's mine.

"Now that Elvira's back," he said after they had ordered,

"and you're not working, I've decided we should go away for a day to Pebble Beach."

"I didn't say I wasn't working. I said I left my job."

"Why doesn't that mean the same thing?"

"Because I took another job, a plum job, the most desirable job in the television writing business," she said.

He wasn't exactly lighting up with glee. "No kidding?" he asked in a measured voice.

"Remember the night we watched *American Dreamers*? The show about the women who start a business?"

"Vaguely," he said.

"It's that show, and it's number one. Charlie thought I should take the job, and since the producer of *American Dreamers* used to be his secretary, he called her and made her read my scripts. And she hired me."

"What kind of hours does it entail?" he asked instead of saying congratulations. For an instant she was tempted to minimize it, to brush off his concerns, but she couldn't lie.

"Long hours, hard work, but it's something I really want."

"Well, then," he said, "I guess you're very happy." They ate their lunch in silence. When the check came, Mark shuffled in his wallet for his credit card, placed it in the tray, and looked at Lily.

"I'm sorry. I handled that badly. But I love you and somehow lately I get the feeling I'm at the bottom of your list."

"I know you do, but it isn't true," Lily said. "I guess I believe that because we love each other we should be happy for each other's triumphs, even if they don't fit in with our personal agendas."

"What if I got a job at the heart center in Houston? Would you be happy for me? Move there with me? Not think of your own agenda?"

She didn't know what to say.

"Be realistic," he said. "Of course I'm thinking about us, the future, the wedding plans that keep getting put off. I'm starting to feel like that character in *Guys and Dolls*. That Adelaide who developed a cold because her boyfriend wouldn't marry her." Lily smiled. "Next weekend," he said, "let's get away. Just us. Does the new employer let you get out of town for a night with a man who's developing a cold?"

"I'm sure she does," Lily said, and it sounded like a welcome idea.

25

The first day of Lily's job at *American Dreamers* was coinciden-
tally the first day of the summer school program Bryan was
taking at his school to make up for the missed time. Lily could
drop him off at school on the way to her office at Fox. Elvira
had packed him a lunch and Lily a snack so she wouldn't have
to eat the food from the commissary. After a few false starts at
leaving the house, the first time because Lily forgot the good
luck pen Daisy had bought her with a plastic lily sticking up
at the top, and the second time so that Bryan could change
sunglasses twice before he had his look just right, they were on
their way.

"What'd I forget?" Lily asked herself out loud as she got on
Sunset heading for school. "Purse, snack; I don't think I need
anything else. You have everything?" She looked at Bryan, who
was grinning at her.

"You this nervous for you or me?" he asked.

"Why do you think I'm nervous?" Lily asked.

"Because the windshield wipers are on and it hasn't rained
since April," he said. Lily laughed and turned off the wipers.
They were at the front of the school. Maybe it was just her
panic, but Lily thought she spotted Kimberly in the crowd of

kids, seeing the car and slinking away. Or maybe that was what had happened in her nightmare last night; she wasn't sure. She held her breath as Bryan opened the door and lowered the wheelchair to the ground, then catapulted into it.

There were kids everywhere, and Lily saw a couple of them stop what they were doing to turn and watch. Then she spotted a skinny girl in denim overalls elbowing her friend to move out of the way to let Bryan through and the friend nervously moved aside. Some people turned away self-consciously, and some stared, and Lily found that while she watched she wasn't breathing. She was waiting for the dig, the hurt, the snide remark. Her hands were clutching the steering wheel and her nails were digging into her hand until a girl with orange-red hair burst out of the building and ran toward the wheelchair shouting joyously, "Oh my God, Bryan's here!" And with a shriek of welcome that cut through the discomfort of everyone else, the girl, the blessed, wonderful, uninhibited girl, jumped onto Bryan's lap.

Lily bit the inside of her cheek trying not to fall apart in front of all of the kids, watching her baby make his way back into his world for the first time. For an instant she thought she saw him turn in the wheelchair to nod to her as if to say everything was all right now, and then he disappeared into the crowd of teens as they moved toward the building.

"He is fine," she said out loud, and realized her hands were aching from clutching the wheel so hard. He is fine, he is fine. She repeated it like a mantra all the way to Pico Boulevard, where she turned in to the Fox lot.

Outside the *American Dreamers* building she saw the sign PARKING FOR LILY BENJAMIN, AMERICAN DREAMERS and hope rushed through her. The number one show wanted her, and she was up to the task. Her brain was brimming with ideas and now she could make some of them happen. Pulling into the space, she turned off the engine and sat for a moment, not sure whether she was elated or afraid. At least, she thought, gathering her purse and the brown bag with her snack in it, nobody will hang me out the window.

She hadn't spoken to Charlie since the day he'd fired her. The night before last Marty had brought all of the boxes containing her supplies to her condo. "The guy's morose," he said about Charlie. "I say he's in a bad mood because he let you go. Bruno figures he let you go because he was in a bad mood. Dave says you can't have that much physical damage and not have some of it affect the brain."

"Want an iced tea or something, Marty?" she had said, hoping he'd stay for a while and talk.

"Thanks anyway, I got to get home." They hugged, and Lily felt a big sadness filling her chest.

"It's kind of like when Pat says good-bye to her kindergarten class every year," Marty said, his sweet eyes holding hers. "She tells them, 'Sad to see you go, but glad to see you grow.' And that's how it is. Harry would be proud. And I can tell you *I* sure am."

"Marty, what if I can't cut it?" she had asked him, feeling suddenly panicked about her own inadequacies. "What if I'm only funny because you think I am, and you laugh at my jokes, and you and the guys support me and prop me up?"

"You're the one who propped up all of us. Even Charlie knows that."

"He does?" Lily asked, surprised that she felt so eager for any drop of information about him. Every day she'd been sure he'd call, if not to apologize then maybe to talk to Bryan. She wanted to hear his voice, to tell him she had decided to take the new job, though she was sure Diane Bennet must have told him. She thought it would be good to say that she didn't hate him for firing her because now she realized he was doing her a favor. Maybe she would even tell him they should try to have some kind of a friendship. No. That would make him laugh. It was too sappy.

Inside the pretty, two-story *American Dreamers* building, it seemed as if everyone was on the telephone. Lily dropped her purse and the snack on her new desk, then walked down the hall to Diane Bennet's office. The door was open and Diane, who was on the phone, gestured for her to find a place to sit. But she kept talking irately to someone on the other end of the line.

"I have to shoot a show at the end of this week," Lily heard Diane say into the phone as she sank into the white sofa behind the dark wood coffee table. Diane hung up the phone and sighed. "I hate to bring you on board on the day a crisis breaks," she said, "but Cathy McCarthy, who plays Ellie, just quit, and we have to replace her by tomorrow or shut down for a week."

"Quit?" Lily asked.

"The messenger delivered the script, she made him wait while she counted her lines, threw it in his face, and said, 'Here's a message to take back to the *American Dreamers*. They're *really* dreaming if they think I'll take this shit.' "

"Poetic," Lily said.

"I thought so," Diane said, smiling through her angst.

"Well, isn't it lucky!" Lily said.

"Lucky?" Diane asked. "This I have to hear. Exactly why is this lucky?"

"I've watched this show and she's without question the weakest link. We've got a chance now to find the perfect person to replace her. Isn't it lucky that it happened this early in the week so we can hustle somebody new into place by the taping?''

Diane was smiling knowingly. ''You *have* spent some time with Charlie Roth, haven't you?''

Lily smiled.

''There's nobody like him.'' Diane said.

''He's demanding, bratty, self-important, and a complete pain,'' Lily said, looking at Diane, who was nodding in agreement, ''and I really am going to miss him.''

Diane sat back in her chair and, forgetting for a moment that she had an emergency to deal with, went off into a reverie. ''He was in love with an actress, a beautiful actress named Liz Mann. Remember her? She was in a few big films, orange-colored hair, green eyes, very intense. And she was in love with him too. She just got him, you know? The freaky way he makes fun of himself, all of it. She lived with him for about a year and then she died. In some really unexpected way. An embolism or something. It was during the first year that I was his secretary, and I remember how it wiped him off the map for months. As if he didn't have enough to contend with.

''After that he was wounded so he struck out at people more. But when I first met him and he was with her, he was the most amazing character. Before I created *American Dreamers* I wanted to write a new sitcom with a leading character in it who had cerebral palsy and model him after Charlie. Naturally the chickenshit networks wouldn't touch it.'' She shook her head, remembering the battles she'd fought.

Lily and her sister Daisy had a code they used between themselves to describe women they encountered over the years who had humor and compassion, whose eyes made it clear that they'd earned their wisdom through years of struggling, women who cared about other women and had no interest in rivalry. The two sisters said of those women, "She's one of us." Lily could already tell that Diane Bennet was "one of us."

"We'd better get on the case," Diane said, standing. "I've called a meeting for ten in the conference room, so let's hit it. We have to decide whether to write her out or just cast someone else in the same role and hope nobody notices."

"They do it in soaps all the time," Lily said, following her out into the hall. "One actress goes into a coma, and when she wakes up she's another actress entirely."

"A coma can do that to you," Diane said, and as the two women walked down the hall to the meeting Lily was already beginning to feel at home.

By the end of the day it had been decided that Cathy Mc-Carthy's character was on an extended vacation, giving them time to search for someone new. Lily assigned a story idea to two of the show's better writers and began to work on one of her own. As the story took shape and the jokes began to flow she said out loud, "Thank you, Charlie."

26

Mark made reservations for the two of them to spend Saturday night at The Inn at Spanish Bay in Pebble Beach. Bryan had Megan, the pretty redheaded girl, visiting every day after school, and when Lily asked if he minded if she went away for a night, he didn't even look up from his homework to say, "Nah."

Driving up the coast with Mark, Lily felt the tension of the last few months slipping slowly out of her body. Mark took her hand, lifted it to his lips, and kissed it. "You've earned this rest," he said. "They have a spa. You ought to go in and order the works."

Lily smiled and thought about the jokes Marty, Charlie, Bruno, and David would make around the idea of "the works." But Mark was right. She needed a day to just sit on the balcony outside the hotel room, staring at the sea. She was working on some story ideas for *American Dreamers* and she'd brought a notebook with her, but she promised herself she'd look at it only if she couldn't sleep.

In the car she nodded off just after they passed San Luis Obispo, and she didn't open her eyes until Mark pulled into the front courtyard of the hotel. Inside the lobby on a round table was a tall floral arrangement of orchids and Lily wanted to cry for happiness at their beauty. Everything made her want to cry. The view of the golf course and the bright blue ocean from the hotel window, and the stunning hotel suite with a fireplace in the corner were such a treat to her senses. She stood on the balcony breathing in the sea air, remembering that the last time she'd done that had been with Charlie the night she drove him home.

Mark was behind her and he put an arm around her and turned her to face him.

"I love you," he said, and she saw his eyes searching hers for something. Some sign of passion maybe. Probably he was hoping they would make love before they went down to dinner. It had been so long and she felt guilty about that. She knew that for him this trip was about getting back to their pattern of sexuality, breaking down the logjam in her brain that stopped her from letting go.

"And I love you," she said, but she heard the hollowness in it. Maybe her indifference was from exhaustion, she thought as he led her into the bedroom and undressed her, and she said a little prayer that she'd be able to drum up some kind of feeling as she let him make love to her. She thought later she would tell Daisy that it was the sex of two people who knew they were paying big bucks for the room so they better make good use of it.

That night when she slept she had a dream that she and Mark were walking down a beautiful, sugar-white beach, soft on her feet. Mark's face was close to hers, he was nuzzling and kissing her. In the dream she was more aroused and full of feeling than she had been when she was awake. But when a noise in the hotel hallway woke her, she sat up and thought about it and knew that it couldn't have been Mark in the dream because her lover in the dream was wearing a Hawaiian shirt and jeans. It couldn't have been Charlie either, she thought, because the man in the dream was well and whole. And then she realized that she had rewritten Charlie for the dream and made him able-bodied and so physically attractive.

Sunday morning as she sat across the table from Mark at a sumptuous room service breakfast she felt as guilty as if she'd actually cheated on him with another man. She picked at a fruit salad and watched, astonished, when a one-legged seagull landed on the railing of the balcony and perched there looking in the window at the two of them.

Last month, she remembered, Charlie had brought Bryan a video of the hysterically funny routine by Peter Cook and Dudley Moore about a one-legged man who was auditioning for the part of Tarzan in a play. Dudley Moore hopped in playing the Tarzan hopeful and Peter Cook interviewed him for the job.

She remembered how the three of them had howled with laughter. What was it Peter Cook had called the one-legged man? A unidexter. Remembering that made her laugh out loud.

"What's so funny?" Mark asked, putting his hand over hers and smiling.

"Just some insane comedy routine," she explained. "Peter Cook and Dudley Moore created it. Ever heard of them?"

"Dudley Moore, the short little actor?"

"Right, well years ago he and another marvelous actor named Peter Cook performed routines together. The two of them did a show called *Good Evening* that was hilarious. You see, in the sketch Peter Cook is casting this part . . ." And then in the hotel room she found herself acting out the whole routine, playing both parts, remembering it from the video, and the only members of her audience were Mark and the one-legged seagull who was still out on the balcony.

When she was nearly at the end, laughing herself as she played out the hopping of Dudley Moore and the deadpan questions of Peter Cook, she could see that Mark didn't think it was the least bit funny.

He was forcing a smile and looking at her indulgently, and when she looked outside and watched the one-legged seagull fly away, she wanted to scream after it, "Don't leave me here alone with him."

Later that day, when she and Mark took a long stroll down the boardwalk that ran along the sea front and had lunch at the hotel's Club Room Grill overlooking the water, she searched every gathering of seagulls, trying to locate her one-legged fan.

When they got into the car to leave for home, she was relieved.

"Well," Mark said. "That was a pleasant respite. Wasn't it?"

"It was," Lily agreed. "Thank you."

She made excuses to herself all the way down the coast about the way she was feeling. She was under pressure with the new job, Bryan was still needy. But both of those were untrue. She loved the new job and knew even after this short time that it was just where she belonged. And Bryan was already so independent he was barely noticing if she was around or not.

At the door of her condo she allowed herself to be kissed by Mark and during the kiss she waited for the feeling she used to get when they parted. The feeling that she wanted him to stay and whip up dinner and be around and affectionate, but all she wanted tonight was for him to go.

"Call me tomorrow," she said.

"I will," he said, starting to walk away, but he turned back. "This weekend really clinched it for me," he said. "I had such a good time and I was so glad because lately, and I know you'll laugh at me . . . but I thought you might actually be thinking of leaving me for Charlie Roth."

"Why would I laugh at that?"

"Well, you know. I guess I thought you'd want to make Bryan feel better, so you might . . . I don't know," he said. "I saw you together and there was this moment . . . never mind. It was just that we'd been drifting apart and every insane thing crossed my mind." He took her in his arms and hugged her, then hurried away to his car.

Elvira was in the kitchen. "Bryan's out with some of his friends," she told Lily. "They took him for dinner, so he said to tell you all his homework is finished and he'll be home by nine." Normalcy. This felt like normalcy. Out with his friends. Lily walked into her bedroom, and without unpacking her suitcase she fell on the bed and lay quietly, with Mark's words ringing in her ears.

In her office the next morning she was tying up some of the ideas she'd thought about over the weekend, very pleased that she still liked them, when her assistant stuck her head in the door. "Sorry to disturb you," she said, "but someone named Marty Blick is on the phone, and he says he has some big news."

Lily grabbed the phone.

"Congratulations," Marty said. She could tell that he was trying to contain his excitement. "We just got word that *Angel's Devils* was nominated for an Emmy not once, but twice. For your literacy show and for Charlie's anniversary show. We're going out for drinks at Adriano's to celebrate at six, you're joining us, and we won't take no for an answer." Now he hollered, "Way to go, Lil!"

"I'll see you there, Marty," she said excitedly.

Lily wanted to jump up and shriek with excitement. An Emmy. Wouldn't it be grand to hear her name called from the stage and to hurry up there . . . but why would she win? Charlie's anniversary show was much funnier and very poignant. He would surely beat her, and there had to be other wonderful candidates too.

"Wow!" she heard someone say outside her door. There was a big uproar out in the hall. She opened her door to see the writers surrounding Diane Bennet and congratulating her. "I was nominated for an Emmy," Diane said, beaming at Lily.

"Me too," Lily said, watching the faces of the writers all turn to her. Diane hurried over and they exchanged a congratulatory hug. The rest of Lily's day was spent fielding phone calls from people who hadn't even called with sympathy when Bryan was shot. Success in Hollywood brought them out of the woodwork, she thought as she looked over a few of the faxes that had arrived after the Emmy nominations had been made public. At five forty-five she looked at her watch, rushed to the ladies' room to fix her makeup, and decided she didn't need much because her cheeks were flushed. She couldn't wait to get to Adriano's.

As she drove up to the valet parking sign she saw Marty, Bruno, David, and Charlie walking toward the restaurant, so she tooted the horn and Marty turned and spotted her. "It's Lil," he said, and he rushed to her car to hug her. "An Emmy," he said as she stepped out of the car. "A fucking Emmy." Lily saw Charlie standing coolly by the restaurant door.

"Congratulations," she said as she approached him.

"And to you," he said, letting her pass him and walk into

the dark restaurant, where a red-jacketed maître d' led them to a big round table. Lily sat with Marty on one side of her and Charlie on the other.

"Champagne for everyone, a straw for the crippled guy, and an iced tea for the broad," David said to a waiter. "She gets weird when she drinks."

"Our show got picked up today," Bruno told her. "That putz Harvey Meyers came in and told us this morning. You and Charlie saved our asses and now I have another year of Writer's Guild health insurance."

"That's great!" Lily said, then turned to Charlie. "You pleased?"

"It reminds me of that joke," he said. "First prize is a week in Acapulco, second prize is two weeks in Acapulco. I win another year with these bozos. How pleased can I be?" But Lily could tell by the way he said it that he was kidding and that he was glad.

The boys were yakking away about how Harvey Meyers had come in that morning right after he'd heard about the two Emmy nominations to tell them that the show was picked up, and they were laughing about what a jerk Meyers was. At the next table was a young couple with their baby girl, who was in a high chair. The baby was smiling an open-mouthed dribbly smile at Charlie, who looked past Lily and gave the baby a wave in return. The baby cocked her head to the side and tried for a wave and then grinned and gurgled at Charlie.

"She's flirting with you," Lily said.

"Babies make pure and instinctive connections," he said. "They haven't learned prejudice yet. Someday I still hope to have a few." He saw her face go soft and thought he had to tell her, "If I make a baby, it won't be like me."

Lily was filled with warmth and wanted to hug him. "You

mean it won't be funny and wise and full of heart?" she asked, but she must have embarrassed him, because he looked away.

Lily knew he might not like it, but she took the chance and threw her arms around his neck in a hug.

"Hey," David said. "She's hugging the competition. Trying to get you to take a dive, boss. Don't do it."

The waiter was pouring champagne into the guys' glasses, and then he put the iced tea in front of Lily as Marty raised his glass to make a toast.

"To Charlie and Lily. Two amazing people who I hope will be very happy. Jeez, I must have pulled out the toast I made at my sister Harriet's wedding. Let me see if I have anything for nominations. Oh yeah, how about this? May the best man win."

"We miss you a lot," Bruno said to Lily after a big swig of champagne. "Nobody bugging us about the smoke or the food or the lousy ideas."

"Thanks, Bruno. I miss all of you too," Lily said, and she looked down at her hand on the seat of the booth and realized she was tightly holding Charlie's hand.

When she got home, Bryan was in his room on the phone, and when Elvira saw her she held a finger to her lips and handed Lily a telephone message. "I'm glad I answered this call. I tore it off the message pad because I didn't want Bryan to see it until you did." Donald. Jesus. The message was from Donald, her ex-husband. She hadn't spoken to him or heard from him in years. Even after the shooting had been in all the papers and she'd thought he'd have enough decency to send a note or a card, anything to the son he had abandoned. And now what on earth could he possibly want?

In her room with the door closed, she called the number Elvira had given her, feeling shaky as she did. "Hello?" he said. He'd always had a sexy voice.

"Donald," she said. She told herself that whatever it was, she'd be businesslike and get it over with fast. This was a bad guy, and she knew that unless something dramatic had happened to him in the last few years, he was up to no good.

"Lily," he said. "How about meeting me tomorrow at Starbucks in Brentwood? I want to talk to you, and I thought we'd best do it in person."

"About what?" she asked, knowing she sounded abrupt and glad that she did.

"My son," he said, and she felt her rage rise. The son he had abandoned and hadn't seen in years.

"Let's talk about it now," she said.

"I'll be in Starbucks in Brentwood at eight in the morning," he said, and clicked off.

"No," she said out loud, and she swore she wouldn't go there, wouldn't play his game and let him control her. But when she got into bed that night she set the alarm for six forty-five, and in the morning she asked Elvira to drive Bryan to school. Then she drove past the freeway ramp she usually took to the Valley, to head for Starbucks.

Donald was still gorgeous. He was sitting at a table outside with his feet up on a chair, his sunglasses perched on his nose as he read the trades. Lily hated that she still was turned on by his looks, and before she said hello she took in every feature and realized how much Bryan physically resembled his father. His lousy, thoughtless father.

"Hey, Lil," Donald said without looking up. "I know your scent," he grinned. Then he turned those turquoise eyes on her, and despite the way she hated him she was flooded with memories of how attracted to him she had been for so long.

"I'll get a coffee and be out in a minute," she said, stalling the conversation and giving her time to compose herself.

The rotten jerk had banked on the fact that meeting in person would be better because he was sure that when Lily saw him he'd have more control than he might have had on the phone. And he was right, she was rattled. She ordered an iced cappuccino and worried that the caffeine might make her feel even more jangled than she was already.

Through the window she noticed a blond at another table giving Donald the eye while he casually perused the pages of *Variety* as if this morning were just another coffee date with just another woman. It was the same cold, detached attitude that had made him capable of leaving one day in the middle of a fight. "I'm sick of your telling me what to do," he'd said in an argument about why he'd bought himself a Porsche when they didn't have enough money to pay the rent.

"That's how I am," he'd said in a statement that was supposed to excuse everything. "I'm impulsive."

To this day she couldn't remember if she had actually thrown him out that morning, which was what he told various mutual friends over the years. But somehow in the muddle of time and temper it seemed to her that he had just sidled out into the Porsche saying, "Let's just call it over." As if he had never sworn to love her forever, or bathed Bryan with kisses in the delivery room, or filmed his son's first run across the room. Something Bryan would never do again.

She took a swig of the cold coffee, then inhaled a deep breath to steel herself before she pushed the door open to the outside. Donald stood and moved the chair out for her.

"I knew you'd come," he said, smiling triumphantly.

"Only because I knew it had something to do with Bryan," she said.

"Of course," he said. He folded the trade paper and shoved it into the pocket of his soft black leather jacket.

"Let's cut to the chase, Donald. What do you want?"

He smiled a white-toothed smile.

"Still the same no-bullshit girl," he said. "That's good, because I want to get right to the point too. I want to see my son."

At four that morning she had awakened worrying that he might say that, worrying what she would reply. Now her stomach felt tight and her heart thumped in her ears.

"Do you have any idea what's happened to your son?" she asked.

"I heard. And I was horrified. I didn't come right away be-cause I thought seeing me might add to his misery. But now I was hoping maybe the timing would be better."

"Donald," she said, trying not to cry, "I have spent the last seven years searching for a role model for this boy so he wouldn't spend his life filled with rage because you walked out. Someone with character, because you've made it clear you don't have an ounce of that, someone with compassion, since you never had a shred of that. Someone that boy can look at and say, 'That's what a man is supposed to be.' "

Donald smirked as if to let her know what she was saying was cloying. "So I guess you found him. I heard you got en-gaged. Who is this sterling character?"

Lily's eyes narrowed. None of his damned business; she wouldn't sully her engagement by discussing it with him. "Never mind who it is," she snapped. Why was she dignifying this meeting by staying any longer?

"Probably a doctor," Donald said. "Your mother's ideal man. I knew when we split that if you ever fell in love again it would be with some hotshot doctor. Am I right?"

She was just about to answer when a Mustang convertible stopped at the corner for the red light. A pretty young woman wearing a backward baseball cap must have been listening to an oldies station and she had the music turned up very loudly. Joe Cocker was singing, "You Are So Beautiful," and Lily heard the words, "You're everything I hoped for . . . everything I need . . ." Then the light changed, and the Mustang squealed away, and Lily stood. And that was when the truth came over her like a welcome tropical shower breaking the heat.

"No," she said, looking after the Mustang and surprising her-self not only with what she was thinking, but what she was telling Donald. "Actually, you're wrong. You're completely wrong. The man I'm in love with is a comedy writer. An eccentric, bonkers, nutcase of a man who sees the world differently than anyone I've ever known. Who appreciates the world more gratefully than anyone you or I have ever met. That's who I love. And you know what else? Your son loves him too." Donald was stone-faced. "Would you like to know why? Because of the time he spends, and the humor he brings, and the trouble he takes and then pretends it was no trouble at all. And the unyielding belief he has in the survival of the human spirit, which he knows about firsthand. And that's why I love him. So much that as soon as I leave here and take care of some important business, I'm going to run to him and tell him so often his head will spin."

"Cool," Donald said, smiling at her patronizingly. "And when you're done, do me a favor. When you get home tonight, ask Bryan if I can call him and . . ." Donald was rambling on about how he had changed and made a mistake and how he hoped she'd at least let him take the kid out to a movie. But Lily didn't hear any of it.

"Good-bye, Donald," she said as she walked away from Starbucks. She would tell Bryan about their meeting tonight, but now she had to figure out what she was going to do about her newfound realization. She knew she had to tell Mark today that it was over for them, had to be over. That even though he was a lovely, honest, kind, and generous man, she didn't feel about him the way she wanted to feel about the man she married.

All the way to the office she glanced at her ring, smiling at the way Charlie had infuriated her by making the joke about the urologist. The same joke his sister made months later. It was a perfect diamond, but what it represented was the flaw.

A marriage she had agreed to for all the wrong reasons, reasons having to do with the way things were supposed to look. Reasons that no longer made any sense to her at all.

Mark, she would say, you are a wonderful man. A man who will make a great husband and father, but you're not the man for me. Was that too cruel? She thought of the joke about the army officer who had to tell young Private Schwartz that his mother had died, but he didn't know how to break the news. So he assembled all of the men in the platoon and said to them, "Everyone in this outfit who has a mother, please step forward." Then he added hastily, "Not so fast, Schwartz."

That's what she would say to Mark, "All men who are engaged to Lily Benjamin, please step forward. Not so fast, Mark." God, she was punchy even letting that thought in. In fact, she was giddy, relieved that she had let herself come to the decision, certain that it was the right one.

Jokes, the God of Jokes. That's who she loved. Charlie Roth, the man she had disdained, shunned, made fun of. He was the one whose soul had touched hers. He was the man who understood her, and now she was going to tell him. Tell him that she loved him, not only because he was so good to Bryan but because he was everything she had been waiting for and praying she would find in a man.

She could walk like she talked. She could see through to his beautiful, tender soul, and she was going to tell him. Not just call him on the phone to tell him or stop by and tell him, but tell him in some special way. She was about to get onto the freeway to go to the Valley when she had an idea, and she pulled over to the curb and dialed her office from the car phone.

"*American Dreamers.*"

"Hi, it's Lily. Put me through to Pam, please."

"Lily Benjamin's office."

"Pam, please tell Diane I won't be in today. I'll finish my script at home and see you tomorrow."

"No problem."

At the next possible turn, Lily got back on the streets heading south to Beverly Hills. Now she knew how she would tell Charlie how she felt about him, and she hadn't been this excited about anything in years. At the Museum of Television and Radio, she found one of the directors and told him what she needed. As he was writing down the request, the young man asked her her name, and when she said "Lily Benjamin," he congratulated her on her Emmy nomination.

Before she sat down to work, she called Mark and asked him if he could meet her at the Coffee Bean and Tea Leaf café just down the street from the museum, at three. When he said he could, she sat down at a cubicle in the scholar's section of the stark white museum, and the director cued up the shows she had requested. One by one, she watched them all, making notes, rolling them forward, and then back to find just what she wanted.

At two forty-five she told one of the attendants to leave everything as it was, and she hurried to meet Mark. He had already ordered two iced cappuccinos. His familiarity with what she would order gave her a pang, but she knew this was the right moment, and she took his hand. He looked pleased, but when he felt her slip something into his hand he opened it and saw the heart-shaped diamond and turned pale.

"You're making a mistake," he said.

"Mark, I know now that what I need is someone fanciful. Someone full of hope and uncharted thinking and whimsy, and I know you'll never be that. But what you do have is so wonderful and someday some other woman will be the luckiest person in the world to get to be with you. Please understand how much I care about you and appreciate everything we've had together."

"Lily," he said, "let me take whatever's wrong and make it right." It was a song lyric, but instead of feeling like laughing, which she sometimes did when he used those, she felt sad for him. Let me be there. That was the name of the song. "I know I get too serious. It's the hazard of being in a profession where life and death are on the line every day. But let me try to change."

"I love you for wanting to try. I'll always love you for being so steadfast and loving and honest. But I can't marry you, Mark."

Mark couldn't reply. He just stood, and then he turned to walk down Beverly Drive. The dark, rich scent of freshly ground beans wafted out through the open door of the shop, and Lily took a whiff and sighed. I am stopping, she thought, to smell the coffee for the first time I can remember. I know what I want and I'm completely delirious with joy.

28

_{◇◇◇◇◇◇◇◇◇◇◇◇◇◇◇◇◇◇◇◇◇◇}

Charlie took a shower, then sat on the deck watching the ocean. It was a perfect Sunday afternoon in Malibu. A group of kids were playing Frisbee with a golden retriever down by the water's edge, and he loved watching them fling the bright pink ring into the sky and then squeal with delight when the dog leapt and caught it in his mouth. That morning one of the brokers from the real estate office had shown the house twice while he had breakfast at the shopping center, and now he could just sit on the deck and read through some of the new scripts. Bruno had done some of his best work, and Charlie couldn't wait to call and tell him that the rewrite notes were minimal, and that his story about Joey's father dying was poignant and well-written.

He had just backed into the lounge chair with his laptop open and on his lap when he heard the doorbell ring. He couldn't imagine who in the hell was coming by on a Sunday afternoon. Natalie and Frank had taken the baby to Santa Barbara to see Frank's mother, so it wouldn't be them. Damn, he thought, moving the laptop and pushing himself off the chaise to stand. The doorbell rang again. "I'm on my way," he hollered, and then opened the front door to find a messenger standing there with a small package.

"It's a good thing the Unabomber is in jail," Charlie joked to the messenger, who was only interested in his signature and didn't seem to get the joke.

He stood in the doorway and looked at the package, and recognized the handwriting on the envelope as Lily's right away. As soon as the messenger was gone, he opened the envelope and pulled out a video. He was so intrigued he didn't even think to close the door behind him, just walked straight into the living room to his large screen TV and inserted the tape into the VCR. First a card filled the screen that said A SPECIAL MESSAGE FROM LILY TO CHARLIE.

Then the clips began. Clips from old television shows were flashing by him, Jackie Gleason and Audrey Meadows as the Kramdens on *The Honeymooners,* Jackie saying to Audrey, "I love you, honest I do." Jean Stapleton as Edith Bunker on *All in the Family,* looking at Carroll O'Connor, saying in her shrill voice, "I love you." Larry Hagman telling Barbara Eden in her Jeannie outfit, "I love you," Miss Piggy telling Kermit the Frog, "I love you." Mary Tyler Moore telling Dick Van Dyke, "I love you." Lucille Ball telling Desi Arnaz, "Darling, I love you." Clips flying by of all of the greats—George Burns, Milton Berle, Alan Alda, Eve Arden.

And each of them were saying the same words, "I love you." This was from Lily to him. This was her way of saying she loved him. That's what the tape meant. What else could it mean? She loved him, and she was sending this tape to him to express it. His eyes burned with tears, and as he felt in his pocket for a handkerchief he heard her voice behind him.

"I do, you know," she said, and he was too filled with the rising emotion to turn around. Surely she would say she was thanking him because he had helped Bryan along, or that she was grateful because he had helped her get the new job. That was all it was, just an exuberant burst of appreciation presented in this creative way because she was so imaginative.

"I watched every one of those shows. I sat in the television museum and laughed and cheered every time one of those stars said 'I love you.' And then I cried because I realized how long I've waited to say a real from-the-solar-plexus 'I love you.' Not a "Maybe-I-love-you,' or an 'I'm-saying-I-love-you-even-though-part-of-me-isn't-sure-I-do.' But a full-out 'Baby, you're the greatest!' And it occurred to me that the one man on earth I wanted to hurry to and offer a blazing 'I love you' was you. So here I am. I love you. I see through to your perfect and beautiful soul, and I love everything about you."

Charlie pressed the handkerchief to his eyes. He could never turn around now and let her see how foolish he looked, bawling like a baby. Yes, she loved him, yes she meant the kind of love he prayed she did. But what could he ever give her in return?

"Please be mine," she said, and now her hands were on his shoulders, "and let Bryan and me roll into your life and be your family, because we both need you so much."

Charlie turned the swivel chair to face her and he saw that she was crying too. She was so beautiful, more beautiful than he had ever seen her look. Her flushed cheeks made her skin radiant and pink and her hazel eyes looked as turquoise as the ocean behind her. He could only get two words out of his mouth, and he hoped they weren't too choked with pain for her to understand.

"Sit down," he said, and Lily grinned and a teardrop fell from her eye and hit the carpet.

"Is this going to be like *60 Minutes* and take you two hours to deliver?" she joked.

"On the contrary," he said. "This is one story even I can give you in thirty seconds."

Lily felt a dark worry come over her, and the light in the room seemed to dim. This wasn't the way she imagined this was going to go. She had hoped as she sat in the Museum of Television and Radio going through hundreds of videos that she would rush here and tell him how much she loved him, and he would take her in his arms and say that she had made his dreams come true. That would be the best case, and in the worst case he would say, "I care about you too, and let's take our time and see if we can work this out."

But the look on his face now told her neither of those two was a possibility. She sank into a chair and held her breath as he began.

"I loved the tape, but there's no deal to be made here."

Lily smiled uncomfortably, hoping he was joking and that there was a punch line to come, but she knew better. She had worked in a room with him long enough to know when what he was about to say was funny and this was not one of those times.

"I've given you and your son everything I had to offer. I got him through the worst fears associated with his physical condition, I helped you deal with him, and played a part in advancing your career. I'm out of tricks. That's all I've got. There's nothing more for me to do for you."

This couldn't be true. She knew he cared for her, that he loved their time together, that he must have entertained the thought of being with her. She was trying not to fall apart. "I don't want you to do anything for me," she said.

"Lily," he said. "I'm very fond of you, but not the way you want me to be. I'm sorry, but I'm not there."

Lily was stunned and then jarred by the sound of a woman's

voice. "Hey, lover. You chilling some wine for me?" she heard the woman call out. And when she turned she saw that nauseatingly pretty blond called Marilee, the one who had come to the office that day to take Charlie out for lunch. She must be going with him, maybe even living with him.

Lily felt sick. Why had she assumed that Charlie didn't have a relationship and would fall all over her with gratitude because she cared about him? Of course she'd thought that, because she was just as narrow-minded as everyone else about the disabled. She had simply figured that he was a poor, lonely soul just hoping that some pretty, able-bodied woman would fall for him. And the truth was that he didn't want or need her at all.

"You remember Marilee, don't you, Lily?" Charlie asked, and Lily nodded and moved toward the door.

"Nice to see you again, Marilee," Lily somehow managed to say before she was out in the courtyard and into her car. She started the engine and then moved into the fast traffic that was zooming down the Coast Highway.

At home, she and Bryan and Elvira were quietly eating dinner when Bryan remarked, "Where's your ring, Mom?"

"I gave it back."

"Whoa. You mean you're not engaged anymore?"

"That's what I mean." She saw Elvira look down at her plate with an expression she'd seen on her face before that meant "I'm staying out of this."

"Did something bad happen?" Bryan asked her.

"No. I just knew he wasn't right for me."

Bryan pushed at the enchilada on his plate and thought about the next question before he asked it. "So, does that mean you're dating?"

"I have so much to do with the new job, I really don't have time to date."

"But I mean, does Charlie have a chance?"

"He doesn't want a chance."

"How do you know?"

"I asked him."

Bryan looked surprised, as if he wanted to ask more questions, but then he changed his mind. Lily felt stupid and sad and embarrassed and she wondered how she would face Charlie at the Emmys, where no doubt he would show up with Marilee.

29

◇◇◇◇◇◇◇◇◇◇◇◇◇◇◇◇◇◇

For the next few weeks she threw herself into her work, writing at the office, having dinner with Bryan and Elvira; when Bryan started his homework, she worked on new scripts for *American Dreamers.*

A week before the Emmy ceremony, she accepted Diane Bennet's invitation to join her at a luncheon for women who worked in television. It was an annual get-together and this year it would be at Shutters by the Sea in Santa Monica. The event was crowded with women she had encountered over the years in the business and it felt great to be among them as the producer of the number one show on the air. The prelunch social hour was on an outside deck above the beach.

A few of the women she spoke with asked how her son was doing and nodded sympathetically when she told them he was doing marvelously well, but she knew their questions were coming from politeness and not genuine concern.

"Oh my God, Lily. Oh, my God," she heard a voice shriek. It was Cynthia Lloyd, across the deck, who hurried over and grabbed Lily's arm and shook it. "Look at that!" She was pointing into the sky, where a plane flew by towing a banner that read MARK LOVES LILY. TAKE ME BACK. For an instant she couldn't take it in, and then she realized that the message was from her Mark and that she was the Lily. Somehow, maybe by calling her office, he had found out that she'd be near the ocean at that moment and he was trying to be whimsical, light, all the things she said she wanted a man to be.

"That is so adorable," Diane Bennet said.

"I had no idea you broke up," Cynthia told her, "or I would have gone after him myself."

Lily smiled. She had to admit it was a valiant attempt, and she would call Mark when she got home to thank him and tell him that she hadn't changed her mind. But she didn't have to make the call because right after the luncheon, when the valet brought her car, before she'd even climbed inside, her car phone rang.

"I was going to parachute out of the plane and land on the beach in front of the party and spell out 'I still love you' in seaweed, but I thought that might be overkill." Cute, Lily thought. Very cute.

"Definite overkill," she said.

"I'm also pricing gorilla suits. I've got my eye on a great-looking one."

"Tell you what," she said, smiling at his guts to hang in and put up a fight for her. "Find a good fit and you can wear it to the Emmys. I have three tickets."

"It'll be an honor," he said.

All the way home Lily thought about what she later told Daisy were "Mark's Greatest Hits." The first night he cooked for her, so eager to please her that he barely touched his own meal because he wanted to watch her take every bite. The way he slid the ring on her finger so gently the night he proposed, watching her face to see if she understood why he'd chosen the diamond shaped like a heart. His nervousness on the first night they made love, telling her through every kiss how much he wanted her and wanted to make her happy. Maybe she was a complete fool to let him go. He was a find; he loved her. Maybe she should leave herself open to the idea of going back to him.

"Looks like you got a visitor, boss," Hugo said, making the U-turn on the Coast Highway and pulling up behind the white Jeep parked in front of Charlie's. The HAHAHA made the vehicle unquestionably Lily's. For some reason she had come back, and now Charlie would have to do another acting job. For the last few weeks he'd been dreading the idea that he'd have to see her at the Emmys, imagining her in some gorgeous gown on the arm of the heart doctor.

"Need any help going in?" Hugo asked.

"I can handle it."

The front gate was open, and she was probably sitting in the courtyard, and he would have to be suitably cool to her and get her to go away. He put a hand up to his hair to smooth it and wondered what she would say this time. Maybe she'd invite him to her wedding, or maybe she wanted to ask some advice about Bryan. To his surprise, it was Bryan who was sitting in the courtyard waiting for him.

"Passed my driver's test last week," Bryan said. "I used the hand controls you got me for my birthday."

"Big-time congratulations," Charlie said, wondering what the kid was doing there.

"She told me she broke up with Mark and now he's managed to wangle his way into coming to the Emmys with us," Bryan told him. "You had that window when you could have jumped in there and gone after her, but you didn't. Why don't you go after her now, today, and admit that you love her?"

"Because I don't," Charlie said.

"You're a lying sack of shit. You drool when she walks into a room."

"I drool when *I* walk into a room."

"What about all the bull you taught me about the way women love a man who has a sense of humor, and guys like you and me bring something special to the party? Admit that you're scared to be with her. Afraid that if you do get to her, one morning she'll wake up and look at you and say, 'Yecchh, you're repulsive. I'm outta here!' Which makes you not just a physical cripple, but an emotional cripple too. Just what you tried to get me not to be. You're a fucking fraud."

Charlie couldn't answer, but he walked around toward the side of the house, where there was a path to the beach and gestured for Bryan to follow him in the chair. Then they moved together toward the shore until Bryan hesitated.

"I can't go down there. Sand gets in my wheels," he said.

"Not as romantic as 'Smoke Gets in Your Eyes,'" Charlie said. "But don't worry, I'll pull you out if you get stuck."

It was a soft, warm evening, and the tide was out, so there was a long stretch of sand ahead of them. Charlie pushed the chair from behind, down a small hill and then toward the shore, where the firm sand made the rolling easier on the wheels.

"My dad called my mom and said he wants to see me. She told me the other day."

"Oh, yeah? And what did you say?"

"I'm not interested. Once a jerk, always a jerk."

They moved south along the water, not talking for a while.

"What's happening at school?" Charlie asked. "Did you try out for the play the way you promised me you would?"

"I talked to the teacher about it, but she said it wouldn't

work. It's Shakespeare, and a wheelchair like mine would be some word like an—"

"Anachronism."

"Yeah."

"Same thing happened to me. I wanted to play the title role in my senior play."

"Just a guess that it wasn't *Little Merry Sunshine?*'" Bryan joked.

"Funny," Charlie noted. "Actually I was perfect for it, but they gave it to some handsome six-foot-four dude who butchered it completely. I was on the stage crew and every night I sat backstage and watched him, thinking I should have played Richard the Third." He moved in front of the wheelchair, raised a finger into the air, and recited Shakespeare with Bryan as his audience.

"Now is the winter of our discontent, made glorious summer by this sun of York . . ."

A couple in purple jogging suits ran by, and Bryan was embarrassed.

"Give it a rest," he said to Charlie, but he could see by the now familiar fire in Charlie's eyes that he was on, theatrical, into his performance.

"But I that am not shaped for sportive tricks, nor made to court an amorous looking glass; I, that am rudely stamp'd and want love's majesty to strut before a wanton ambling nymph; I that am curtailed of this fair proportion, cheated of feature by dissembling Nature, deform'd, unfinish'd, sent before my time into this breathing world, scarce half made up, and that so lamely and unfashionable, that dogs bark at me, as I halt by them . . ."

A brown standard poodle had stopped in its tracks to listen

to the speech and was now behind Charlie, crouching and re-
lieving itself, and the sight of that made Bryan fall apart with
laughter. He was laughing too hard to speak so he pointed, and
Charlie turned to look. "Your audience speaks the truth," Bryan
managed to say through his giggles.

"Thou thinkest so?" Charlie asked in mock anger. "Then I
must fling thee into the briny foam," and he hurried behind the
wheelchair, grabbed the handles and in his best run pushed it
toward the surf, with Bryan shrieking above the roar of the
waves. When the wheels accidentally hit a piece of driftwood
the chair tipped and both of them hollered as Bryan was thrown
into the wet sand and Charlie fell with him. For a long time
they sat there together laughing, each of them fighting hard not
to cry.

30

♦♦♦♦♦♦♦♦♦♦♦♦♦♦♦♦♦♦

It was the day of the Emmys but Lily was in the office. One of the *American Dreamers* stories wasn't working, and two of the writers had a family crisis in New Jersey, so Lily was left to finish their episode. Pam had been in the reception area on the phone calling the tailor who was hemming Lily's dress for the evening because Lily was starting to panic. The ceremony was in four hours.

"I'm running over there to pick it up," Pam announced. "Back in ten minutes."

Lily was just starting the second act when she heard her office door open. She didn't turn around because she assumed it was being opened by Pam.

"How does it look?" she asked over her shoulder.

"Lily," she heard a woman's voice say, and she turned the chair to see Charlie's sister Natalie. "Natalie Gold. Remember?" she asked.

"Of course I do," Lily said. "Is something wrong?"

"Something's very wrong," Natalie said.

The first thing Lily thought was that Charlie must be dead. Yes, he was dead, and his sister was here to tell her what had happened to him. Lily braced herself for the worst.

"The day we met I told you how special my brother is to all of us. He's such a bear, he'd slay me if he knew I was here, but I couldn't live another day with what I know and you don't."

Lily couldn't imagine where this was leading and she was glad to see through the now open door that Pam was back and carrying a garment bag, which meant that as soon as this woman finished her seemingly urgent story, she could hurry home to get dressed for tonight. She had rented Bryan a gorgeous tux and when he tried it on for her she could tell that he loved how handsome he looked.

"I was making a video of my daughter a few weeks ago at Charlie's house. I'm a techno-moron with the camera, so when I ran up to change the baby's diaper I mistakenly left the damn thing on. The other day I was looking at the video and I showed it to Frank and he was laughing at me for leaving it on and getting a video of Charlie's wall. We were still giggling at my stupidity when we discovered something I think you ought to know. So I had it transferred and brought it to you." She handed Lily a video.

Lily stood and walked to the VCR in her office, and Natalie handed her the tape. Lily cued it up; first she saw that adorable Francie playing in the sand. Then for just a second she saw Charlie in the distance talking to someone on the beach who looked like it could have been Mark wearing a suit.

Then there were some jumpy shots of some steps up to what might have been Charlie's back deck, and then nothing until she heard what was unmistakably Mark's voice.

"I came here to say that I think that Lily Benjamin in her idealistic way believes that by loving you, she can prove to Bryan that someday a wonderful woman will love him too. And I understand that. You're an extraordinary man, and your accomplishments against all odds have been remarkable. I can't tell you how much I admire you. That said, you and I both know that's not a good enough reason for her to give up what she could have with me."

Mark. It was Mark, in Charlie's house. Mark, who had to know all along that she and Charlie were so right for each other, that their getting together was inevitable, and that the only way he could stop it was to go to Charlie and ask him to back off.

"That's Mark Freeman," Lily blurted out over Mark's continuing speech. "He and I—" But Natalie shushed her and turned up the volume.

"I've dropped all pretense and pride to come here and fight for her because I love her so much. And I know she loves me too, but her terror for Bryan's future is getting in the way. You're a hero to Lily and Bryan now. An example of how to be, and I'm glad that they have you. But Lily's mind is clouded."

Lily looked at Natalie and shook her head. "I don't believe this," she said, but Natalie put a finger to her lips as if to tell her there was more to come.

There was a long silence on the tape and then Lily heard Charlie say as clearly as she had ever heard him say anything, "What about the fact that I love her too? More than I ever thought I could."

Lily gasped. He said it, he loved her. Oh God, he loved her. Then why hadn't he told her, said so, admitted it when she ran to him that day with the "I love you" video?

"The best way for you to prove that love," she heard Mark tell Charlie, "would be for you to unselfishly insure that she'll have the kind of life she deserves, and let her go."

Lily snapped off the video and looked into the eyes of this woman she barely knew.

"Thank you for this," she said.

"I had to bring this," Natalie said. "I knew the day you were at my house that you cared for Charlie. I also knew that he would probably be afraid to tell you how much he cared for you. So I needed you to hear it for yourself."

The two women embraced.

"You've changed my whole life," Lily said. "Now all I want to do is rush out and change Charlie's." But then she moved away and looked closely at Natalie's face. "One question though. Who is Marilee?"

"Isn't she your worst nightmare?" Natalie asked, grinning. "She's a real estate broker who was looking to list Charlie's high-priced beachfront house."

Lily sighed with relief, then happily embraced Natalie again. With one arm holding her new dress and the other around Natalie, she headed for the parking lot.

From her car phone she tried Mark's house and left a message on his voice mail. Then she called his office at the hospital, but his assistant told her that he'd already left. Then she left a message on the machine at his house. "Please call me. It's about tonight."

While Elvira helped Bryan get dressed, Lily washed her hair and blew it dry, took the time she never took during the week to apply her makeup, and then slid into the long, black-sequined slip dress and was pleased with the way it looked. She never bought clothes like this dress, but she had loved the slinky feel of it on the hanger in Saks and was impressed with the way it fit. It was just the dress she imagined she'd wear if she were ever lucky enough to be nominated for an Emmy.

She and Bryan met in the hallway, and his good looks made her stop and smile, then hurry to find the camera. She was rummaging through the desk drawer where she'd last seen the camera when the doorbell rang. She stood, afraid but resolved, and walked into the living room to open the door. Mark was there, resplendent in his tux, smiling at her warmly.

"Got your messages, but didn't have a second to call you back. And by the way, I want you to know that I tried to rent the Oscar Meyer Wienermobile to drive us there, but it was booked." Bryan rolled into the living room just then, and Mark lit up. "Hey, friend," he said, putting out his hand for Bryan to shake. "Glad we're all going together." Then he caught the look on Lily's face. "Is there a problem?"

Lily handed him the video. "Mark," she said, "Charlie's sister was making a video of her daughter the day you went there to talk him out of being with me. I saw you in it on the beach. I also heard everything you said to him about me. It's all on this tape." Mark's face was flooded with embarrassment. Lily felt Bryan's presence behind her, and she weighed her words as she went on. "I know you went out there to say those things because you love me. But it was hurtful and a terrible thing to do to Charlie. Now that I know he loves me, all I want to do is to run to him and convince him to be mine forever."

Mark was pale.

"More than my seeing through his outside to his inside, he sees through to mine, and that's why I need him so much."

"I guess I ought to just head home then," Mark said.

"Probably best," Lily said as she moved past Mark. Bryan followed.

"Take my car," Mark said as the three of them stood in front of the building, where a black limo waited at the curb.

"We have a car," Lily said as the white Cherokee was backed out of the garage by their driver for the night, Elvira.

*   *   *

Pasadena Civic Auditorium was bustling with the TV elite and Lily and Bryan moved out of the car and up the red carpet to the lobby. There were already hundreds of people inside. Men in black tie and women in bright, glitzy, high-fashion gowns. Lily spotted some of the writers from *American Dreamers* in a group with Diane Bennet at its center, but she was looking for Charlie. It was Bryan who, even from the lowered height of his chair, managed to spot the *Angel's Devils* writers across the room and pointed them out to Lily.

"Go for it, Mom," he said. "I'll catch up."

Marty and Bruno saw her coming toward them, looked behind her for Bryan, and made their way toward him as Lily pushed through the jostling crowd to where Charlie was standing talking to a man Lily didn't recognize. She was nearly there when Harvey Meyers stepped out of the crowd and grabbed her hand.

"Hey, big-time writer. I still love you even if you did leave my network." Then he looked down at her hand. "Whoa, no engagement ring anymore? Does this mean I can take you to dinner one night?"

Lily forced a polite smile at the slimy man and kept walking, but now the lights were blinking as a signal to get everyone inside. She could see Charlie move toward the auditorium door, but she put on a burst of speed and was at his side with her hand on his arm as he looked at her with surprise. It was noisy, much too noisy, and maybe she wouldn't be able to get him to hear her words, but she had to try. Even as the crush of people threatened to separate them she moved her mouth close to his ear and said, "You love me."

He looked at her with surprise, and it seemed as if he were about to shake his head no. "Yes, you love me. I know it, and I know that Mark came to you and told you to give me up."

Charlie couldn't hide the surprise in his eyes. "Please," Lily said, wishing they were somewhere else, anywhere else so she could get through to him. "I'm begging you not to do what you think is some noble favor by staying out of my life. You must know that I love you and need you so much." Before Charlie could say a word, Lily found herself being moved along by Diane Bennet with the *American Dreamers* group, and she saw David hurrying Charlie toward the seats where the *Angel's Devils* writers would sit.

The show began, but all of it was a blur to Lily, who craned her neck, trying to spot Charlie across the auditorium. Bryan had transferred into the aisle seat and his wheelchair sat folded next to him. He seemed to be enjoying the show, laughing and applauding, and every now and then patting the nervous Lily happily on the arm.

Now Jerry Seinfeld was at the podium. "Nominations for the best episode of a comedy are Diane Bennet, 'Waiting for the Test Results,' *American Dreamers*; Norman Steinberg, 'Jason Pollock' episode of *The Cosby Show*; Charlie Roth 'And the Angels' Sing' for *Angel's Devils*; Lily Benjamin, 'ABCs of Love' for *Angel's Devils*; And the winner is . . ."

Lily thought she was going to be sick, throw up, or faint, the way her heart was beating much too fast. Her face was hot, and she realized that she'd never even written a speech because she knew there was such a slim chance of her winning over those other writers, but what if she did win? What would she say? Jerry Seinfeld had pulled the card out of the envelope and was grinning.

"Yes," he said. "He's the man. He's the God of Jokes. Charlie Roth!"

As she saw Charlie stand, Lily realized Charlie had been sitting very close to the front of the theater. Thank heaven somebody had been smart enough to put him on the aisle in the second row. She felt the people behind and in front of her jumping to their feet in an ovation for him, and she stood too. Charlie was making his way to the stage and Marty and Bruno were following him as if they were his bodyguards. The audience was cheering, and Lily realized as she watched that Charlie was going to have to climb several stairs to get to the stage.

He took the steps very slowly, and when he stopped on the third one and looked for an instant as if he might tumble backward, Marty and Bruno grabbed him and lifted him under each arm to fly him onto the stage. The flying made him laugh and walk to the mike with the ovation still thundering. When it died down, he spoke.

"It's good to know I'm not just another pretty face," he said, which got an enormous laugh.

Lily felt Bryan's hand take hers and she knew it wasn't in sympathy because she hadn't won, but in shared pride for Charlie.

Charlie was smiling a big, open smile as he said, "They told me I had forty-five seconds. It takes me longer than that to blink." That line got another big laugh, and Lily settled back in her chair, knowing Charlie felt comfortable and safe up there. "At the risk of taking comedy too seriously," he said, "I'd like to tell you a brief story."

Lily knew the director must be going crazy in the booth. They always liked to think they had these shows timed properly, but someone like this who walked so slowly and talked so slowly had to be a problem. Right now, the director was probably cueing the orchestra to play some music that would remind Charlie to say a fast thank-you and get off the stage. Yes, she could see the conductor raise the baton. He was about to cue the music, and Lily held her breath. But then Charlie spotted the baton too, and said, "Hold the music, Ray. I've been waiting for this moment all my life."

The audience applauded and whistled at that, and the monitors showed the conductor laughing, not only putting the baton down, but taking off the headset that connected him to the control booth, where Lily imagined the director was probably apoplectic thinking he'd have to put up with a speech from this slow-talking writer.

"One day a man walked by a tree and spotted a cocoon with a hole in it just as the butterfly was about to emerge," Charlie said. "Wanting to help the butterfly, the man breathed hot air on the cocoon, hoping to hurry the process. But he was horrified when the emerging butterfly died in his hand."

Lily looked around the auditorium to see that everyone was rapt, listening to Charlie slowly make his way around the words to the story.

"What the man realized, to his dismay, was that it's the very act of gradual and steady beating of the wings against the inside of the cocoon that builds the power of the wings and gives the butterfly the strength to fly."

There were monitors everywhere, and Lily looked from one to another, watching Charlie's wonderful, funny face and wondering where the story was going, amazed at the total silence everywhere in the auditorium.

"I wanted to tell that story because it's about seasons and cycles and growth and patience and allowing things to happen in their own time. For example, I know that last year I never could have written a show about a man's heart opening to the deep and abiding love of a woman. I had to wait until it came into my own life."

Bryan squeezed Lily's hand, and she looked at her son. His eyes were full.

"Which is why," Charlie said, "I ask that you indulge me while I use this podium not for political gain, or some career agenda, but probably for the first time on live television . . . pure romance."

Then he stepped away from the podium and descended slowly to one knee, which took him a long time, during which a group smile of acknowledgment fell over the audience as they realized what he was about to do. And when he looked out into the auditorium and asked, "Lily, will you marry me?" people rose to their feet to cheer him on.

The heat of surprise burned through Lily, and her jaw dropped. Bryan was laughing, and the *American Dreamers* writers all turned in astonishment to realize that she was the one. Cameramen with handheld cameras were searching the auditorium trying to locate the woman, and Lily could hear her name in the buzz of voices. Benjamin, it's Lily Benjamin, where is she? There, over there.

Her feet pushed into the floor, and she stood and found Marty and Bruno flanking her now, moving toward the stage as the audience spotted her and the cameras found and followed her, and dazed, she managed to get to the steps and then up the steps where she rushed to the arms of the most perfect man she had ever hoped to find.

Epilogue

✦✦✦✦✦✦✦✦✦✦✦✦✦✦✦✦✦✦✦

Lily Benjamin and Charlie Roth married at Christmas. Lily's sister, Daisy, wore a black tux to the wedding, at which her mother did not appear. The groom's sister Natalie and his brother-in-law Frank nudged their daughter, Francie, down the aisle so she could be the flower girl, and Bryan happily gave away the bride. One year later, Lily gave birth to a beautiful, healthy, eight-pound baby girl. Lily and Charlie named their daughter Gracie.